Cover design by Natasha Brown

Book design by Giacomo Giammatteo

This edition was prepared by Giacomo Giammatteo gg@giaoomog.com

Print ISBN 978-1-940313-88-7

Electronic ISBN 978-1-940313-87-0

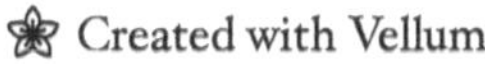 Created with Vellum

THE GOOD BOOK

GIACOMO GIAMMATTEO

Inferno Publishing Company

Chapter One

ANOTHER VISIT WITH THE SHRINK

Tip's alarm went off at 6:00 AM. He got dressed, said hi to the dogs, got the paper off the porch, and then read it while coffee brewed. He figured he was one of the few people left on the planet who still read a real paper instead of reading it online.

He hated getting up early, but he had to see the psychiatrist today, and he hated that more than getting up early. He drove to the station, facing little traffic, then stopped at the coffee room for tea. A cup of tea might sit well before a meeting with Doctor Nutbag.

About fifteen minutes later, Tip walked down the hall and knocked on the doctor's door, then he went in and sat down when invited.

"Good morning, Detective Denton," the doctor said.

"Not so good if you ask me," Tip said.

"And why is that? Does it have anything to do with you being shot?"

"Not really, no. It has a lot more to do with me being here instead of on a case."

The doctor made a few notes in a tablet sitting atop his desk. "You've been in here before, Detective Denton."

"Damn if you're not right. Son of a bitch, but you're sharp. No wonder they made you a shrink."

"According to this file, the last time you were in here it was for the reverse; you had shot someone else."

Tip shrugged. "Shooting someone or getting shot. Doesn't make much difference. It's all part of the job."

"Really? Did you know that going in?"

When Tip didn't answer, the doctor continued. "Even if I said I agree, they're both traumatic experiences."

"Call it what you will, but to me, it's not much different than getting punched in the nose. Fact is, I've had punches in the nose that hurt more."

"I can't imagine that," the doctor said.

Tip smiled. "I'm sure you can't, but it's true. I imagine you've never been hit in the nose by my old nemesis, Hap."

"Detective, why do you insist on being antagonistic? I'm only trying to help."

"Because I don't buy into your psychological bullshit. You're always wanting to put somebody in a box, categorize them as one thing or another. That's not always the case."

"Detective, I have found that that is usually the circumstance."

Tip shook his head. "Yeah, but usually and always are not the same thing. Just like in my line of work. It's usually the case that the murdered person knows the person who committed the murder. But it's not always the case. Sometimes people are just crazy. Or just mean. And not because their mama yanked them off her teat too early."

Tip leaned back in the chair and folded his hands behind his head. "I had a dog once that used to bite wheels. Anything with wheels—cars, lawnmowers, chairs, wagons…didn't matter. If it had wheels on it, he bit it. Now I'm sure a psychologist would say it was because somebody beat him with a wheel or ran over him or some such nonsense, but it wasn't the case. Fact is, he just didn't like wheels."

"And how do you know that, Detective? Perhaps—"

"No, I'm sure. He didn't like wheels. Plain and simple."

The psychologist sighed. "Detective, you told me previously that the dog was adopted from a shelter. There is no way for you to know for certain."

"I know because he told me."

"Who told you?"

"The dog," Tip said.

"I think we're done here," the doctor said as he stood. "And I don't mean for just the day. I'll be making a report to your superior before the end of the week."

"Sounds good to me," Tip said, and reached his hand to shake. "Nice meeting you, Ralph."

As Tip walked out of the room, he nodded. *Looks like I've managed to piss off another one.*

Tip was walking back to his office when he passed Captain Cooper.

"Denton, did you see the shrink?"

Tip smiled. "I believe I did, yeah."

A frown formed on Coop's face. "You believe you did? What did he say?"

Tip leaned close. "I don't want you to take it hard, Gladys, but he said despite all your problems you have a chance to be a good boss."

Captain Cooper shook her head as she walked down the hall. "I don't know why I bother with you. You're hopeless."

Tip raised his voice as Coop walked away. "I'm guessing you'll recognize that pretty soon. Maybe then you'll leave me alone. At least that's what I hope. And based on what that shrink said, there's a reason to be optimistic."

Coop waved her hand in the air. "Go to hell, Denton."

"Okay," Tip said. "But don't expect me back before lunch."

Coop continued down the hall shaking her head.

Chapter Two

JUSTICE SPOONS

Justice looked up at the sky. Not a cloud was in sight, but that didn't stop him from wishin' it would rain. It had rained not far from here, so maybe it would come his way. He wished for it. He wished it so bad it hurt. But then again, a lot of things hurt Justice. He'd been hurtin' all his life.

Justice had been a frail little boy, but he'd grown into a hard-nosed man. Everything about him was hard. His mama made sure of that. He didn't have no daddy, leastwise, none he knew of. The one time he asked his mama who his daddy was, his mama beat him so bad he never asked again.

Not knowin' who his daddy was, itched under his skin, so he kept trying to find out—but not by asking her. No sir. He might not be much educated, but he wasn't dumb. Even a dog knew what drew a beating. Even so, from time to time, Justice tried getting clues.

On the few occasions that his mama had guests over, he listened from his room down in the cellar to see what she said. He put his ear to the ceiling and listened as hard as he could. The only thing he ever heard was her saying his daddy was a cur, and it was better he went where curs were supposed to go.

When he got older and could read a little—and when he had a light to read by—Justice looked up that word "cur." He found it had two meanings. One meant a dog—and he didn't much reckon his daddy was a dog—but the other meant a coward.

Justice often thought about it, and he reckoned he would rather his daddy have been a dog, knowing how his mama felt about cowards, that is.

Sometimes, when his mama had her "guests" over, they would get into a conversation and suddenly start laughing. Justice listened to what they said, but he never understood what was so funny. It tended to confuse him, though if given to consideration he wasn't much for laughter.

The few times he tried laughing, the noise echoed off the concrete walls and bounced around. It kind of made him feel like the walls were laughing at him. Justice didn't like that; in fact, he didn't like cellars, and he often wondered about them. From what he could hear of the other kids, they didn't have cellars. Only Justice and his mama were lucky enough for that. That's what she said.

When his mama left the house, which was often, he would stand on the old milk box, with its four splintered slats, and peek out the window.

It was dark 'cause the windows were taped up, and nobody could see him, but he could see the kids playing through the holes in the tape. If he'd have had a nickel to bet, he'd put it down that they were laughing, he just hoped it wasn't at him.

And he could see it rain through the holes in that tape, sometimes he could. Not often, though. It didn't rain much out in that part of Texas. Leastwise, that's what mama said.

It was a shame, 'cause Justice liked rain. He liked the sound it made after the puddles formed, and the raindrops splashed and splashed over and over again. Sometimes the other kids would play in it. He saw them through the holes in the tape too.

He wondered why they wanted to get wet. At first he thought them stupid, but the more he watched them, and the more he heard them laugh, the more he wanted to play too. He'd wouldn't mind getting wet if he could laugh about it, even if Mama beat him.

A loud thunderclap brought him to focus on the present. He pressed his face against the side window of the van, stained with splatters from the mud-slicked road he'd encountered on the drive over, and he stared at the kids in the street. Rain had begun, like he prayed for, and it was causing the kids to scatter and run for home.

A moment later, Justice saw what he was looking for, a calico Manx, conspicuous for the lack of a tail, and he stepped out of the van and scooped it up. He opened the side door and tossed the cat inside, then climbed back behind the steering wheel.

The rain was really coming down now, but he sure wished it would rain harder.

A good rain always took away that crazy feeling he got when he killed someone., and he might have to do that before the night was over.

Chapter Three

KC IS MISSING

Karen Hendricks parked her car in the drive, grabbed the milk and bread from the passenger seat, and took the laundry from the hook behind her. She walked briskly toward the front door. Sweat beaded on her forehead before she got the keys into the lock. For a second, she thought about taking a dip in the pool to cool off, but she had to finish her taxes before the deadline, and that happened in six or seven hours.

Mid-April and it's already 95 degrees. What the hell!

She laid the laundry across the back of the dining room chair, set the bread on the kitchen table, put the milk in the fridge, then kicked off her shoes as she called for the cat. "KC, where are you?"

When he didn't come, she called again. "KC, get out here. It's time to eat."

Karen took the clothes from the chair and put them into the closet, hanging them next to her work outfits, then she changed into jeans and a light-green tank top. She thought about which shoes to wear but opted to go barefoot. When she got back to the kitchen, she was surprised that KC's bowl was still full.

Where the hell is he? "KC! Where are you?" Her tone had taken on a bit of impatience, even irritation.

"Tommy, have you seen KC?"

Where is that damn cat?

She got no response from Tommy, not unusual for a seven-year old, so she walked toward his bedroom. *What is it going to be like when he's a teenager?* The thought frightened her. She flung the door open and stared, hands on hips.

"Thomas Hendricks!"

The use of the double name must have caught his attention. He broke off from his video game and looked up.

"Hi, Mom. I didn't hear you."

"Turn that thing down."

"Sorry, Mom."

"Have you seen KC?"

Tommy got up quickly, abandoning the game. "Not since I left for school this morning. Where is he?"

"I don't know. I just got home." She followed her son down the hall. "You have some responsibilities around here, you know. Feed the cat, pick up clothes, sweep the porch."

"I know. I know." Tommy poked his head into a spare bedroom. "KC, where are you, boy?"

Karen stopped being angry and grew more worried. Tommy doted on KC, and he was probably upset not knowing where the cat was, especially after just getting him back from being lost for a week. She didn't want to go through another week like that. The damn kid had put her through hell, and the way her life was now, she didn't need more to worry about.

She put two baked potatoes in the oven, then called a few neighbors. "Sylvia, have you seen KC?"

"No," she said. "How long has he been gone?"

Karen sighed. "I don't know. I came home to find him missing. That damn cat just returned after being gone a week. I should just get rid of the damn thing."

"I wouldn't worry," Sylvia said. "I'm sure he'll be back soon."

"I'm not worried myself, but Tommy is. You know how he loves that cat."

"I'll keep my eyes open," Sylvia said. "He's bound to show up soon."

"Okay, thanks. See you later." Karen hung up the phone then called Emily and went through the same questions. She got the same responses too. Neither of them had seen KC.

She continued preparing dinner while fending off Tommy's questions, and she repeatedly went to the back and front doors to call KC.

On the way back from one of her checks, the phone rang. "Hello?"

"Ma'am. My name's Connor Jackson. I just moved here from Oklahoma. The long and the short of it, is I found a cat on the highway, and it had this number on the tag."

"Oh, my God. Is it KC? Does it have a tail?"

"A what?"

"A tail. Does it have a tail and what color is it?"

"No, ma'am. It's got no tail. And as far as color, I guess it's some kind of spotted."

"What does the tag say his name is? Does it say KC?"

"I don't know. I didn't pay attention to that. Let me look." There was a moment of silence, then, "Yes, ma'am. It has KC written on it. Just like you said."

"Thank you, sir. Let me give you my address. If you could bring him, I'll gladly give you a reward."

"Aw shoot, ma'am. I don't want no reward. I just want the cat to get back to you. But I won't know how to get to wherever you are. I just moved here from Oklahoma."

Justice did his best to imitate an Oklahoma accent. Okies talked slow. Slower than anyone Justice knew, stretching out words like they were bubble gum or talking with a mouth filled with jelly.

"How about Stuebner Airline Road? Do you know where that is?"

There was a long pause, then, "No ma'am, but I know where the mall is. I work by the mall. Are you close to it?"

"Do you mean Greenspoint Mall?"

"I guess. The one by that I-45 or something."

She laughed. "That's Greenspoint. Okay, good. I'm not far from there. I'll meet you in the parking lot behind the mall, across from the hotel in half an hour. How about that?"

"I think I can make that. What are you driving?"

"I'll be in a black Mitsubishi convertible, and I'll be standing outside of it waiting for you."

"Okay, see you in about half an hour. Make sure you're on time because I got to get to work."

Karen looked at her watch, wondering what kind of work he did if he had to start at this time. "I'm sorry to put you to this trouble, but don't worry, I'll be there."

"And tell KC we're coming to get him," Tommy yelled from behind her.

When the man didn't respond, she said, "Oh, and by the way, I'm about 5' 6" with brown hair pulled into a ponytail."

"Okay, see you then." He hung up the phone and smiled.

Don't worry. I know exactly what you look like.

Chapter Four

UNCLE DOMINIC

I sat at the kitchen table, staring out the living-room window. I was waiting on Tip to pick me up for work.

It wasn't often that I was ready and waiting before he started his incessant horn-beeping, but I couldn't sleep last night; the thought of what happened to Carlos Cortez still haunted me. It wasn't like I cared about him or that he died—it was how he died and who I thought had done it that bothered me.

I was almost sure it was Uncle Dominic—actually the men who worked for him. I wasn't positive, but I felt pretty damn sure; in fact, I had made up my mind that I was going to confront him about it, among other things.

I took another sip of espresso to calm my nerves. Espresso wasn't supposed to do that, but it always worked for me. I guessed it was my upbringing. Being served espresso since you were in kindergarten would do that.

Why am I nervous? He's the one who did wrong.

It was easy to reason that out, but a lot more difficult to make reason a reality. He might have done the wrong, but he probably didn't see it that way, so he wouldn't lose a minute of sleep worrying about it. I—on the other hand—hadn't done anything, but I felt embarrassed that he may be involved and that his actions would somehow taint me.

I glanced at my watch again, wondering where Tip was when my cell rang. "Tip? Is that you?"

"No, this is a serial killer using your partner's phone."

"Stop with the shit," Connie said.

"Then stop asking stupid questions. Anyway, I'm calling because I'm running late. I'll probably be another thirty minutes. Something's wrong with Sacco's back leg; in fact, I may have to take him with us and drop him off at the vet."

"No problem," I said. "I'll be here. Hey, wait a minute, I thought your vet was in the other direction, north of here."

"He is," Tip said. "But he's on vacation and won't be back for two days, so if I take Sacco in, I'll take him to my old vet."

"Okay. Got it," I said, then hung up the phone and got up to make more espresso. With thirty minutes on my hand, I decided I may as well get it over with and call Uncle Dominic. He was an hour ahead of me anyway.

"Pronto."

I almost froze, hung up, and went about my morning. But with the next breath, I found myself saying "Buon giorno, Zio Domenico."

"Concetta! How nice to hear your voice. How is my favorite person? And why are you calling your old uncle?"

I closed my eyes and sighed. I hated to confront him when he was being so nice. "Uncle Dominic, I have a question I need to ask and…"

"So ask."

"You might not like it so much after I ask."

"Concetta, remember the saying I taught you? The one I learned from my mother. 'You'll never know what's in the drawer until you open it.' The same holds true for questions; she was never talking about the drawer. We never had anything in drawers worth knowing about."

I laughed. "Okay, then. Here goes. Uncle Dominic, did you kill Carlos Cortes?"

"No. How could I do that? You know I was in New York."

I frowned. I forgot how crafty he was. "Let me rephrase it then. Did you have someone kill him?"

"Ah, now we're getting somewhere. I could plead the fifth, but I wouldn't do that with you, so I'll tell you. Yes, I did have him killed."

I gasped. "You can't say that. I'm a cop."

"But you asked. I'm not going to lie to you."

"Uncle Dominic, you can't do those things."

"But I did. He was going kill you. He had already tried to kill you twice, and he tried to kill your partner. The man deserved to die."

"That's not for you to decide."

Dominic sighed. "Concetta, if someone attempts to break into your house, would you shoot them?"

"Probably."

"What I did is the same. He was trying to hurt you, so I had him killed. He wasn't going to stop until one of you was dead. In that situation, I chose you."

"But you can't do that."

"I don't think you understand. I did do that. And I will continue doing it. And no one is going to stop me."

"Uncle Dominic, there are laws."

"My dear Concetta. There are a lot of laws prohibiting a lot of things. That glass of wine you probably had with your dinner last night would have been against the law at one time. And gambling is still against the law in most places, yet the government sells lottery tickets at almost every corner store and gas station. There are hundreds of other things against the law, but that doesn't mean they are wrong; it just means that the people in power have not found a way to make money from those things yet. You wait, though, when they do, the laws will change."

"Uncle Dominic, you're cynical."

"No, Concetta, I'm a realist. Keep your eyes open, and you'll see. Most crimes involve greed or sex or power. But if it's only a crime technically, then someone might be acting out of good will."

"What the hell are you talking about?"

A pause ensued. "Imagine three cars are stolen. One was for the purpose of stripping it down to sell the parts; one was for some kids to have a joy ride; and the other was because a parent's child was hurt, and they needed to get that child to the hospital right away."

I heard him sipping espresso. "But they all stole a car," I said.

"My point exactly. Technically they are all guilty of the same act, but when circumstances are taken into consideration, there is quite a difference. The first two examples are not excuses, but the third is —a child's life was at stake."

"Some people don't see the difference; they're all against the law."

"Then I feel sorry for those people. What a pitiful life they live. A man—or a woman—should be judged by their intent."

"That's not the way the law works, Uncle Dominic. We can't live by your rules."

"That's a shame. I live that way, and I won't live any other way. I know I've told you this before, Concetta. But in the village where I grew up, if a man stole food to feed his family, he was forgiven, provided with more food, and sent on his way. If he stole for greed, he was exiled, never to return."

"All right, enough of this, Uncle Dominic. I have another question."

"Ah, another drawer to open. Go ahead, then."

"Are you my father?"

Dominic laughed. "Where did that come from? No, I'm not your father."

"And you're not lying?"

"Concetta, I just admitted to you that I had a man killed rather than lie to you. Why would I lie about this?"

"I don't know. Some things don't add up. And Carlos said—"

"Ah, Carlos said. Now we get to the heart of the matter. You would believe Carlos instead of me?"

I was quick to respond. "It's not that, Uncle Dominic. It's that there are questions, things that don't add up. I looked into this before, and I couldn't find any record of Mom giving birth. Not anywhere. Not any of the local hospitals or churches. And nobody knew my father. The only people they remember are Mom and you."

Dominic laughed. "Concetta, the world was a different place back then. We had advanced in some respects, yes, but in other ways, no. In the community where you were born, many women still gave birth at home, attended to by a nursemaid. As long as there weren't complications, all was well."

"And that's what happened with me?" I asked.

"I wasn't there when you were born, but I was shortly afterward, and you were safe and sound in your room; in fact, your father was there with you."

"So you're not my father?"

"No, Concetta. I wish I were. I love you like a father, but I'm not you're father."

"And you said my father died from a drug overdose?"

"I don't know exactly what caused his death, but I suspect he died as a result of complications associated with drug abuse, although I can't be sure."

"Uncle Dominic, it's not like you to not be certain about something."

"That's the way life is sometimes, Concetta. Now, get yourself another cup of espresso and thank God you're alive."

I smiled. "Okay, Uncle Dominic. Thanks for talking."

"Prego," he said. "And don't forget to call your uncle more often, and don't forget to keep opening drawers."

That made me laugh. "Deal," I said. "Ciao."

"Ciao," Dominic said. "Ti voglio bene."

"I love you, too, Uncle Dominic," I said, and hung up the phone.

LOOKING FOR A CAT?

Justice sat in the van toward the back of the parking lot. The cat sat in his lap as he stroked its head and back.

Justice waited about twenty minutes, then put the car in gear and drove to where he was supposed to meet Karen. He placed KC into a small cat carrier, put it on the back seat, then drove off. She should be there by now.

Sure enough, as he rounded the corner at the mall, he saw her standing outside her car, leaning against the hood. Little Tommy stood alongside her.

Justice pulled beside her car, making sure to tug his mask down so she couldn't see him. At the same time, he pushed the button and opened the side door that faced them, displaying KC in a small cat cage.

"KC!" Tommy yelled, and raced for the open door of the van, climbing inside when he reached it.

Karen ran to grab her son. "Tommy! Get out of that car. You have no business..."

She never got to finish her statement. Justice placed a cloth which had been soaked in chloroform over her mouth and held it tightly.

She struggled a little, but not much, although Justice had to keep the cloth applied firmly, covering her mouth and nostrils for several moments. It was not like in the movies, where a few seconds would do.

By the time Karen succumbed, Tommy had exited the van holding the cat. "Mom, look," he said, then must have seen her slumped in Justice's grip. "Mom! Hey, mister, what are you doing to my mom?" he said while setting down the cat carrier.

Justice opened the door to Karen's car and set her inside. All the while, Tommy was pounding on his back and yelling.

He turned, grabbed Tommy by the collar and shoved him into the van. "Take care of the cat," he said, then climbed behind the steering wheel and removed his mask.

"What are you doing? Where's my mom?" Tommy yelled.

"Not to worry, boy. You'll only miss her for a few days. Then it will be all right. Besides, KC will be with us."

"Where are we going? Where's my mom?"

"I can't tell you where we're going, but your mom will be fine. She's going to wake up in a few minutes, and she'll be as good as new. Just sit back and relax. Enjoy KC."

About thirty minutes later, Justice pulled off the freeway, concerned at first that Tommy might know where he was going, but then Justice realized it would make no difference. Tommy would never be able to tell anyone even if he did recognize where he was.

After exiting the freeway, he turned right onto a small, two-lane road and followed it until it stopped at a dead end. He continued, driving down an unpaved section, then turned the van into an old barn, hit a button, which opened up a hidden compartment underneath, and then parked the van so it was out of sight.

Not many houses in Texas had rooms under the ground, but Justice had this built special with the money he had gotten from selling his mama's place.

He placed the car in "Park," then got out and opened the side door for Tommy and KC. "Get the cat," he said.

Tommy grabbed the handle of the carrier and, through tears, said, "Where's Mom? Is she coming?"

Justice put his hand on Tommy's shoulder and patted his back. "Not yet, Tommy. Not yet. But there will be plenty to do. Just come with me."

He walked down a dark corridor, then through a door that had light shining from under it. When he opened the door, they were greeted with a rousing cheer from three kids about Tommy's age—two boys and a girl. Barks could be heard coming from the rear of the room, followed by two young dogs racing into the room. A kitten leaped at Tommy from atop a sofa.

Tommy laughed when the dogs knocked him over and licked his face. "What the heck?" he said.

Justice leaned down and picked him up, shooing away the dogs. "Leave him alone," he said. "You were too rough."

Justice brushed Tommy's clothes off, straightened his shirt, then offered him a comb. "Fix your hair," he said. "Those dogs messed it up."

For the next two hours, the other kids and Tommy joined Justice in playing games at a table set up in the corner of the room. They played Chutes and Ladders, Find the Rabbit, and a favorite of Tommy's called Pass the Pigs.

After they were done, Tommy sat on the couch and petted KC's head. Justice sat next to them and rubbed KC's back. "I think he likes it here," Justice said. "Do you?"

Tommy nodded. "I guess. But I'd like it more if Mom was here."

"There's time enough to worry about that," Justice said. "For now, just have fun."

Chapter Six

WE'VE GOT A CASE

The tires of Tip's car screeched as he turned the corner and pulled to the curb. Before he had a chance to beep the horn, Connie walked out the front door.

"About time you got here, cowboy. I could have walked to work by now."

"You should've done that. I wouldn't have stopped you."

She opened the passenger door and slid into the seat. "Screw you, Denton. Just be on time from now on."

Connie turned her head and glanced to the back seat. "I see Sacco's not here. Was he better?"

"I'm not sure about better, but slightly improved," Tip said. "He was able to walk outside and do his business. He limped a little but not much. I figure if he's still limping tomorrow, I'll take him in."

"What brought it on?"

"I don't know. Might have stepped in a hole and sprained it. Or it could have happened jumping a fence. That damn dog is forever jumping."

"Hopefully, he'll show more improvement tonight," Connie said. "In the meantime, let's see if we can catch a case. I'm tired of loafing."

"We could always go out and kill somebody," Tip said. "I know some good prospects."

Connie laughed again. "Tip, maybe we should wait for a real case to come in. I'm sure some nut will drop a body before long."

"If you say so," Tip said.

Twenty-five minutes later, they walked into the station. Orange-haired Julie, who used to be purple-haired Julie, met them at the top of the stairs. "Where in God's name have you been? Captain Cooper is looking everywhere for you."

"Sounds like I'm gonna need more coffee," Tip said. "Better get workin' on it."

Connie and Tip walked to the end of the hall, where Cindy showed them into Coop's office. "Good morning, Captain," Connie said.

"Damn I hate your cheerful morning voice," Coop said. "I'd almost prefer that piece of shit partner's dreary good morning."

"Really?" Connie asked.

"I said *almost*. I'm not an idiot. Yet."

Tip frowned and plopped into one of the chairs opposite her desk. "And a happy 'shit in your hat' to you too, Gladys."

Connie sat in the chair beside Tip and crossed her legs. "What's up, Cap?"

" 'What's up' is we've got a case, and I need quick action on it."

"Who got killed?" Tip asked.

"Nobody got killed yet. At least that we know of, but a young boy is missing, kidnapped from his mother in the parking lot of the mall."

"Which mall?" Connie asked.

"Greenspoint, from the parking lot across from the hotel."

"Gunspoint? Should've known," Tip said. "Nothing good's happened at that mall since it opened—unless you want to count the carnivals that go there about every week."

"I need you to find this boy and find him before the press picks up on it. We don't need them involved. And you know how the press is, if they smell the opportunity to yank a tear out of someone, they'll milk it. So find this kid before they get wind of the story."

"Any ransom notes?" Tip asked.

Coop shook her head. "Not yet anyway."

"Parents divorced or together?" Connie asked.

"Divorced," Coop said. "I put Julie on it this morning, and from what she told me, the ex-husband is living in Corpus. And the divorce was not pleasant."

"We'll have to push that end," Connie said. "You know how it goes with divorced cases."

"Yeah, I know," Coop said. "But I don't see this one falling on that side of the fence. According to the mother, whoever snatched the kid had previously taken the boy's cat, then he arranged to meet her at the mall. He arrived wearing a mask and chloroformed her, then took the kid."

"Chloroformed her?" Connie asked. "You're right. Doesn't sound like an ex to me."

Tip chewed on a toothpick and rolled it around in his mouth. "Captain, when did this happen?"

"Last night, and yes I know that doesn't rule out a ransom call, but it makes it unlikely."

"I agree," Connie said. "We'll interview the mom and let you know when we finish."

"See Julie when you leave here. She'll give you the address and all the other particulars. Then get your asses on top of it. Like I said, I want this done quickly."

Connie got the information from Julie, then she and Tip headed out. "Don't think I'm riding with you," Connie said. "The lady lives in the north part of town, so I can go home straight from there." She handed Tip a slip of paper with the address written on it. "I copied this for you. See you there."

"Did you forget you rode in with me?" Tip asked.

Connie laughed. "Oh, shit. I guess I did. Then take me to get my car, so I can drive."

"Where's the lady live?" Tip asked.

"By FM 1960 and Steubner-Airline, not far from Bammel-North Houston."

"Not the best neighborhood," Tip said. "It's not the Fourth Ward, but it's not Champions either."

"We all can't be born with a silver spoon stuck up our ass," Connie said.

"The world would be a pretty sad place if we were," Tip said. "Anyway, I'll take you to get your car, then see you there."

Tip arrived on the scene before Connie, so he sat in the car and waited. It wasn't the worst neighborhood, but it wouldn't win any awards either.

Connie pulled up and got out of her car. Tip met her curbside. "Ready?"

"Always ready. Let's find out who took this kid."

"Let's do it then," Tip said, and he started toward the door.

WHERE'S THE KID?

Tip was about to knock on the door when I stepped in front of him. "Let me," I said. "The lady's just had her child taken. She might feel more comfortable talking to a woman."

Tip shrugged. "Go ahead. Whatever works best."

I knocked on the door, which was answered a moment later by a slender-looking woman who appeared to be about my age. She wore jeans and a beat-up flannel shirt and had her hair tied in a bun.

"Ma'am, I'm Detective Connie Gianelli, and this is my partner, Detective Tip Denton. We understand that your child is missing."

"Oh my God, yes. Come in."

She sat in a recliner alongside the sofa and gestured for Tip and me to have a seat on the couch, but she stood before we sat. "I don't know where my manners are," she said, extending her hand. "My name is Karen Hendricks. Do either of you want something to drink? Water, coffee, iced-tea?"

"I'm fine," I said, and Tip echoed that. "Just sit, ma'am. We need to ask a few questions."

"Of course," she said, and sat in the chair, hands folded in her lap. "What do you need to know?"

"Why don't you start off by telling us your son's name, how old he is, and anything else you can think of that would help identify him."

"Tommy's seven years old. He's got brown hair and blue eyes, and he's normal as all get out. He plays video games, watches super heroes, and loves his cat KC."

Karen got more animated then, raising her hands and waving them. "Oh my God, that's another thing. His cat KC was taken too. The guy had him. He had him in a van. That's how he got me to the mall, telling me he had the cat."

I reached forward and placed my hand on her arm, to try and calm her. "Okay, ma'am. Why don't you start from the beginning? When did you first notice that Tommy or the cat were missing?"

Karen took a swallow, then reached for a can of Coke she had on the table and took a sip. "I had gone grocery shopping, and I stopped to pick up clothes at the cleaners. When I got home, I went to feed KC and couldn't find him. I asked Tommy if he'd seen him, and he said no. I called a couple of neighbors, and they said they hadn't seen him either. It's not like they wouldn't notice. KC is a Manx cat, so it has no tail. It's harder to miss."

She took another swig of Coke, licked her lips to wet them, then continued. "Anyway, about two hours later, someone called. I—"

"What time was this?" I asked.

Karen seemed to think for a moment, then said, "About seven. I'm pretty sure it was about seven o'clock."

I made note of the time in the unlikely event the phone company could tell us anything about the call, though I felt sure that it would have been from a burner phone and it was likely untraceable. "And what happened next?"

"A man was on the phone. He said his name was Connor Jackson. I remember that because I have a cousin named Connor and it's not a common name." Karen took another sip of Coke.

"Anyway, he told me he'd found a cat and gotten our number from the collar. When I asked if it was KC and if it had a tail, he said that it didn't have a tail, and when he checked the collar, he said it had KC etched on it."

"What else?" I asked.

"He said he could meet me at the mall. Oh, and he said he was new in town, that he'd just come here from Oklahoma. He sounded like it too."

Tip leaned forward. "What happened after he asked to meet? Did you call anyone or just go meet him?"

"I just went to meet him," Karen said. "I didn't have much time. And he sounded okay. Besides, he had KC."

"Did you recognize his voice or his accent at all?" Tip asked.

She shook her head. "Definitely not the voice. He said he was from Oklahoma, and from what I remember about that accent, it sounded right. Either way, it was a slow, long drawl. Very pronounced."

"Then what happened?" I asked.

"I went to the mall and waited in the parking lot, like I said I would. A few minutes after I got there, he showed up."

"What was he driving?" Tip asked.

"A van. I'm not good with cars, but I think it was maybe five or six years old. And it was green. I know that much."

"What color green?" I asked. "Was it a light green? Dark?"

"Dark green," Karen said. "Definitely dark. It almost looked black. And it was dirty. Like it had dust all over it."

"Go on," Tip said.

Karen thought a moment, then said, "He got out of his van, then he said he had the cat and started walking toward the back of the van. When he did that, the side door opened. Then he..."

She shook her head. "I should've seen something. He reached into his pants pocket and pulled something out. The next thing I knew, he was holding something over my mouth, covering it with some kind of chemical. Chloroform, I'm guessing."

I sat on the edge of the sofa. "Chloroform? You're sure?"

"No, I'm not sure, but I think so. It smelled like raw alcohol or something like that."

I looked to Tip. "We may be able to trace that. There can't be too many places that sell chloroform."

Tip made a few notes in his book. "Got it. We'll check on it."

"Anyway," Karen said, "In a minute or two, I passed out, and when I woke up, he was gone." Karen started crying, her hands covering her eyes. "And so was Tommy. It was the last I saw of him."

"Have you heard from the man since?" I asked.

She shook her head. "Nothing. And I've been by the phone the whole time, and my cell has been with me."

"How about your husband, or ex-husband?" I asked. "Where is he?"

She shook her head. "He lives in Corpus Christi. He's been out of the picture since Tommy was four. And no, there's no way Vince could have done this. He wouldn't."

"Vince?" Tip asked.

"Yes. Vince Hendricks. I kept his name." Karen pursed her lips. "He isn't a bad guy; he was just a bad father and an unfaithful husband. But he would never do something like this."

"You're sure?" I asked. "What was his relationship with Tommy? Were they close?"

"No. Even when Vince lived at home, he was more interested in chasing skirts than anything. I finally had enough of it, so we got a divorce."

"How did the divorce go? Were things civil?"

Karen looked over to me. "Very civil. And he's been good since. Child-support payments arrive every month, on time. And he calls once a week to talk with Tommy." She started crying again. "Or at least, he did."

"What did they talk about?" Tip asked.

"Everything. Homework. Baseball. Video games. Vince could have been a good father if he tried. He's been better after the divorce than before."

"Anyone else you can think of who would want to harm Tommy, or who has a grudge against you?"

"Nobody. No one would have a reason to."

"And you've had no ransom request?"

"None," Karen said. "I already said that."

"Ms. Hendricks, even if the person instructed you not to tell the police, you have to do it if you want Tommy back safely. We can help."

Hendricks squeezed her hands as if wringing them dry. "I know that. If someone had called, I would have told you. I'm not an idiot."

I grabbed her arm. "Ms. Hendricks, we don't think you're an idiot. We just wanted to make sure. Some people are intimidated when facing a situation like this. We were just checking."

"I understand, but no need to check further. No one called."

"Anything else you can tell us?"

"He smelled."

"What?"

"The man. He smelled like KC must have peed on him."

"Peed on him? Are you sure?"

"I should know. I've smelled it enough. If you want to know what it smells like, whiff the chair by the kitchen."

Tip stood. "Ms. Hendricks, we're gonna get your son back. Don't worry about that. You sit tight and tell us if anything happens. Anything."

Karen stood and walked toward the door. "I'll let you know about things on my end, but you keep me informed too. And I mean about everything."

"Will do, ma'am," I said. "We should be in touch in a few days whether we have something or not."

"Okay, thank you," Karen said, and swung the door wide.

As Tip opened his car door to get in, he turned to me. "Come on up to the house. We'll eat something and maybe drink something and figure all this out."

"I've got a few things to do, but I'll be up afterward. Probably around seven."

"See you then," Tip said.

ELENA RETURNS

I got to Tip's house a little before seven. Another car was already in the driveway. As I wondered whose it was, recognition hit me—it was Mollie's. It had been a while since I'd seen Mollie, or should I say *heard* her. Mollie was one of those people who never shut up, even if you asked her to.

I walked in the back door, said hello to Sacco, placated Flash with pets so she would stop her snarling, then headed to the kitchen to sit at the table.

Mollie was at the counter, preparing the condiments for fajitas.

"You need help with that, Mollie?"

She scooped some guacamole into a small dish and diced tomatoes into a small bowl sitting next to it. "I'm good, baby doll. But thanks."

"Let me know if I can do anything, Mollie."

"Baby doll, the day I can't handle fixin' a few fajitas is the day I quit. So you sit there and enjoy your beer and figure out how you and that no-good partner of yours will solve whatever crime it is you're workin' on."

"Who said we're workin' on a crime?"

"Ha. I might be stupid but I ain't dumb. You don't come up here unless you two are workin' on solving something. So go on about your business and get done whatever you need to get done. I won't bother you."

"You're a character, Mollie."

"I've been told that once or twice, so tell me something I don't know." She returned to removing the meat from the container where it had been marinating and then sliced it very thin. "Beginning to think that the only reason Tip invites me up here is to get my help. The Lord knows he needs it."

I smiled but hid it from Mollie. "I'm sure Tip will fill you in when he feels the need to. In the meantime, I'm bound by secrecy. I can't say anything."

Mollie kept working. "All right by me. If that fool wants to pretend I didn't help him solve the last two cases, that's up to him. But if he hopes to solve any more cases, he better ask for help."

Mollie finished chopping an onion, put it in a small bowl, then said, "So what are ya workin' on? Who's gone and gotten killed now?"

I grinned. "Nice try, Mollie. But I still can't say anything. You'll have to ask Tip."

"Ask Tip what?" Tip said as he walked in from the other room.

"Mollie wants to know what we're working on," I said.

"Well shoot, I'm workin' on gettin' a cold beer," Tip said. "I don't know about you."

"Fine by me," Mollie said. "If you don't want my help ..."

Tip sat in a chair across from me. "We got a young kid missing, Mollie. A little boy about seven years old."

"One of the parents?" Mollie asked.

"We don't think so," Tip said.

"Just one kid missing?"

"So far," Tip said. "I hope it stays that way."

"When did it happen?"

"Just yesterday," I said. "And no, no one has asked for ransom money. So we think it's sex motivated or a pervert of some kind. Nothing to indicate the boy's mother is a target."

"Either way. I intend to find the son of a bitch responsible for this. And when I find him, I'll make him pay," Tip said. "Trust me."

"All right. In the meantime, I hope you're hungry, because I got a lot of fajitas here, and I hate to waste food."

"Serve 'em up, darlin'. I'm hungry."

"Keep your trousers on. They take a minute to cook."

"Tip, Sacco still doesn't look good. He didn't even get up to greet me. Not that he's animated, like Flash, but he usually gets up."

"Yeah, I know," Tip said. "I might have to take him in tomorrow."

The front door opened, and Tip leaned to the side to see who it was.

A few seconds later, Elena walked through the dining room and into the kitchen. "Hello, Tip. I missed you."

"Elena! What the hell are you doing home? I wasn't expecting you."

She laughed. "The best kind of surprise is a real surprise, the kind you're not expecting." After she said that, Elena walked across the room and into Tip's arms. "I've missed you," she said. "It's been too long."

Tip squeezed her hard and kissed her. "About time you got home. I half missed you."

Elena smacked him, then pulled out a chair and sat next to Connie. "Connie, have you been keeping him in line while I was gone?"

"Trying," I said. "But you know how difficult it is. Besides all the women he chased, there were—"

Elena yanked on Tip's arm and pulled him to her. "Women chasing, huh? That may eliminate what I had in mind for the night's activities."

Tip sat on her lap, then leaned over and kissed her. "And they were pretty girls too. Not ugly ones like you."

Mollie looked over while shaking her head. "You gonna put up with talk like that from him? I'd teach him a thing or two if I were you. Get up and leave, that'll teach him. Ain't no decent woman who'd have him." She plopped a bowl of salsa on the table alongside a bag of chips. "That's what I'd do," she said.

Elena looked into Tip's eyes and smiled. "Hear that? I might have to hire Mollie as an advisor."

"Might as well hire a rattlesnake," Tip said. "It'd be nicer and not as venomous."

"Huh. Might be nicer if it was cooked up nice. Fried dark brown with some jalapeños and onions."

Tip shook his head vigorously. "There you go again, reverting to your roots. There's nobody in the world who would give you a plug nickel for a rattlesnake, that is except the restaurant in that redneck town you came from."

Mollie threw the fajita meat into the frying pan and started cooking. "There you go again, runnin' your mouth when it don't know what it's talkin' about. I got half a mind to cook you up some rattlesnake, then wait for you to tell me how good it was before I tell you what you ate." She shook the pan and shifted the meat to one side. "Got half a mind to do it," she mumbled.

"I think you should," Elena said, hiding an obvious smile. "Just don't do it when I'm here."

"Speaking of rattlesnakes," I said. "Who do you think took this kid, Tip? What kind of scum snatches a little boy?"

"We can check on the ex," Tip said, "But I don't think he was involved. We need to make sure there aren't any suspicious boyfriends, and we need to canvass the neighbors too."

"And check phone records, especially around the time she said he called. See what other numbers have been called. And look for dark-green vans."

"And people who smell like pee," Tip said.

I laughed. "Yeah, let's not forget that." Then I thought of something else. "And the cat. We can't forget the cat. I've never heard of a kidnapper who took animals. What do you think that's all about?"

Tip cocked his head to the side. "Not sure. I guess we'll have to give that some thought—or wait for the cat to show up dead and see if we get any clues."

"I guess so," I said. "Or wait for the kid to show up."

Tip lost his smile. "Yeah. Or that. I was thinkin' the same thing, just didn't want to say it."

Mollie plopped a plate of sizzling fajitas near the center of the table, then surrounded it with all the fixings: guacamole, onions, sour cream, diced tomatoes, shredded lettuce, and jalapeños. Then she brought a plate of hot tortillas. "Eat your fill," she said. "Plenty for everyone."

"Sit down, Mollie. Join us," I said.

"Not me. I gotta get home and clean. Besides, I don't like hearin' about no missing kids anyway. Gives me the shivers."

"I'm with you on that, Mollie. I didn't come all the way from Paris to hear about kids who've been taken."

"Well, shoot, Connie. I guess you went and ruined the night with your big mouth."

"Me? You're the one who started it."

Tip finished wrapping his fajitas in a tortilla before taking a bite. "Just like you New Yorkers to blame an innocent man," he said.

Mollie grabbed her purse, hung it from her forearm, then headed for the door. "You two can stay and listen to his nonsense all night if you want, but I'm goin' home."

"All right, Mollie. See ya," I said.

"Call me if you need me," Mollie said as she closed the door.

Chapter Nine

WHO TOOK THE CAT?

Tip picked me up as usual, and we headed straight for Ms. Hendricks' neighborhood. "Might as well get an early start on it," Tip said. "We're probably gonna miss half of the people anyway."

We knocked on the door of Ms. Hendricks' neighbor to the left and waited for a response. Before long, a heavy-set Hispanic woman answered.

I showed my badge and said, "I'm Detective Connie Gianclli, and this is my partner, Tip Denton. Do you have a minute?"

There was a long pause before she said, "What is this about?"

"It's not about you or any of your family," Tip said. "A little boy was kidnapped, and we want to know if you saw anything."

She raised a hand to cover her mouth and said, Dios mío. Who?"

Tip pointed to the house next door and said, "The Hendricks' boy. Two nights ago."

She blessed herself quickly, then invited us inside. "I'm sorry I wasn't so friendly at first," she said.

She extended her hand and said, "My name is Yessenia Rosario. I was hesitant to talk because my daughter is dating a man who is in the country without papers. He plans on getting them, but he doesn't have them yet."

I smiled. "Thank you for saying that, ma'am, but we don't care about anyone's immigration status. We're only here about the kidnapped youngster."

"Would you like coffee? Or tea?" she asked.

"No thanks," Tip said. "If you could tell us what you saw two nights ago. Was there anything unusual? Or did you see anyone different?"

Ms. Rosario leaned back into a cushiony chair and said, "It was raining that night. I remember that. And I remember seeing a van parked across the street."

Tip perked up. "A van? What kind of van?"

"I don't know who made it, but it was a dark-green van, and it had letters on the side. An electric company."

She rose from the chair and started toward the kitchen. "Wait here. I wrote the name down because I need an electrician to fix some things."

Ms. Rosario returned a moment later and handed me a slip of paper. "There is the name and number that was on the van."

I looked at the note.

Clausen Electric. (281) 654-5555.

"This will help a lot," I said as I put the note away. "Anything else you remember? Was there anyone in the van?"

"There was a young man sitting behind the wheel, but I figured he was waiting for the rain to stop. He wasn't doing anything."

"Where was he parked?" Tip asked.

She walked to the window and pointed across the street. "Right there, in front of the Campbell's house, the one with green shutters."

"Did he ever get out of the van?" Tip asked.

Ms. Rosario shook her head. "If he did, I didn't see him, and I look out that window a lot. I didn't see Tommy either. He's usually outside playing, almost like he doesn't have a mother, but I didn't see him that night."

"What do you mean by that?" I asked.

"Like I said, he's always out on his own. His mother seldom even checks on him." She lowered her head and shook it. "I shouldn't say anything. I guess a lot of the younger mothers are like that. When I raised my kids, they never left my sight."

"Same with me," Connie said. "I was lucky to even get outside to play. My mother watched me like a hawk."

"The way it should be," Ms. Rosario said. "Anyway, you should talk to the Campbells. Maybe they saw something else or got a better look at the van."

We talked to two more neighbors—who saw nothing—before knocking on the Campbell's door.

A man answered, wearing a pair of faded jeans and a white T-shit. "Mr. Campbell?" I asked.

"That's me. What do you want and who's askin'?"

Tip pulled out his badge. "I'm Detective Tip Denton, and this is my partner, Detective Connie Gianelli. We're here about a kidnapping that happened the other night."

Mr. Campbell seemed to perk up. "Oh, you mean little Tommy. I heard about that." He swung the door open wide and stepped aside, then said, "Come on in."

"Does anything strike you as having been unusual that night?" I asked.

He seemed to think for a moment, then said, "I've been thinking about this ever since I heard about it, and the only thing that comes to mind is that there was a van parked in front of my house for probably half an hour or more, a green van, and it had writing on the side, but for the life of me, I can't remember what it said."

"Can you describe the van any better?" Tp asked.

"I'm not sure, but I think it was a Chrysler, and like I said, it had a sign on the side panel. Hang on. It's coming to me now ... something Electric. It was a name, a person's name."

"Do you remember the name?" I asked.

He thought for a minute, then said Clawson, that's it. No, wait a minute, it was Clausen, Clausen Electric."

"You're sure?"

He scribbled something on a notepad, looked at it, then said, "Yeah, now I am. Now that I look at it."

"Ever heard that name before. Or do you know anyone around here who was having electric work done?"

"Never saw the name. And I know my neighbors on either side of me weren't having work done, and if it was anyone else, why'd he park here? Why not in front of their house?"

Tip wrote something down. "Good question."

"I was gonna ask him myself, but it was raining so damn hard that I was waiting for it to stop before going out. Once it did stop, the van was gone."

"You think it could have been somebody who just pulled over to wait out the rain?" I asked.

Campbell shook his head. "I don't think so. You can't tell, but I don't think so."

We talked to two more people, neither of whom saw the van or anything suspicious. Afterward, we got in the car to leave. "What do you think?" I asked.

Tip slid behind the steering wheel. "I think whoever was in that van, snatched the cat, then used the cat to lure the mother and kid to the mall. That's what I think."

"Where's the cat?" I asked.

"I hope it's with the kid," Tip said, "And I hope they're both still alive."

"Hang on a minute," I said. "I'm going to call that electrician's number." She dialed her phone and listened to a message that said the number wasn't in order. "Tip, what was that number again?"

"What number, the electrician's?"

"Yeah, the one Ms. Rosario gave us."

Tip pulled his notebook out and handed it to me. "Look it up. You know you should take better notes."

I flipped through his pages until I came to it: (281) 654-5555, then I checked the 'recently dialed' list on my phone. "Same damn number. It's fake."

"At least now we know we've got the vehicle pegged," Tip said.

"Ms. Kendricks didn't say anything about a sign on the van. We need to ask her about that."

FUN WITH THE KIDS

Justice parked the car, got out and went inside. Once situated, he walked to his bedroom, opened the closet door, then accessed the secret door near the back, the one he'd had built special when he constructed the house.

He turned on the light, then walked down the stairs. "I'm home," he said, and waited, but heard nothing. "I'm home," he shouted again.

With no response, he walked slower, moving to the large bedroom built into the corner. He used his key to open the door, then stepped inside.

Four young children sat on a long sofa watching TV. "What? No hellos?" he asked.

"Hey," one said, without looking.

"I'm hungry," said another one.

"Me too. And thirsty," said a third.

The fourth didn't speak. Justice walked over to him and placed his hand on the boy's shoulder. "What's the matter, Sean?"

The boy shrugged off his touch. "My name's Tommy. And I want to go home."

Justice tousled his hair. "Don't worry. It takes a week or so to get used to something new, but before long, you'll think of this as home."

"Never," Tommy said. "I want my mom."

"Your mom isn't coming. She doesn't care about you. Besides, you've got KC. Remember him? He's the one who cares. He's the one who never left you alone."

"He left for a whole week," Tommy said.

"That wasn't his fault," Justice said. "That was your mother's fault. The cat wouldn't have run away if it had been taken care of."

"She fed him," Tommy cried in defense.

"There's a lot more to caring than feeding someone," Justice said. "You'll see."

Justice walked over, turned off the TV, then sat in a big chair facing the kids. "Let's play a game," he said. "I'm going to make a noise, and you see if you can guess which animal I am."

"Yeah," one of the boys said. "I love this game."

Justice pretended to be a dog, a cat, a cow, a chicken, and anything else he could mimic the sound of. It began with only one of the kids partaking, but by the time he was halfway through, they all had joined in, even Tommy.

When he ran out of animal options, he did a few other sounds, like a train whistle or the horn of a car, and when he finished with that, he said he'd go upstairs and make his own brand of Play-Doh, which the kids all loved.

About fifteen minutes later, he brought down a huge bowl of self-made Play-Doh and plastic containers to store it in. Along with it was a bag filled with small plastic animals—farm animals, jungle animals, even dinosaurs.

Soon, the kids were building castles, making swamps and mountains, and using fake trees to create forests. Shortly after that, they were pretending that the baby animals were stuck in the swamps, or lost in the woods, or trapped on a remote mountain pass.

Through it all, Justice played along with them, mimicking the pleading cries of the baby animals calling for help.

The play lasted for almost two hours, after which, Justice said he had to leave. "I've got to get up early," he said.

"Not yet," one of the kids yelled.

"Stay for a while," another said.

Justice had already stood to leave. He placed his hands on his hips and said, "It's up to Sean. If he wants me to play, I will."

"Come on, Sean. Please?"

Tommy had a frown on his face, but it quickly disappeared. "My name's Tommy. But okay." He turned to Justice and said, "Will you play some more?"

Justice stared for a moment as if considering, then said, "Okay. Hang on, and I'll get some Legos."

Then he walked across the room, opened a cabinet, and took out a large bag of Legos, enough for them all to play.

Within fifteen minutes, all the kids were building houses and castles and bridges over their make-believe swamps, complete with animals crossing them. Before long, wars broke out.

Justice played with them long into the night, until they were almost falling asleep while playing, then he said it was time to quit.

"Before we go to bed, we need to read a good-night story," he said, and he sat on the sofa and opened up the book. "This is the Good Book," he said. "My mama used to read it to me."

The kids gathered around, taking places on the floor and in chairs surrounding the sofa. After a couple of stories, the yawns started, and they soon spread around the room.

Justice finished reading, then shut the book and put it aside. He stretched and stood. "Guess it's time for bed," he said. "I'll see everyone tomorrow bright and early. And in the meantime, don't forget—do unto others as others do to you."

"I don't think that's how it goes," Sean said.

Justice turned to look at him. "Why do you say that?"

"My mother told me. She said it was—"

"How old is your mother, Sean?"

Sean shrugged. "I don't know, about forty."

Justice smiled. "My mama was almost twice as old when she died, and she told me what the Good Words were. She said they came straight out of the Good Book. I reckon that's good enough for me."

Sean nodded. "Sorry, Mr. Justice."

"No problem," Justice said. "Now let's get this place cleaned up before bedtime."

The kids helped put the toys away, then climbed into their beds. He covered them up, turned off the light, then went back up the stairs.

It had been a fun night. Sean even said he had fun.

Chapter Eleven

SACCO GOES TO THE VET

I got a call while I was sipping my first cup of espresso. "Yeah, Tip? What do you need?"

"How'd you know it was me?"

"Because no normal human calls someone this early."

"I called to tell you I wouldn't be driving today. I've got to take Sacco to the vet. And Umlang's back, so I need to drive him to Conroe."

"I figured as much. No change in his leg?"

"None. If anything, it's worse this morning. He can barely get up. I had to help him outside."

"Okay. Good luck. Let me know what the vet says. And don't worry. I'll get started on the case."

"Thanks, Connie."

"Hey, wait a minute. This isn't some ruse because Elena is back is it?"

"Damn, I wish. If I'd have thought about that, I'd have done it."

I laughed. "Okay, see ya later. Give Sacco a pet for me."

Tip helped Sacco into the car, then made the drive to Dr. Umlang's clinic so he could look at Sacco. By the time he got there—half an hour later—the dog couldn't get out of the car.

Tip picked him up and carried him in. The receptionist was behind the desk. "Betty, I'm gonna need a room for him. He can't even stand."

She got up from her chair and rushed down a hallway, pointing ahead to an open door. "In there. Set him on the larger table. I'll tell Dr. Umlang you're here."

Five minutes later, Umlang walked in followed by a tall, thin, young man who looked to be in his mid-twenties.

Umlang reached over and rubbed the hind leg. "This the one?" he asked.

Tip nodded. "He was just limping last week. Now he can't even walk."

The assistant moved closer and began rubbing Sacco's back leg gently. At first, the dog flinched as if he felt pain, but then he calmed down and lay still.

Tip was about to say something when Dr. Umlang spoke. "Tip, this is my new assistant, Spoons."

Tip turned to him and extended his hand to shake. "Spoons?"

The assistant smiled. "Yeah. I know. And I've already heard all the utensil jokes—like stick him with a fork, he looks done, or he's not the sharpest knife in the drawer—but feel free to use them. I don't mind."

Tip moved aside, and Spoons stepped closer. He massaged the back leg and leaned in to kiss the dog. When he did so, he whispered, "It's gonna be all right, boy. Don't worry."

Spoons continued massaging the area, then turned to face Tip again. "I think he might have torn a tendon.

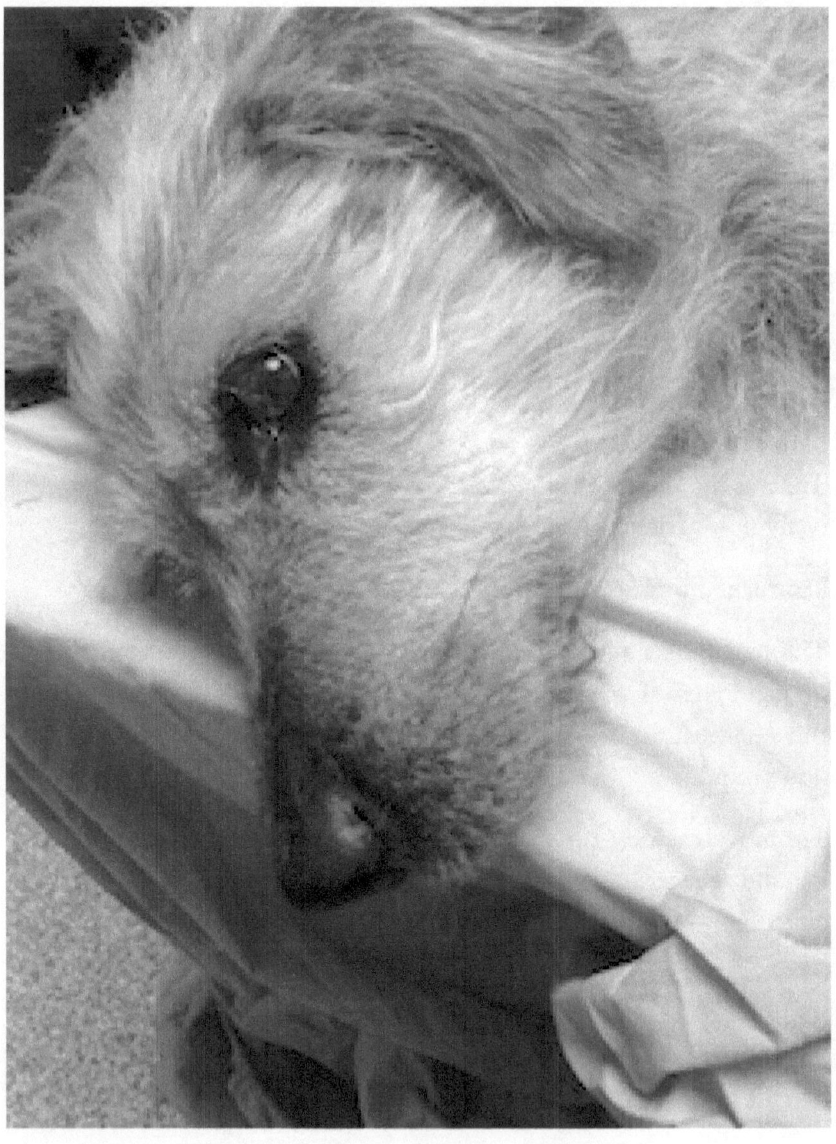

Maybe stepped in a hole when running or jumping. If that's what it is, he's gonna need rest. And his leg should be iced if you can."

"You sure that's what it is?"

"Not *sure*, but pretty sure. You can order some imaging tests that would confirm it, but I think Dr. Umlang will tell you that I'm usually on target."

Tip looked to Umlang. "That right?"

Umlang nodded. "Hate to say it, Tip, but he's right. At first, I used to double check him using X-rays and MRIs. Now I take his word for it. Kid's got a knack. It's costing me some money if I don't do the tests, but it's saving the customer a lot more."

"Okay, tell me what I gotta do, and if I need a prescription."

"Already told you what you need to do," Spoons said. "Let him rest and put ice on his leg. Bandage him if you can. And give him time. Maybe a couple of weeks. Try to keep weight off the leg while you're at it. It'll make it heal faster."

Tip glanced at Umlang, who was nodding. Then Tip said, "Okay, Spoons. I appreciate it. Should I crate him?"

"You don't have to, unless he won't stay still. If he'll rest on a couch, that would be perfect. If not, a carpeted floor. Anything that would cushion his leg would be good."

Tip laughed. "I guess we're good then. That dog's hard to get *off* the couch." He reached down to pick Sacco up, then nodded to Spoons. "Thanks for your help. I appreciate it."

Spoons smiled. "No problem. Let me know how you make out with him."

Tip left, dropped Sacco off at his house, then headed in to work.

Connie met him at the top of the stairs. "How'd it go?"

"Good. Umlang's got a new kid working there who seems like he knows his stuff. Told me what to do in no more'n ten minutes."

"You going to tell me?"

Tip laughed. "Rest and ice is the main thing. Hell, even I can handle that."

"So nothing serious then?"

Tip shook his head. "Thank God, no. He thinks he might have torn a tendon in his back leg. Maybe stepped in a hole or something."

"Sounds about right," Connie said. "Now that your personal life is taken care of, let me fill you in on the case."

"Shoot."

"I checked out the ex to cover our tracks, but like we figured, there doesn't seem to be anything there. His phone records show him in Corpus that day and that night, and he has witnesses that will vouch for him. Besides that, he seemed genuinely concerned over the boy's disappearance."

"What else?"

"So far, there doesn't seem to be any reason to suspect a boyfriend. There aren't any in the picture. I say we head out there and talk to more neighbors to see if anyone spotted anything suspicious, or see if anyone remembers seeing a dark-green van."

"Then we better get our asses moving," Tip said. "I'll drive."

"Like hell," Connie said. "I had a peaceful ride to work this morning. I think I'll enjoy a peaceful ride home. Meet you in front of the house."

"I'll probably be done by the time you get there," Tip said

"I'm counting on it. I might even stop for a coffee."

Tip was sitting in his car out front of the Hendricks' house when I pulled up. I tapped on his window and motioned for him to follow. "No sense wasting time. You've been loafing long enough."

We walked up to the first door, a neighbor of Ms. Hendricks, and knocked. A moment later, a young Hispanic-looking woman answered. She didn't look anything like Ms. Rosario though.

"I'm Detective Connie Gianelli, and this is my partner, Tip Denton. We had a few questions about the disappearance of your neighbor Tommy Hendricks."

She blessed herself while saying, "Dios mío."

"Do you mind if we come in?" Tip asked.

She swung the door open and stepped aside. "¿Por favor?"

"Do you speak English?" Tip asked. "¿Habla inglés?"

She shook her head. "No, señor. No está bien."

"Shit," Tip said. "Connie, no sense in staying here. We'll have to get Delgado to stop by for us."

"You think he'll do it?"

"He doesn't live far from here. I'll ask him tomorrow." Tip faced the woman again. "Gracias, señora."

We went to the next house, where the woman spoke English, and asked our questions. "Did you notice anything at all that day—Monday—when Tommy went missing?"

She shook her head. "Nothing. And I was outside until it started raining. I even saw Tommy go inside after I hollered to him. I knew Karen wasn't home yet, so I told him to get his butt inside."

"Did you see his cat? Or a strange van?"

"No. Usually, KC is right with him. It's kinda odd, but that cat follows him like a dog. Never saw anything like it. But I didn't see him that day. And the only strange car I saw was an electrician's van in front of Campbell's house over there." She pointed across the street.

"An electrician's van? How long was it there?"

"I don't know. Maybe half an hour. It was a green van with a company name on it, but I don't remember the name, just that it was an electrician's van."

"What else can you tell us about the van? Remember any numbers from the license plate? Was it light green?"

She shook her head. "No, it was a darker green, and I didn't get a look at the license plate. Not a single number."

"Okay, thanks," I said, and turned to leave.

"Oh, wait a minute," she said. "There was a name on the side of the van. It was…give me a minute, and I'll remember."

She tilted her head back and closed her eyes. "Clausen!" she hollered. "It was Clausen Electric."

"You're sure?" I asked.

"No question," she said.

Tip and I thanked her and moved to the next house. There was a disabled man in this house, who said he hadn't seen anything—not Tommy, the cat, or the van. He said he doesn't get outside and hadn't looked out the windows.

No one answered at the next house, but the one after that had a young woman and two kids.

"I remember seeing the kid," she said. "He was out playing with one of his friends. After it started raining, he went inside. I didn't see the cat, but I did see a van. It was plumber's van, I think. Parked over there," she said, pointing to the same spot the other woman had. "Must have been there an hour or so."

"A plumber's van?" Tip asked. "You sure it wasn't an electrician's van?"

"I don't know. It might have been. It was some kind of worker's van. I know that."

We went across the street and questioned the residents in four of the houses. They all recalled seeing the van but not Tommy or the cat. And no one was having electric work done.

We finished the day questioning everyone on the street. Two people weren't home, and we had one who didn't speak English. Other than that, the stories were pretty much the same; seven of them had seen the van, but no one saw anything after the rain started. Looked like we still had work to do.

Tip said he'd call Ribs on his way home to ask about questioning that woman in Spanish.

"Want to get together and grab a beer?" I asked.

"I'd love to, but Elena and I are going to dinner. And then, if I'm lucky, we'll be busy afterward."

I laughed. "Good luck to you, and God bless Elena," I said. "See ya tomorrow."

"Yeah. See ya."

Chapter Twelve

CARNIVAL BAIT

I got in early, but not early enough. A note from Coop was waiting on my desk. Tip wasn't in so I headed down there myself.

"Where's Denton?" she asked.

"He's not in yet, Captain. I think he had a late night."

"Late or not, tell him to get his ass in here. We had another kid taken."

"What? Where? When?"

"Greenspoint Mall again, at a carnival. And the when was last night. Ten years old."

"Parents?"

"Just the father was with him. He was getting a drink, and when he returned, the child was gone."

"Okay, Captain. I'll get right on it."

"Get that partner of yours on it too. This case needs both of you." Coop reached for a folder on top of her desk. "There's not much here, but it'll give you a start. Names and addresses and such. Get on it."

"Yes, ma'am. I'll get back to you tonight."

"I'll be waiting. Anything new on the other one?"

I shook my head. "Nothing yet, but we're working it."

"Then get out of here and get busy."

"Yes, ma'am," I said again, and left the office.

I called Tip on my way down the hall. He answered immediately. "On my way, for God's sake. Have patience."

"No sense in coming down. Meet me at Greenspoint. We got another grab."

"Aw, shit. Not another kid."

"Yep. This one's ten. Took him right from the carnival while his dad was getting a drink."

"Okay, meet you there in twenty minutes."

"You can be there in twenty if you want, but it'll take me thirty or forty. See you then."

I got to Greenspoint, found Tip, and then we headed to the address Coop had given us. It was an apartment east of the mall.

The father was home when we arrived, and he was accompanied by more than a few friends. I introduced myself at the front door. "I'm Detective Connie Gianelli, and this is my partner, Tip Denton. We're here about the disappearance of Mr. Williams' son."

A man in his thirties, wearing shades—even though he was inside—and sporting dreadlocks that hung below his ears, let us in after examining the badges twice. Music was blaring, and we could barely hear.

"He's in the living room. You heard anything?"

"How were we supposed to hear anything?" Tip asked. "We don't even know what happened yet."

The guy led us to the living room, where Williams was sitting on the couch. "Mr. Williams, I'm Detective Gianelli. We're here about your son."

He stood and walked toward the front door. "Let's go into the hall so we can talk without shouting."

Once in the hall, Tip said, "Why don't you tell us what happened. Don't leave anything out because no detail is too small."

"I had my son for the night, and he wanted to go to the carnival. It was the first night back, so as soon as it got dark, I took him."

"Hold on a minute," I said. "You mentioned you had your son. Does your wife work, or are you divorced, or what?"

Williams hesitated a moment, then he said, "My wife was out for the night, so she left Michael with me."

I nodded. "Okay, go on."

"Anyway, I took Michael to the carnival. We went on a couple of rides together, and he went on a few by himself, then I went to get us a drink. Iced tea for me and a Coke for him."

Williams began tearing up. "When I got back, he was gone. Nowhere. I was only gone a couple of minutes. There wasn't even no line at the food stand."

I waited a moment, then said, "How far away was the food stand from where you were? Fifty feet? A hundred?"

Williams looked down the hallway, then pointed to the stairway. "About as far as those steps," he said. "I'm not good with estimating distance in feet, but I can tell you by looking."

"No problem," Tip said. "That looks like it's about fifty or sixty feet."

"Anyway, I told Michael to stay put, then I went to get drinks. When I came back, he was gone. I looked everywhere but couldn't find him. And it was only a minute. I mean, goddamn. It wasn't a lot of time."

"Is there anyone who would have a reason to take Michael? Or a reason to want to hurt you or your wife?" I asked.

Mr. Williams shook his head. "Nobody I can think of."

I made note in my book, but something about the way he said it left me wondering. I put a question mark next to the note.

"Was your wife working?" Tip asked.

"Yeah. Working," he said.

"Where does she work?"

Williams looked to Tip with defiance showing in his eyes. "Odd jobs. Here and there. Nothin' steady."

"Where was she working last night?" Tip asked.

"I don't know. She said she was working, so Michael and I went to the carnival."

"What time did your wife get home?" Tip asked.

Williams snapped. "How the hell do I know. It was late. Maybe eleven o'clock." He leaned toward Tip and said, "What the hell difference does that make? She didn't take the kid. And she didn't have nothin' to do with it."

"I'm sure she didn't," I said in an attempt to placate him. Then I tapped Tip on the arm. "Let's go, Tip. I think we have what we need to get started."

As we walked to the car, Tip said, "What the hell was that about? That guy knows something. I don't know what, but something."

"I know that, but we weren't going to get it from him. Let's check around with friends and neighbors. See what we can find out."

"Something's going on. I guarantee that. His place looked like they were having a party, not worrying over the loss of his son."

"Yeah. And where was the wife? If my son went missing, I'd have been there regardless of work."

Tip stopped and looked at me. "Are you thinking what I'm thinking, that we should go back and question a few neighbors?"

"We've gotta do it sooner or later," I said, then turned and started heading back.

Chapter Thirteen

WHAT DO THE NEIGHBORS KNOW?

I knocked on the door of the neighbor at the end of the hall. If anyone was going to talk, it would probably be the neighbor farthest away.

A woman who appeared to be in her forties answered. She wore skin-tight jeans that looked to be several sizes too small. "Can I help you?" she asked.

"Do you know Mr. Williams, in 209-B?"

She leaned to one side, cocking her hip. "I know who he is, but I don't *know* him. Why? Did he do something? What do you want to know?"

"I don't know if you were aware of this, but his son Michael was taken last night while Mr. Williams and he were at the carnival in the parking lot of Greenspoint Mall."

"Why did you ask if he did something? Should we suspect him of doing something?"

"If you were half a cop, you'd expect everybody did something and suspect them of it. But yeah, you might expect him more than others."

"What should we suspect him of?" Tip asked.

She switched and leaned to the other side. "You expect me to solve this whole case? Damn. Ask around. He pimps his wife out. I'm sure that's done pissed somebody off. I don't know if it's enough to snatch a kid, but I wouldn't be surprised. Low-life scum that they are."

I stepped a little closer and lowered my voice. "You're saying he pimps his wife out?"

She shook her head. "I don't know how much clearer I got to say it. He...pimps...his...wife...out. Every goddamn night. As soon as it turns dark, she's gone. Outta here wearin' clothes meant for a woman twenty years younger and twenty pounds lighter. And she's showin' enough skin to make a man look twice, even the ones who shouldn't be lookin'."

"And who would be upset by this?" I asked.

"Goddamn. You people don't know shit, do ya? Rasta."

She must have seen the lack of recognition in my expression.

"Rasta. Rasta from down by West Road. From what my husband says, Rasta runs all the whores. And that no-good son of a bitch should know; he's sampled enough of the goods. Anyway, Rasta was probably pissed off that Williams was runnin' his wife without him gettin' his cut. Maybe he did somethin' about it."

"You know anything about Rasta?"

"Already told you, he runs the whores from West Road. I'm guessin' you can find out on your own from there."

"We can," Tip said. "Thanks."

I took that as a cue that Tip had what he needed, so we said our goodbyes and made a final trip to the car. "You know Rasta?" I asked when we exited the building.

"Not him, but I know enough people who will know him. Get in the car, and we'll take a drive to West Road."

"I've got my car here."

"Don't worry about that. Just get in."

Tip got to West Road in less than twenty minutes. Considering the traffic, that was pretty good. Two young women were hanging around the intersection where West meets I-45. They looked to be who Tip was looking for.

He pulled into the parking lot, rolled down his window, and said, "Hey, young thing. I need an hour of your time."

The thinner of the two women headed his way, swaying the whole time. When she leaned forward, she must have noticed Connie. "My name's Tarif, but I have to tell you, three-ways are more expensive."

Tip showed his badge. "I'm not concerned with how expensive they are, darlin'. I want to know where to find Rasta."

Tarif straightened. "I don't know any Rasta."

Tip laughed. "Come on, Tarif. I think we both know you do. I'm sure you see him every night to give him his share of the day's take."

She started to walk away. "I don't know what you're talkin' about."

"Don't make me have to run you in on a prostitution charge to get what I want. Look at it this way; if I lock Rasta's ass up, you'll be getting all the money until he gets out. And from what I hear, that may be years."

Tarif turned around, placed her palms on the car door, and leaned inside. "Show me that badge again."

Tip flashed it to her. "Write the number down if you want."

"I don't need that, but if I give you what you want, you'll owe me."

"I'll give you a walk on minor things, but nothing major. No drugs or felony robberies."

She nodded. "Don't need that. But a walk would help. Give me somethin' to write with, and I'll get you his address."

Tip handed her his notepad, and she scribbled down an address. "Don't tell him where it came from. I mean it. And if you need me to testify about anything, that'll be extra."

"Got it," Tip said. "I'll let you know." Then he handed her a card. "That's got my cell number on it. If you get in trouble, call me."

Tip drove west until he hit Steubner-Airline Road, then he turned right and entered a subdivision soon afterward. Rasta's house was the fourth one in.

Tip parked across the street, about half a block down, then he and Connie waited and watched. Before long, a stocky guy of medium height pulled up and entered the house.

That was what they'd been waiting for. They got out of the car and walked down to Rasta's house. Connie walked toward the back of the house while Tip knocked hard on the front door.

It only took a moment for Rasta to try making a break for it out the back door, but I was waiting. I drew my gun, pointed it at him, and yelled, "Stop right there, Rasta, or I'll plug your ass."

He continued to run, so I put a shot into the ground and yelled again. "Next one goes in your back. And I don't miss."

He must have believed me because he stopped and put his hands in the air. "I didn't do nothin'," he said.

"Then why run?"

He shrugged. "It's what you do down here. I didn't know who you were."

"Now you do," I said.

Tip must have heard me shoot and came rushing around the house. "Cuff him," I said.

We put Rasta in the back of the car, and I stayed with him while Tip went to check the house. Less than twenty minutes later, Tip returned with a kid—it was Michael Williams.

"Looks like you're going away for a long time," Tip said. He opened the back door. "Climb in, Michael, and we'll take you home. Don't mind the scum next to you. If he does anything, my partner will shoot him. And that ain't no shit. She'll put one in his eye."

I pulled my piece out and pointed it at him. "He's not lying. I will."

Traffic was bad on the way north, so it took us almost forty minutes to get to Michael's home. His father was in when we arrived.

"Michael! Damn, son. I'm so happy to see you. What happened?"

I grabbed hold of Mr. Williams' arm and pulled him into the hall. "Mr. Williams, I think you know *exactly* what happened to your son, and I think you knew all along. Just so you know, I think it's disgusting what you do with your wife, and now that we know about it, we're gonna be watching. We're going to lock both your asses up as soon as we can, and we'll place the boy with child services."

"You can't talk to me like that."

"I just did, Mr. Williams. Keep it in mind."

We walked back to Tip's car, chatting about the case. "I can't believe he does that."

"Believe it," Tip said. "It happens more than you think. The sad part is it took us off a real case while we played with this one."

I nodded. "Well, we don't have time to waste, so let's get moving on this." I walked to get my car. "See you tomorrow."

"Yeah, see ya," Tip said.

Chapter Fourteen

WHOSE DOG IS THIS?

Justice shifted his seat on the bleachers. He was now right behind the little boy whose shirt proclaimed him to be Ryan, at least according to the name imprinted on the back.

Based on Ryan's cheering, Justice could tell he was rooting for the team wearing the dark-blue jerseys. Not that Justice cared who won, but it was good that the dark-blue team was winning.

After a kid who appeared to be about twelve smacked a triple, driving in two additional runs, Ryan got up to go to the concession stand. Justice followed at a safe distance.

Justice was two in line behind Ryan when he leaned to the child directly behind him. "Do you hear that? It sounds like a dog barking."

"I don't hear anything," said the kid.

Justice straightened and cocked his head to the left. "I swear I hear a dog. It might be that one I saw earlier. Anyone missing an Australian Shepherd, black, about two or three years old?"

Ryan perked up. He turned and looked at Justice. "I am, why? Did you see one?"

"I saw a dog like that on the way here," he said. "Now, I hear a dog barking. I wonder if it's the same dog."

Ryan stepped out of line. "Where'd you see it?"

"It was up there," Justice said, pointing toward the road. But never mind, get back in line before you lose your place.

"No. If it's my dog, I need to find him. Can you help me look for him?"

"I'm not getting out of line to look for a dog," Justice said.

Ryan tugged on his sleeve. "Come on, mister. Help me find him."

"All right," Justice said. "Hang on a minute. At least let me get a Coke. You want one?"

"Sure," the kid said. "But we gotta hurry before he leaves."

"Okay. Okay," Justice said, then placed his order. "Two small Cokes, please. Extra ice." He paid the lady, handed a Coke to Ryan, then they walked toward the street.

"Where are your parents?" Justice asked.

"My dad is working, and my mom will be here soon. She had somewhere to go. My brother is playing baseball. That's why I'm here."

"Oh, I see," said Justice, then he picked up his pace. "Come on, if we're going to find your dog, we better hurry."

Justice went up to a white van parked by the side of the road, and he peered inside, using his hands to shield his eyes from the sun. "I think he's in here. I hear something."

Ryan ran up next to him and stretched to look inside. "Marcus! Marcus, is that you?"

Justice pulled out a keychain with numerous keys on it. "Let's try some of these. They might work."

He pretended to insert different keys into the lock. On the third try, he slid the side door open. "It worked," he said.

Ryan ran up to the van's door. "Marcus! Where have you been?"

Justice pushed Ryan inside and closed the door. Then he got in and tied Ryan's hands and feet and gagged him. "It won't be long now," he said. "And don't worry, nobody's going to hurt you. Marcus either."

Justice exited the freeway, and five minutes later he was pulling into the barn behind his house. Once inside, he hit a button, which opened up the hidden compartment underneath. Then he parked down below, next to the other vans, and went back up and closed the ramp. It would be a cold day in hell before anyone would find his vans.

Justice walked to the house with Ryan trailing behind him. Marcus was alongside Ryan, but Ryan's head hung low.

"Don't worry," Justice said. "You'll get used to things. Besides, Marcus is with you. That's nice, right?"

"I want my mom."

"I know. But your mom can't come right now, and besides, it takes a week or so to get used to things. After that, you'll love it."

Justice led Ryan down the steps and into the playroom. He used his key to unlock the door. Four kids were inside. They cheered when he opened the door.

"Hey, Mr. Justice," one said.

"Can we play games?" another asked.

"I'm thirsty," a third one said.

Justice held up his hand. "Hang on a minute. I've brought someone home," he said, then gestured to Ryan. "This is Quentin."

"My name's Ryan," he said.

Justice patted his shoulders. "I know, but we give out different names here, and it's all based on what your name was before. So if your name started with the letter 'T' like Tommy, then we'd give you a name that starts with the letter 'S.' Whatever letter your name used to start with, we make a new name using the letter before it. Since your name began with 'R,' we gave you a name that begins with 'Q'—Quentin."

"Hey, Quentin," Sean said. "Nice to meet you. My name's Sean."

The rest of the kids introduced themselves, then introduced their pets also—KC, Brutus, Frisco, and Cookie.

Justice reached down and petted Marcus' head. "And this is Marcus," he said. "Marcus is a good boy."

For the next hour, Justice played games, built castles with Legos, and shaped an assortment of landscapes using Play-Doh—his own brand of Play-Doh. Before Justice finished playing, Quentin had joined in and was even laughing. And Marcus was getting along great with the other dogs and even with KC. Things were going just as Justice hoped for.

Chapter Fifteen

SACCO RETURNS

Tip walked into the kitchen to make coffee, and he almost tripped over Sacco. "What the hell are you doing on the floor?"

Sacco didn't move, simply lay there and looked at Tip with sad eyes.

"Come on. Get up and get on the couch," Tip said. When Sacco didn't respond, he knelt next to the dog and felt his back leg. "Has that gone bad again? Huh?"

Sacco whimpered when Tip touched his leg. Tip shook his head and pulled out his cell phone. He hit the button to speed-dial Connie.

"Hello?"

"Connie, I need to take Sacco back to the vet, so you better drive yourself in. I'll probably be a while."

"Okay. Take care, and let me know what's going on with Sacco."

"Will do. See ya later."

Tip made the drive up to Conroe with Sacco on the seat beside him. Once he got there, he parked in front of the building and carried Sacco in. "Betty, got a hurt dog again. You want him in the room down the hall?"

Betty got up from her desk and looked down the hallway. "Yeah, Tip. Put him on the table in the last room on the left. But I have to tell you, Dr. Umlang isn't in yet. He had to stop at a farm out in Huntsville before coming in."

"How about his assistant. Spoons or something?"

"He's here. You want him to look at Sacco?"

Tip nodded. "Yeah. He did a good job with Sacco last time. Send him back here."

While Tip waited, he noticed a flyer sitting on the desk against the wall. It was of a cat that looked suspiciously like the one Ms. Hendricks had a picture of.

Reward for missing Manx: $200

The flyer went on to describe the coloring of the cat, the size, the name (KC) and other features. It concluded with Karen Hendricks' name and address.

Tip realized as he looked at it that this was a flyer from before, when Ms. Hendricks said the cat was missing for a week.

Spoons came into the room a few seconds later. "What's the matter, Mr. Denton? What's up with Sacco?"

"I don't know. I woke up this morning, and he was on the floor. He couldn't move. So I thought I'd better bring him in here."

Spoons got busy massaging Sacco's back leg. "I'm guessing he sprained it. Worst case, he tore the ligament."

Sacco whimpered and jumped, and Spoons said, "You're gonna need to do what I told you before, but you're gonna have to make sure he stays still."

"That's hard to do when you're at work every day. I've got to let him have access to go outside to do his business, but if I let him out, he can run and step in holes."

Spoons kept massaging Sacco's leg, then he said, "All right, I'll make you a deal. You leave him here for two weeks, and I'll watch him."

"You'll watch him? How?"

"I can walk him during the day, and we can put him in a pen at night, so he can't run and hurt himself. By the end of two weeks, I think he'll be healed enough to go home. And don't worry about him being away from home. It takes a while to get used to things, but after about a week he'll be fine."

"You'd do that, Spoons? Walk him, I mean?"

"Of course. No problem. You can leave him here today and pick him up in two weeks. And no charge from me. If the doctor charges you for boarding, that's between you and him."

"Well all right then. I appreciate it. I'll call you to see how he's doing, but you call me if anything goes wrong." Tip handed Spoons a card. "I mean *anything*."

Before Tip left, he looked at Spoons. "You sure he's gonna be all right?"

Spoons laughed. "Don't worry. Sacco will do fine. Like I said, it takes a week or so to get used to something new, but once he does, he'll be great."

"All right," Tip said. "Take care of him. I'll be calling."

Tip left and started the drive back to the station. It was a long drive, and he needed something to think about, but he tried his best to avoid thoughts of his long-dead mother.

The problem was "trying his best" wasn't good enough. Before he got to the Woodlands, he found himself wondering once again not only who would kill her, but who would pay fifty thousand dollars to kill her. He presumed that was the amount because that's how much The Ranger was rumored to have charged, and if the little bit of information he had was correct, The Ranger was who did the killing.

Knowing that much created a lot of confusion. The Ranger was a notorious killer who charged a fortune to do his work. If it really was him who killed Tip's mother—why'd he do it?

And why was she killed? Who would pay that much money to kill her? What the hell was she mixed up in?

For the next twenty miles, Tip tossed possibilities around in his head, but he couldn't make heads or tails of the facts. Nothing made sense. His mother had been a waitress for God's sake. Who would pay that much money to have a waitress killed?

He pulled into the parking lot and parked, then went into the station and straight to his desk. Connie was sitting across from him, buried in paperwork.

"Sorry I dogged you, Connie. But I had to get Sacco taken care of."

"No big deal," she said. "I'd have done the same with Hotshot. How'd it go?"

"He's gonna stay there for a couple of weeks and see if he can get rest. Umlang's new assistant said he'd watch him. Hell of a nice guy."

"Nice guys come at a price," Connie said.

"No, that's the thing. He said he'd do it for nothing. I'm telling you, he's a nice guy."

"If you say so," Connie said. "Anyway, just so you don't think it's my cynical attitude at work—we've got another kid missing."

"What? Shit! What the hell is going on? We haven't had three kids snatched in three years, now we've got three in one week, counting the Greenspoint one, that is."

Tip punched his desk. "Where was this one?"

"Meyer Park, right by the sheriff's office on Cypresswood Drive. It was still light out too."

"This son of a bitch is brazen. We've got to stop him."

"If we plan on stopping him, I suggest we take a trip to Meyer Park and talk to a few people."

Tip looked at his watch. "It's late. Let's get our ducks lined up and meet there in the morning. Better yet, let's go to the kid's house in the morning. We'll see what the parents have to say."

"Fine by me," Connie said. "Here's the address." She handed Tip a piece of paper.

"No need for that," Tip said. "I'll pick you up, and we'll ride together."

Chapter Sixteen

ANOTHER MISSING CHILD

I waited patiently at the kitchen table while sipping on my second cup of espresso and enjoying every moment of it. Having a second cup of espresso made me crave a biscotto or even a scone, but my figure couldn't afford either one. I'd succumbed to too many indulgences of late, especially the box of zeppoli that Uncle Zeppe had delivered overnight—a dozen of them—and from my favorite bakery.

I finished the box in two days, and I felt sure my butt was showing the effects. It may have been in my head, but my jeans seemed more difficult to put on, and they were more difficult to zip up. Damn Uncle Zeppe.

Thinking of Uncle Zeppe made me ponder my situation again. If anybody knew anything about my mother or Uncle Dominic in the early days, it would be Zeppe.

I thought for a moment, then said: "What the hell" and picked up the phone to dial.

He answered after a few rings in typical Zeppe fashion. "Yeah?"

"Zio Giuseppe, it's me, Connie."

"Connie! What are you doing calling me? Everything all right?"

"Fine. I was sitting here drinking my espresso, and I thought I'd give you a call."

"As much as I'd like to believe that, I don't, so tell me why you really called. If Dominic taught me anything after all these years, it's not to be gullible. I used to be, but I'm learning."

"You're too cynical, Uncle Zeppe."

"Not according to Dominic. He even suspects the mailman of having an agenda."

"Uncle Zep, what was my father like? Did you know him well?"

A long pause ensued, then, "Connie, you can't ask me things like that."

"Why not? You knew him, right?"

"Yeah, I knew him...but I can't say anything."

"Why can't you say anything?"

"Because Dom would kill me. Maybe literally kill me."

"Uncle Zeppe, what is it you're not telling me? What would Uncle Dominic get mad about? And why would he?"

"I can't say anything, Connie. I'm sorry. I just can't."

"Okay, Uncle Zeppe, let's move on to something else. Like how are the kids? I haven't seen them in ages."

He laughed. "I know. They ask about you all the time. I told them you'd probably come for a visit this summer. You will, won't you?"

"Probably. If only to see my two favorite uncles. I'll let you know beforehand, though. By the way, are the kids home? I'd love to see them. We could connect using Facetime."

"Aw, shit. No. They're not here, but call back tonight or tomorrow night. They'll be here then."

"Okay, Uncle Zeppe. Ti voglio bene."

"Ciao, Concetta. Ti voglio bene."

I got up to pour another espresso since Tip still hadn't shown, and while I did, I pondered what I'd just learned. Zeppe hadn't told me anything specific, but he did let it slip that there was something to hide and that Uncle Dominic was the one who wanted it hidden.

I sat down at the table again and slowly sipped the espresso. Now, all I had to do was figure out what he was hiding and why.

I finished my third espresso, and Tip still hadn't arrived, so I cleaned the table and decided to go outside to wait. My next door neighbor, Ted, was coming out just as I was going down the steps.

I sat on the bottom step and leaned against the wall. "Hey, Ted," I said as he passed.

"Waitin' on your boyfriend?"

"Boyfriend? I don't have a boyfriend."

"Really? I see some guy pick you up most days, and I thought...my mistake."

I laughed. "That's all right. He's just my partner picking me up for work."

I heard a car turning the corner, and when I looked, I saw it was Tip. "In fact, here he is now. Finally."

"Okay. See ya later, Connie."

"Yeah. See ya."

I opened the car door and climbed into the passenger seat. "Keep this up, and I'm gonna start calling you nine-o'clock Tip."

"Real funny. Some people have more to do than sit around and drink coffee."

"You mean like drink tea?"

Tip laughed. "Exactly what I mean. Anybody worth anything knows that drinking tea requires more intelligence than drinking coffee."

"Really? There are about eight million people in New York who would disagree."

"That's because they're not smart enough to know better, and that's because they don't drink tea. Anyway, let's get down to this kid's house. What's his name again?"

"Ryan. Ryan Salerno."

"Salerno. Is that Italian?"

"I don't know. It sounds like it, but you don't have many Italians in Texas. I'm thrilled though. At least you didn't say 'Eye-talian.'"

"That's from all the tea I've been drinking."

I laughed. "Shut up and head down Veteran's Memorial. He lives south of 1960."

"South of 1960? What was he doing playing ball so far north?"

"I don't know. I guess we'll have to ask the parents."

We kept going south after passing 1960. A few miles later, Tip pulled into an older subdivision, one that had seen better days, though it was holding up well.

The house was a detached ranch with a big tree in the front yard.

We walked up and knocked on the door, and didn't have long to wait for a young woman to answer. She appeared to be Latino, although I couldn't tell, as she had a great command of English.

I showed my badge and said, "I'm Detective Connie Gianelli. This is my partner, Tip Denton. We're here about the disappearance of your son."

She stepped aside, leaving us room to enter. "Please, come in. I've been waiting for someone to show."

"Why don't you start by telling us what happened?" I said.

She took a seat in a chair next to the sofa. "Ryan rode to the game with his friend Pablo. Pablo plays third base."

"You weren't there?" Tip asked.

"Not at first. I never got there until...until he was gone," she said, and broke into tears.

"What time did you get there?" I asked.

She sobbed for a moment more, then dabbed her tears and said, "It was about halfway through. I remember the score was five to three when I got there. My oldest son, Ricky, was in the outfield."

"And that's when you noticed he was gone?"

"I went to get a seat in the bleachers, and when I looked for Ryan, he wasn't there. That's when I panicked. I ran to the concession stand, then to the other bleachers, but I couldn't see him anywhere."

"If you don't mind me asking," Tip said, "Why was Ryan playing ball that far north? Is that normal?"

She paused, then said. "No. We use one of his cousin's address so we can send him to St. Ignatius', on Cypresswood Road. The park is just down the road from there."

"And you're sure he was there, at the game?" I asked.

She nodded vigorously. Pablo's mother dropped them off. And Ricky saw him between innings. I think he said after the third. Besides, Ryan wouldn't go anywhere. He's a good boy."

"Where was his father?" I asked.

She sighed. "His father doesn't live with us anymore. He left two years ago."

"You think—?" Tip started to say.

"No way. He's in town, but he doesn't give a shit about the kids. He's got two more of his own now. Besides, I doubt if he even knew Ricky was playing, let alone where."

"You know anyone who would want to hurt Ryan? Or take him?" I asked.

She shook her head again. "I've been wracking my brain, but I can't think of anyone. I mean, come on, who the hell would take a person's child? It's not right. It's just not right."

Tip set his notepad on the table and looked at her. "I understand what you're saying, Ms. Salerno. But stuff like this happens all the time. Is there anyone else we should talk to? Anyone who might have information that would be helpful?"

She began crying again. "I can't think of anyone. He's a good boy. Why would anyone take him?"

I placed my hand on her forearm. "We're gonna find that out, Ms. Salerno. I don't often make that kind of promise, but I will this time. I'm gonna find out who took your boy."

She reached over, put her arms around me and cried on my shoulder. "Please do," she said. "I can't lose my baby. Not him."

Tip had a disapproving look on his face, probably due to my promise, but I didn't care. I wasn't going to let this woman suffer the loss of her child. I hadn't promised the Hendricks woman, but in hindsight, maybe I should have.

Ms. Salerno broke the embrace, then began walking out of the room. "Let me get a picture of Ryan. I'm sure it will help. It's a recent one."

She returned a moment later and handed one picture to Tip and one to me. "These were taken at school," she said. "I think it was two months ago."

"What was he wearing yesterday?" I asked. "Do you remember?"

"Of course. He had on his jeans with a dark-blue jersey, the same color as his brother's team uniform."

"This is great," Tip said. "And ma'am, if you could give us his friend's address, we'd like to talk to Pablo's mother. It more than likely won't help much from what you said, but we'd still like having it."

"Of course," she said, having reverted to sniffles. "I'll get that for you now." She stood and walked into the kitchen, returning a moment later with a slip of paper in her hand. "Here's her name and address and phone number, cell and home phones. Tell her I said to talk to you." Ms. Salerno looked at us both. "She's a little leery of talking to authorities. I think she may be illegal."

"That's not our department," I said. "And we don't much care about it. We're focusing on finding your son."

Ms. Salerno reached forward and squeezed my hand. "Thank you," she said. Then she walked us to the door.

Chapter Seventeen

THE NEXT GAME

We interviewed Pablo's mother, and, as Ms. Salerno had said, she was reluctant to cooperate, but after we explained why we were there, and what we wanted, and that we had no interest in her immigration status, she opened up.

We also spoke to Pablo, who told us where Ryan had been sitting.

"But you weren't with him?" I asked.

"I was at first," Pablo said. Then he glanced at his mother with what appeared to be an embarrassed look. "Then I went to play in the park."

"You what?" she asked.

He lowered his head. "Juan and I went to play in the park. I got tired of watching. It's no fun."

She rushed over and hugged Pablo. "*Dios mío.* You could have been stolen."

"But I wasn't," he said.

She playfully smacked him on the butt, then said, "Go on. Get out of here."

We asked a few more questions, and before leaving, we found out the next game was that same evening—at Meyer Park also.

I looked at Tip, and he nodded. We planned on attending. With any luck, some of the same people would be there. Aside from the scheduled game information, Pablo's mother had little to give us as Ms. Salerno had said. We worked on the Kendricks' case, made a few more calls, then went to eat an early dinner and headed out to Meyer Park for more questioning.

The spectators were arriving as we got there, and the bleachers were getting full. "Little League draws a hell of a crowd, doesn't it?"

"Shit. All the sports draw big crowds down here. Not hockey, but baseball, basketball, and football. You should see the crowds football draws. Friday nights at a high school game looks almost like a professional game's attendance."

On the way to the park, Tip took a two-block detour to show me the size of the local high school stadium. I had to admit, it was impressive. It wasn't as big as a pro team's facility, but it approached some college facilities.

Fifteen minutes later we arrived at the park. Tip pulled to the curb, then we walked to the location where Pablo had told us Ryan was seated. Once there, we began questioning people, asking if they had been at the previous game.

"I was here," one guy said. "The whole family was here. Our boy was the starting pitcher. He held 'em to only three runs too. Would've shut them out if that one kid hadn't gotten lucky and hit a homer."

I thought we were in danger of getting a replay of the whole game when Tip stepped closer. "I don't mean to interrupt," he said, "but we have a missing boy, and we need to get moving."

"Oh, I'm sorry. What do you need to know?"

Tip showed him a picture of Ryan. "Did you see this boy during the game? He was sitting right in these bleachers, on the second row."

"I don't think so," the guy said.

"Before you say no, take a look at his picture." Tip showed him a picture of Ryan, then said, "He wouldn't have been wearing the clothes in the picture. He had on jeans with a dark-blue jersey the same color as the team's jersey."

The guy looked, then showed it to his kids. "Y'all remember seeing him last night?" he asked.

They all said no. Tip took the picture back, and we moved on, asking more people the same questions.

After about an hour, we had nothing, so Tip walked onto the field, stopping to grab a megaphone from one of the umpires. He moved toward the pitcher's mound, then shouted. He was so loud I wasn't sure he needed the megaphone.

"Listen up, y'all. I'm a detective with HPD. A young boy was kidnapped from here last night, and we need help locating him. I want all of you to start thinking, then come down and talk to me or my partner, who is over there." He pointed in my direction.

Almost immediately, people began the descent to the bottom, waiting in line to talk to us. Still, after another half an hour, we had nothing. Then a man nodded when I showed him the picture of Ryan.

"I saw him," he said.

I got excited. This was the first person who remembered seeing him. "Where was he sitting?" I asked.

"Wasn't sitting anywhere. I saw him walking toward the street. Headin' up from the concession stand."

"Was he alone?"

"No, a man was with him. Tall guy. And thin."

"Is that all you can tell us? Any other features? Was he white, black, Latino? Did he have blond hair, black hair, brown hair? What kind of clothes was he wearing? Jeans, slacks, shorts?"

The guy seemed to think for a moment, then said, "He was a white guy or maybe a Latino, and he had brown hair. Oh, and he had a funny way of holding his head, like a chicken does when it's pecking the ground."

"Like a chicken?"

"Yeah, I just remembered that."

"Anything else? Clothes? Glasses?"

The guy shook his head. "I don't remember. It was raining pretty hard at that time. I was more concerned with staying dry. I don't think he wore glasses, but I can't be sure."

"You notice a van on the street? Maybe with a Clausen Electric sign on the side panel?" I asked.

"No, nothing electric, but I did see a van; it was some plumber's van."

"How do you know?" I asked.

"Had the name on the side."

"What color was the van?"

"White. I'm sure of that. It was a white van."

"Okay. Thanks," I said.

My initial excitement faded as I moved on to the next person, asking the same questions.

We had just finished up when the game ended. "We better catch the people at the concession stand," I said. "If we don't, they'll be gone."

As Tip finished up his questions. I walked over to join him and suggested we talk to the guys at the stand.

Tip walked over, showed his badge, then asked if they'd seen anyone that stood out, and in particular, if they'd seen Ryan.

The guy managing the stand shook his head. "We were busy. I didn't see anything."

"Come on, this is a missing kid here. Think harder."

"I already told you, we were busy. I wouldn't have noticed if my mother was in line—and she's been dead for three years."

"Yeah, all right," Tip said, then mumbled, "Son of a bitch."

We ended the evening talking to a few stragglers, who gave us nothing new, then walked to the car. "You believe this shit?" Tip said. "Nobody saw anything."

"Still better than Brooklyn."

"How can it be better? We didn't get anything."

"That one guy talked to us. We even got a description, remember?"

"Yeah, I remember. The guy is tall and thin. He's either white or Latino. And he may, or may not, be a chicken."

I laughed as I opened the car door. "So what do we do with that, partner?"

Tip reached behind him and grabbed a hot beer and popped it open.

I sneered. "You're not going to drink that, are you?"

"Better than nothin," he said, and slugged his beer. "And if you want to know what to do with that description, put out an APB. How many Latino chickens do you think there are? Not many. I'll tell you that."

"And how do you spot them?"

"Come on, Connie. You've been down here long enough," Tip said. "You gotta listen to them cluck. They do it with an accent."

I laughed despite the seriousness of the situation. "You want to go to your house? We can work a little on this."

"Not tonight," Tip said. "The vet is open late tonight, so I'm stopping by to check on Sacco. I don't want him to think I abandoned him."

"You are a sucker," I said. "Not to mention a slacker."

"You better get your beauty rest," Tip said. "After tonight, you're gonna need it."

"Just take me home, cowboy. I'll get some work done myself. And say hi to Elena…I mean Sacco."

Tip laughed. "You son of a bitch. I'm serious. I'm gone to visit Sacco. Elena's working herself."

"And I'd bet she's not coming over till…what nine?"

"None of your goddamn business, Yankee."

Fifteen minutes later, Tip pulled to the curb. "I'd walk you to the door if I were a gentleman, but I'm not. So get going."

I laughed. "See ya tomorrow, Tip."

"Yeah, see ya," he said.

Tip drove to the vet's office in less than half an hour. Considering the time of day, that was good time.

He walked in, but Betty wasn't there. She must have gone home already. Tip didn't see anyone. "Hello," he called. "Anybody here?"

A few seconds later, Betty walked up. "So you didn't go home?" Tip said. "I thought you were gone."

"Just powdering my nose," she said, and giggled. "What are you doing here, Mr. Denton?"

Tip leaned on the desk. "Came to visit Sacco. See how he was doing."

"You could have just called. He's doing great; in fact, Spoons has him out for a walk right now. He should be back any minute though. He's been gone a while."

Tip looked at his watch, then said, "All right."

While he waited, he caught a glance at a few pictures of young kids on the desk. "What are these about?"

Betty looked over, then said, "Oh, they're the kids that were kidnapped. They haven't found them yet."

"What? Kidnapped? When did this happen?"

"Must have been about three weeks ago. Three of them. Two boys and a girl."

"Son of a bitch! Son of a bitch," Tip said, then he headed toward the door. "Betty, tell Spoons I stopped by, and I'll call tomorrow. I gotta get on this right away."

"Yes, sir, Mr. Denton. I'll make sure to tell him."

Tip was on the phone to Deputy Rawlins before getting out of the parking lot. "Rawlins, this is Tip Denton. Why the hell am I just finding out about these kidnappings?"

"I guess because you don't read anything but the Chronicle. If you'd have even glanced at the Courier for the past month, you couldn't have missed it."

"And you never thought to call me to see if we had anything like it going on?"

"Well, do ya?"

"Yeah, you goddamn buffoon. I got two kids kidnapped in the past few days. Maybe if we'd have been working this, it wouldn't have happened."

"And maybe it would've. Don't get your pants pulled up too tight. Call my office in the morning, and we'll send you what we've got. You do the same for me."

Tip hung up without saying goodbye. He dialed another number and was connected to Samantha Roberts, reporter for the Chronicle.

"What's up, Tip? I haven't heard from you in a while."

"I'll tell you what's up. I've got an exclusive for you on a rash of kidnappings—all little kids. And it's happening In Harris and Montgomery counties."

"What? How many?"

"Five that I know of. Call me tomorrow, and I'll have more information. I just wanted you to reserve a front-page slot. We need to let people know what's going on. I don't want any more kids nabbed."

"You got ransom notes? How much are they asking?"

"None down here. I don't know about Conroe yet."

"No ransom? What the hell does he want?"

"Don't know yet, but I intend to find out."

"Where are you now?" Roberts asked.

"Too far away to do you any good. I'm just crossing the San Jacinto and traffic's bad."

"How about we meet tomorrow then? Sometime after breakfast and before lunch."

"You got it. Call me around nine-thirty. I should have information from Conroe by then."

Chapter Eighteen

WHERE ARE THE KIDS?

Tip called Connie early in the morning. "You're going to have to get your lazy ass up. I'm meeting with Roberts around nine-thirty."

"My lazy ass? I've been up forever. To quote a ridiculous Texan, I know—'I was up before the crows.'"

"Before the crows? Damn, that's early, girl. Anyway, I'll be over in about twenty minutes."

"And I'll be waiting—as usual."

Tip picked up Connie, and on the way to the station, he filled her in on what he'd learned from Deputy Rawlins.

"I can't believe they didn't call us sooner," Connie said.

"Tell me about it. I'm supposed to call his admin this morning to get more details. I'll do that when we get in."

"What the hell do you think this is about, Tip? If the kidnapper hasn't asked for a ransom, what's he doing with the kids? And why is he taking them?"

Tip shook his head. "I don't know. I wish I did."

"You think it's a sex operation? Is he shipping them off to Mexico?"

"Forget shipping them off to Mexico. Mexico is a great place to get kids, but the market for selling them is in the United States."

"Sex trafficking? Here?"

"No doubt about it. You may not think it happens, but California alone has three of the biggest sex trafficking areas—Los Angeles, San Diego, and San Francisco. Add Dallas, Seattle, and New York to the list, and you've got an epidemic."

"And they get the kids from Mexico?"

"Mexico supplies a lot of the people as well as Eastern Europe, China, and Africa, but they're abused here."

Tip's cell rang while he was driving down I-45. "Denton."

"Tip, it's Rawlins."

"Well, the prick of the north. What do you want? You callin' to tell me you had another kidnapping? I promise I won't shoot you—at least not today."

"Screw you, Denton. You'd have done the same thing. When was the last time you called me about a case you were working?"

"I don't remember the last time, but I know there won't be a next time unless I get some good information."

"We got three kids grabbed in one week, either from their neighborhoods or another public place. One was a shopping center, one a restaurant men's room, and one from in front of the church. In all cases, no one saw anything. I don't know how that's possible, but that's what everyone said."

"Don't feel bad, Rawlins. We've got the same thing. We had a kid snatched from a Little League game which must have had a thousand people attending, and we got nothing."

"Did you check the parents?" Rawlins asked.

"Yeah, but it doesn't look like they're involved. In two cases, the fathers were estranged but seemed to check out."

"Same here," Rawlins said. "And if that's the case, you thinkin' what I'm thinkin'?"

"I don't know what you're thinkin', but if it involves sex trafficking, then yes. I suspect these kidnappings have something to do with it. They must. I can't see any other reason for so many kidnappings in such a short time span, especially with no ransom demands."

"You've got no ransom demands either?" Rawlins asked.

"Not a one," Tip said. "What's the gender of your kidnappings? We've got young boys, younger than twelve."

"We've got two boys and one girl," Rawlins said. "But the same age. I think two were ten and one eleven."

"Shit! I don't like the sound of it," Tip said.

"Me neither," Rawlins said. "Let's make a deal. I'll keep you informed of anything up here, but you need to do the same."

"I should tell you to go shit in your hat, but you'd probably do it. So, okay. You got a deal. Call Julie to get what information we have, but it isn't much."

Tip drove like a normal person the rest of the way in. And he only made one call—to check on Sacco.

After he hung up with Spoons, Connie asked, "Does Elena know about your relationship with that dog? I'm beginning to wonder."

"Eat shit, Connie. I'm just checking on the dog. Poor baby didn't have much of a life before Papa Tip got him."

Connie laughed. "Oh, now it's Papa Tip? Damn, what's next?"

"Shut the hell up. You're worse than I am with that damn cat of yours. The thing doesn't even have four legs."

"And that makes him all the more lovable. Besides, he's a hell of a lot smarter than those oafs you have."

Tip turned off the freeway onto McKinney and headed south. "It's a good thing we're almost at work."

"Why? You gonna challenge me to a game of Jeopardy?"

"Keep it quiet, Yankee. We've got work to do."

Connie and Tip barely had time for coffee before he got a call from Roberts. "All right," Tip said. "Be there in ten minutes."

He turned to Connie and said, "Time to go. Roberts is meeting us at the Starbucks on Smith Street, by Louisiana.

Tip sat at the table across from Roberts.

Connie took the seat next to him. "How are you, Samantha?" Connie asked.

"I'm fine. And either you have a good memory or Tip reminded you of my name on the way over because it's been a long time."

"Too long," Connie said. "But I blame my partner for that."

"He's to blame for a lot more than that," Roberts said. She turned to look at Tip. "How's it going, Tip? Been a while since we've spoken in person."

"Yeah. Elena told me it's not fair to mingle with other women. Just me being close by makes them go a little crazy."

Roberts laughed and said to Connie. "I see he's the same old Tip. How do you put up with it?"

"My uncle once told me that everybody has a cross to bear on Earth. I figured Tip was mine."

Roberts laughed. "And that's a heavy cross to bear."

She sipped her coffee, then stared at Connie and asked, "What have you got on these kidnappings? And, more importantly, what do you think I can do to help? I know you and Tip wouldn't have called me if you didn't need help."

Tip leaned forward. "Roberts, I…never mind."

"What? What were you going to say?" she asked.

"I was gonna say I knew there was a reason I liked you, but then I realized there wasn't."

Connie laughed. "See what I mean about that cross on Earth?"

"I'm beginning to," she said.

"Okay, seriously," Tip said. "Let me tell you what I think. And I'm looking for ideas here. Nothing is etched in stone."

"Go on," Roberts said.

"To bring you up to speed, we've had two kidnappings north of the city, and Montgomery County has had three. All of this has taken place in the past few weeks. And the kicker is that no one has seen a damn thing."

"How can that be?" Roberts asked. "How can you kidnap a child in front of so many witnesses and not be seen."

"He must fit in, blend with the crowd," Tip said. "Based on that, I'm figuring he's an ordinary-looking guy, nothing unusual. Not excessively tall or fat and not too short either. He's gonna be average or slightly outside the parameters of average, but nothing drastic."

"The bigger question is how does he know who to grab?" Connie said. "I know if my uncle is out somewhere with his kids, he watches them like a hawk. Never lets them leave his sight."

"Damn, I never thought of that," Tip said. "I guess not being a dad I didn't think that way."

Roberts nodded. "I agree. If you've got kids, and you're in a crowded place, you *never* take your eyes off of them."

"That means he knows who he's after *before* going to the site," Connie said.

Tip set his cup down and pointed. "You're right, Connie. He's *got* to know. But how?"

"While you two figure out how he knows who to grab, let's work on deciding what this article should discuss. Are we trying to make the public aware of what's going on? Let the kidnapper know we're onto him? Tick him off? What?"

"All of the above," Tip said. "And it'll be easier than you think."

"How's that?" Roberts asked.

"We'll alert the people by letting them know what's going on, and that will piss him off because he'll have to work harder. Then we bluff him by saying we've got DNA evidence from when he kidnapped the kid at Greenspoint Mall. And finally, we tick him off by calling him a sexual pervert and a deviant."

"And how is that going to work in our favor?"

"It may make him try harder to outsmart us—which he's already doing, though he doesn't know it—but once he starts trying harder, he's bound to make a mistake. And he only gets one chance. The first mistake he makes, his ass is mine."

"And you think spreading this all over page three will cause him to make a mistake?" Roberts asked.

"Hell no," Tip said. "I think spreading it all over page one will, not page three. This isn't a damn pickpocket we're dealing with."

"Give her a break, Tip. She's trying to help."

Roberts nodded to Connie. "Thanks. Nonetheless, I'll see what I can do regarding page one. If I can catch the boss in a good mood, I'll convince him."

"Then take him a case of whiskey or Scotch or whatever the hell it is he drinks and throw a spiel at him. We need a break if we're gonna catch this son of a bitch."

"That bad?" Roberts asked.

"Worse," Connie said. "We don't have a clue after two kids missing. And Montgomery County said they have nothing after three."

Roberts stood to leave. She wore a smile. "The boss drinks expensive Scotch."

"That figures," Tip said. "I was hoping he drank beer, but I should have known. Just get it done. I don't care what it costs. Get it done and send me the bill."

"You got it. And thanks." She turned as she was leaving. "Can I cite you as the source?"

"I insist," Tip said. "I want to do everything I can to piss this guy off."

"I'm sure you will," Connie said. "You're good at pissing people off."

Tip threw a five on the table and started to walk out. I stopped, staring at the table. "You know you don't have to leave a tip at the coffee shop?"

"Why not? They work their asses off same as everyone else," he said, and continued toward the door.

"You're a goddamn softie; you know that?"

"Tell that to the son of a bitch who took these kids after I shoot him full of holes."

Tip drove back to the station in silence. Connie seemed to have her own thinking to do, which kept her silent as well. As he pulled into the parking lot, he finally spoke. "I don't know if I did right by asking Roberts to run that story, but we had to do something."

"I'm not complaining," Connie said. "If anything, I may have taken a harder stance than you did. I guess we'll have to see what happens."

"I hope it's nothing bad for the kids."

"I think we all hope that," Connie said. "Let's get together tonight and start planning because sure as shit, we're gonna need to. You know he's going to try again now that you've challenged him."

"Make it after seven," Tip said. "I'm dropping by to see Sacco."

"You're more of a softie than I thought. Does Elena know?"

"No, and don't say a thing or I'll kick your ass."

"Yeah, like that would happen," Connie said as she got out of the car. "See you tonight."

Chapter Nineteen

A NIGHT OF PLANNING

I got to Tip's house a little before seven, and Mollie's car was still there. Not that it surprised me to see her car, but I began to wonder if she ever went home.

Tip's car wasn't there yet, which I presumed meant he was still at the vet's or on his way home. Either way, he was gonna get ragged. I wasn't about to let his tardiness slide without comment.

I walked in the back door, greeted by Flash's snarls and enthusiastic hello, then I made my way to the kitchen. Mollie was busy cooking when I entered.

"What're you cooking, Mollie? Smells good."

"Onions. Cookin' onions always smells good. Maybe better than they taste." She laughed as she stirred the pan with a wooden spoon. "Anyway, this is for bratwurst. Picked some up fresh at the butcher's today. Tip told me you were coming over, so I stopped by special."

"Well, thank you, Mollie, but you didn't have to do that."

"I know I didn't have to, but a person can do something once in a while just to be nice. Besides, what they sell at the grocery store don't compare. Tip likes his to be veal, and this butcher gets his cuts fresh every day."

"Veal? Tip barely knew about veal before he met me."

"No shit?" Mollie laughed. More of a cackle than a laugh. "Fat chance you have of gettin' him to admit that. He says it like he's been eatin' veal brats all his life. But that's Tip. A liar if I ever saw one."

"Mollie, if Tip is so bad, why do you put up with him?"

Mollie stopped stirring the food and looked over to me as if I'd cursed. "Bad? Never said he was bad. I said he was a liar, and I ain't takin' that back; that's what he is. But bein' a liar don't make a man bad, it just makes him a liar. Hell, Tip kept me out of prison when I shot my husband. I owe him for that. Not many people would've done that. Gave me a job too."

Mollie cackled again. "He acted like he needed help cleanin' this place, but I never saw a man who kept a place as clean as he did. I could tell. No dust on the furniture, even in places where things had to be moved. No dirt under the sofa and no cobwebs in the corners of the unused rooms. Ain't many people that can claim that, let alone a man living by himself."

"So you're doing this—coming over here—for Tip?"

Mollie went back to her cooking. "If I don't do it, who will? Damn fool's got to have *somebody* to take care of him. Sure as hell ain't gonna be either of them damn dogs. They don't even know enough to not shit on the floor."

I laughed. I knew Mollie felt she was right, and I had to agree with her. Despite what Tip might say, he was a fanatic about keeping things clean. Even his car was immaculate.

Tip sat in the lobby waiting for Spoons. "Hey, Betty, you got any good coffee?"

"I don't know about the good part, but we've got coffee. You want a cup?"

"Do you use it to put animals to sleep?"

Betty laughed. "It's not that bad. You want it or not?"

"I guess if it won't kill me, it can't be as bad as some I've had. So, yeah, please."

About ten minutes later, Betty returned holding a styrofoam cup of steaming coffee. "Here you go, Tip. Hot and bad."

Tip walked over and took it from her. "Thanks, Betty. I appreciate it."

"By the way," she said. "Spoons isn't back yet with Sacco. I think he's walking him in the woods behind here."

"Gonna goddamn spoil that dog is what he's gonna do. I only get to walk him on the weekends, if that."

"Spoons will do that. He takes to the animals right away, and the animals love him too."

Tip was looking down at a stack of faxes while Betty talked. Each one mentioned a missing animal, as well as location, date it went missing, and description. They were just like the fax he saw the last time he was here. He was about to walk away when he noticed a fax on the Hendrick's cat.

He riffled through the stack, stopping at a notification about five pages down. "Isn't this the dog that went missing with that kid up in Conroe?"

Betty stepped over and leaned close. "Looks like it."

Tip picked up the pile of notices and continued looking. "He pulled out the Hendrick's cat flier, then continued." By the time he finished going through the pile, he'd identified two more animals that had gone missing from the Conroe cases. "That's four of them so far, one in Houston and three in Conroe."

He looked to Betty. "Where do these come from? How do you get them?"

Betty sat at her desk again. "There's a service down in Houston that faxes out missing animals every day. If you have an animal missing, you go there and pay about twenty bucks, then they fax the information to all vets in a fifty-mile radius. For an extra twenty-five, they'll post the flyer on bulletin boards at local churches and grocery stores."

"And it works?" Tip asked.

"Seems to," Betty said. "We get a lot of response."

Tip shook his head. "That's better than what we have set up for kids. I'm impressed."

"What works?"

Tip turned to see Spoons walking up the hall with Sacco—and Sacco was walking normal, no limp. "He's feeling okay?" Tip asked.

"Seems to be," Spoons said. "I just had him out in the woods, and he did fine. Even ran after a few squirrels."

"Well, shoot. I guess I'll take him home then."

Spoons bowed his head. "Mr. Denton, if you don't mind, I think it would be better to let him stay a few more days. There'll be no charge," Spoons was quick to add. "Just that I'd like to keep an eye on him. Make sure he's doing okay."

Tip shrugged. "If you think so. How long are you talking about, though?"

"If he keeps up this level of healing, a few more days. No more than that. And don't worry. He'll love it here. I take him for walks a couple of times a day, and he has fun."

"Okay, how about I come get him on Friday? That's three days. That way I can spend the weekend with him."

Spoons smiled. "Sounds good. I'd like to take the weekend off anyway."

"Deal then," Tip said, and he smiled and shook Spoons's hand.

He started for the door, waved goodbye to Betty, and said, "Betty, I'm gonna call you tomorrow or have someone else call. I'll want those four flyers." Tip had his hand on the doorknob, then turned. "Hell, you might as well copy the whole damn pile and Fed-ex it to me. Send an invoice along with it."

Then he walked out. "See y'all on Friday."

I was still sitting around chatting with Mollie when I saw head-lights coming down the driveway. "Looks like Tip's gonna finally make it home," I said.

"About time. I'm gettin' tired of waitin' on that man. Acts like all I got to do is wait on his sorry ass."

I almost laughed, but I managed to hold it in. Besides, Tip's car was just turning into his parking spot. I looked out the window but didn't see Sacco. "I guess Sacco had to stay."

"Figured as much," Mollie said. "He could have found out that much with a phone call. Some damn detective he is."

A moment later Tip walked in the back door. Flash was already snarling and racing to greet him. "Good news," he said. "Gettin' Sacco on Friday."

"I hope they taught him how to cook," Mollie said. "I'm gettin' tired of cookin' for people who don't show up."

Tip walked across the kitchen, squeezed Mollie from behind, and kissed her on the cheek. "Hush up, you old windbag. If you don't stop yakking, I won't kiss you no more."

Mollie laughed. "Better watch out. The last man who kissed me, I had to kill."

Tip laughed. "I remember. But that was a lucky shot. Besides, you'd never shoot ol' Tip."

Mollie went back to cooking, then Tip said, "By the way, Mollie, can you stay late on Thursday. I invited Gino and Ribs over to eat."

"I'm guessing that means you want me to cook something?"

"Well, be better than eating garbage."

Mollie shrugged. "I guess so. I don't mind Gino so much, but that Ribs—"

"—Is like a tick," Tip said. "He grows on you."

Mollie laughed as she scooped the fried onions onto a plate. "Reminds me of what my grandpappy used to say back up in Tennessee. We used to swim in the crick, and sometimes the leeches would get on you. I would come home and say 'I hate those darn leeches.' And grandpappy would say 'They're not so bad, they just have to grow on you.' " Mollie laughed after she said it.

Tip said, "It's not that funny, Mollie. A lot of people down here in Texas don't know about leeches, but ticks they do. And besides, it's a creek, not a crick."

Mollie shot Tip a sneer. "Creek or crick. How the hell would you know? You probably ain't never stuck your foot in one your whole life."

I laughed.

Mollie glared at Tip. "You can go to hell and take Connie with you."

I raised my brows. "Me? What did I do?"

"Nothin'," Mollie said. "That's the thing. You sat there and kept your mouth shut when you knew damn well you should have told him what an ass he was."

Mollie walked toward the sink, mumbling. "Crick, creek. Shit, the man don't know a tick from a dick."

Tip couldn't stop laughing, but a few seconds later, he managed a few words. "All right, Mollie. Calm down. I was just funnin' with you."

"Funnin'? You know less about having fun than you do ticks. Just go on back to your business and let whoever's doin' the killin' keep on doin' it. You'll never catch him anyway."

"I'm gonna catch him," Tip said. "And besides, we don't know if he's killing them."

"Ya ain't got no ransom notes have ya? If he ain't killin' them, then he's selling 'em for sex. 'Cause sure as shit stinks ya can't hide that many young kids without 'em being seen."

"Yeah, yeah. I hear you, Mollie. You just go on home, and when you solve the case, come tell me."

Mollie finished placing the dinner plates and tossed her towel on the counter next to the sink. "That does it for me. I'm done for the night. Hell of a thing when you got to do your own job and somebody else's too."

Tip laughed. "I wouldn't be much of a detective if I didn't recruit the best."

Mollie smiled back at him. "Well, at least you got that part right."

She then headed for the door, reached down to pat Flash on the head, and said, "See y'all tomorrow."

"Okay, Mollie. Thanks for dinner."

"You're welcome," Mollie said. She stopped and stared at Tip. "You're welcome too, you old shit."

Tip almost choked from laughing. "Thank you, Mollie. You're a sweetheart."

Chapter Twenty

JUSTICE PLANS TO GET EVEN

Justice turned the burner on to boil water for coffee, then walked outside and down the drive to get his morning paper. He knew he was one of the few young people who still had a morning paper delivered, but it was something he enjoyed and had no intention of giving up.

The pot was coming to a boil as he re-entered the kitchen. He fixed coffee and took it outside along with the paper to enjoy his morning routine.

As he sat in the chair on the front porch, he glanced at the headlines.

SEXUAL PREDATOR ON THE LOOSE IN HOUSTON

Sexual predator? The nerve of them referring to him as such. He went on to read how the cops had obtained his DNA from the kidnapping at the mall, and that—according to them—it wouldn't be long before he was apprehended. The article went on, quoting a "high-up source" but not naming that source.

Whoever is responsible for these kidnappings needs to stop right now and return the kids to their parents. It's their only way of coming out of this intact; otherwise, I'm going to hunt them down and take them out. I'll make sure they regret the day they came to Harris County.

Is that right? Justice thought. *Make me regret the day, will you? Maybe I'll make you regret the day you made that statement.*

Furthermore, for the person who is behind these kidnappings, I don't expect you to take me up on this, but if you ever find your courage—which I'm sure you lost sometime around puberty—let me know where, and I'll meet you and settle this like real men do.

Detective Tip Denton

Detective Denton? So he's the one working this? Interesting. This makes things far more exciting.

~

Justice went to work that day as usual. He never missed work. Afterward, he came home, ate dinner, read some, then went to bed.

Hours later, the sound of the rain hitting the roof woke Justice. It didn't much matter as he couldn't sleep anyway. He'd been dreaming about hearing those good words, the ones he had heard all the time when he was young—when he had been chained up and stuffed in that little closet. He hated that closet—and the darkness—but most of all he hated that little bucket he had to go in, the way it stunk and how it tipped over sometimes in the dark.

When it did that, he'd have to be real still, or he risked getting himself messy. If it was a long night, his legs would cramp, even his back. A couple of times he couldn't take it and had to sit in it. He cringed and covered his eyes, but it didn't do any good. He could still smell the stench, still feel the mess on him.

It was during those times when he lived for the words, waited all day to hear them, prayed they would come to bring him peace. And lo and behold, after dinner, after she would make him eat even while he was messy, he would hear her repeating them over and over. He usually didn't remember the words right off, but once she got him started, he recalled every word—every single word. "Do unto others as others do to you."

He walked to the kitchen, stopped, and listened. The rain was coming down harder now, pounding the roof and pooling on the sidewalk.

"I guess it's time," Justice said to no one, and he packed what he needed and left. Today would be the day.

Later that night, Justice sat in the van and waited. He knew it wouldn't be long. He'd been here before and observed the children play. Three of them had mothers who watched their every move, peeking out kitchen windows, sitting on the front porch, working in the yard. They did a variety of things, but the one thing they had in common was they watched.

But not Shane's mom. Justice once sat for more than an hour and never got a glimpse of Shane's mom. If he didn't know better, he'd have wondered if he even had a mom.

He squeezed his hand until the knuckles turned white. What he wanted to do, what he should do, was walk up to her door, knock on it, then kill her when she answered. It would serve her right. It might even teach her to pay attention to what mattered. It might, but she'd be dead.

He heard a thunderclap and smiled. Perfect. Once the thunder started, he didn't have long to wait. The rain came within minutes, and with the arrival of the rain, the other kids scattered.

Shane, alone now, started for home. All the way, he called his dog's name. "Poncho, Poncho. Where are you, boy?"

From the back of the van, Poncho whimpered. He must have heard Shane calling him.

Justice rolled down the window when Shane was about fifty feet away. "Hey, boy. You lookin' for a little dog?"

"Yeah. A black one," he said.

"Thank God. He's right in here. I saw him trapped in the rain."

Justice got out to open the side door of the van, and when he did, he looked up and down the street, then shoved Shane inside. Afterward, he taped his mouth and tied his hands.

"Don't worry," Justice said, as he drove off. "Everything will be all right."

Poncho licked Shane's face the majority of the drive. Finally, Justice got to his house and unloaded Shane and the dog. Shane struggled to break free, but he was tied too tightly.

"Take it easy," Justice said. "I'll untie you in a minute. Then you can play with the other kids."

Justice spent the night playing games with the kids and trying to get Shane acclimated to the group. "You'll like it here eventually," he said. "Everyone has fun. We play games. Build with blocks. Wrestle with the dogs. Everything."

"I want to go home," Shane said. There were tears in his eyes.

Justice patted him on the back and tousled his hair. "I know you do. But you won't feel that way for long. It takes a while to get used to things, but everybody likes it here."

"What about Poncho?"

"Poncho is staying here too." Justice pointed to the other side of the room, where Poncho was playing tug-of-war with another dog. "You see how much fun he's having. You'll feel the same way soon."

The kids played games for about two hours, then Justice made popcorn, and they all sat down to watch a movie. Afterward, he said goodnight, and went upstairs, locking the door when he left.

In the morning, Justice cooked pancakes for all the kids, then joined them for breakfast. "I have to go to work," he said to Shane. "But you be good and ask for help if you need it. Everybody knows the routine."

Shane nodded. "What time will you be back?"

"Later today. But don't worry. The other children know what to do, and they'll be here to have a good time with. And the dogs will be here to play with too."

Justice went back upstairs and made more coffee. He went and got the paper while he waited for the water to boil. Once the coffee was made, he walked to the front porch to drink it and read the morning paper, setting the glass on the table next to him. He shuddered when he opened to the front page.

Sexual Predator Strikes Again

Sexual predator? The nerve of them. They have no reason to call me that.

Justice continued reading, but the story got worse. By the time he finished reading, he was more angry than upset. What to do about it was the question.

He pondered the situation for a moment, then decided. He'd have to show that bitch the error of her ways. He wasn't going to sit by and let her print lies.

Chapter Twenty-One

CHILD NUMBER THREE

Tip picked me up at the usual time, and as usual, I was waiting, sitting on the steps leading up to the apartment. I got up and walked to the curb when I saw him turn the corner, then opened the door and got in.

"Glad to see you've put priority on work for a change," I said. "No hurt dogs. No shit on the floor."

Tip laughed. "Buckle up and be quiet, Connie. But preferably in reverse order so I don't have to listen to you any longer."

"Testy this morning?" I asked as I fastened the seat belt.

"Did you get a call from Coop? We've got another kid missing."

"Son of a bitch," I said. "No, I didn't hear the phone ring. Maybe she called when I was in the shower. Where's this one?"

"Over by Aldine-Westfield Road. Not too far from I-45. This makes six kids now. Something's up. This isn't normal."

"I agree," I said. "In fact, I was giving this thought last night. Something that Mollie said got me wondering. If these kids are alive—and we're assuming they are since we've got no bodies—then where the hell are they? It's pretty difficult to hide six kids from the prying eyes of neighbors."

Tip shrugged. "I don't know."

"Come on, Tip. The other day when I was waiting on you, my neighbor asked me if I was waiting on my boyfriend. I said *no*. And he apologized, saying he thought that I had a boyfriend because he always saw me waiting on you."

"You trying to make me feel bad?"

"No. The point I'm making is he noticed that I'm usually out there waiting for you. If my neighbor—whom I barely know—notices that, how are six young kids going to go unnoticed?"

"Unless he's selling them as sex slaves, and they're no longer around." Tip drove in silence. He seemed to be thinking. "Or unless he still has them, but there *are* no neighbors. Like he owns a damn big piece of property."

"That's what I was thinking. If that's the case, it should narrow the search."

"Not enough," Tip said. "There are a lot of people who own acreage in this city. Hell, up on FM 1488, there are whole communities where you have to own at least five acres. Five acres is a big space, and it would be hard to see kids, especially if the guy had some trees. "

"I understand that, but I think we can narrow it down to the north side and ignore the other areas. All the kidnappings have been north of the city, and we've got the ones that happened in Conroe, which is even farther north. I'm guessing the guy lives somewhere between here and Conroe."

"I might tend to go along with you, but on the other hand, driving fifty miles to kidnap someone wouldn't be out of the question."

"Based on that reasoning, he could live almost anywhere in the city."

"My point exactly," Tip said. "Even though I agree that he probably lives in this part of town, I don't want to stop looking anywhere yet."

We passed by Greenspoint Mall, and soon after that, Tip exited the freeway and took a left. Five minutes later we were parking in front of the kidnapping victim's home.

"Mrs. Kimmler's the name," Tip said.

We walked up to the door and knocked. I never liked interfacing with the victim's family, especially when young kids were involved. Still, it had to be done.

A moment later, a woman about my age answered the door. Her hair was a mess, and a cigarette dangled from the corner of her mouth. She was dressed in a skimpy bathing suit and nothing else.

"We're here about your son," I said.

"Oh yeah, come on in," she said. Then she took a long drag from her cigarette and tossed the butt over Tip's shoulder into the front yard.

We followed her to the kitchen, where she gestured to a couple of chairs. "Have a seat. Want a beer?"

I raised my brows. The way she asked if we wanted a beer was as if she expected a positive response. "No thanks," I said, and wondered who in God's name would start drinking at this time of day.

While we waited on a glass of water, the sliding door opened and a man about the same age walked in. He wore a pair of cut-off jeans and no shirt. He nodded to Tip and me as he slid the door closed.

Tip got up to shake hands. "I'm Detective Denton," he said. "And this is my partner, Detective Gianelli."

"Are you Mr. Kimmler?" I asked.

He shook his head. "Can't blame me for that one. I probably got some rug rats out there somewhere, but not him."

A scowl formed on Tip's face. I figured the guy was about two comments away from Tip smacking him. "And *your* name?" I asked.

Mrs. Kimmler brought the water and set the glasses in front of us. "That's Rudy. He's a friend of mine. We were just outside tanning when you came."

"Kind of an odd thing to do when your kid's been taken, isn't it, Ms. Kimmler?"

"What do you want me to do? Die? I feel bad, yeah, but I'm not gonna waste my life."

"I'm sure she don't mean that," Rudy said. "Kaylee dotes on that boy. Pays more attention to him than she does to me."

"That's how it's supposed to work," Tip said, the left side of his face was twisted into a snarl. "What's your name again?"

"Rudy. Rudy Santiago. Like I said, I'm a friend of Kaylee's."

"Where were you last night?" Tip asked.

"You mean when it happened? Probably on my way over here. I got here about eight, then we watched some TV and drank a few beers."

"Watched TV and drank beers? Was this *after* you realized Shane was missing?"

"At that time, he wasn't missing, he just wasn't home yet," Rudy said.

"When did you notice him gone?" Tip asked.

"About nine," Kaylee said. "I went outside to call him, but he never came in."

"What did you do after that?" I asked.

"When he wasn't home by ten, I called the neighbors, then when I still didn't find him, I called the cops."

"Have you had any ransom demands?" Tip asked.

"Ransom? No way. If they're expecting a ransom out of me, they're shit out of luck. I ain't got no money for no ransom."

I kicked Tip under the table and said, "Okay, Ms. Kimmler, I think we have what we need for now. We'll contact you with more questions, I'm sure. And let us know if you hear anything."

"Will do," Rudy said.

I handed my card to her. "Then you might need this card. It has my number on it."

I started to leave, then turned back. "Where did you say you were, Rudy? Before you got here, I mean."

"I was at work at Drilco. Then I stopped for a couple beers. Then I came here."

"And you've got people who can vouch for you?"

He furrowed his brows. "I guess. I hadn't thought about it. But I'm sure somebody at the Ice House saw me."

"Which Ice House?" Tip asked.

"Buffalo Fred's. Inside the loop. I got there about six."

"You got there at six, and you didn't get here till nine? Damn, Rudy. You could've called me," Mrs. Kimmler said.

"Okay, thank you," I said.

Tip and I walked back to the car in silence. Once we got inside, Tip started the engine, and I said, "You want to question the neighbors?"

Tip shook his head. I don't want to know anything else about either one of them. They're both disgusting. I don't feel so bad for the kid now. He's probably with somebody nicer."

"At least someone who treats him better," I said. "That Rudy guy gave me the creeps."

"The mother didn't do much for me either. Between the two of them, I wouldn't have them babysit a dog."

"I'm with you on all of that. But you didn't answer my question. You want to question the neighbors?"

Tip sighed and turned off the engine. "Guess we might as well. We're gonna have to do it sometime."

We started at the house next door and were greeted by a teenage boy who looked to be about fifteen.

"Is your mother or father home?" I asked.

"Who wants to know?"

Tip stepped forward and flashed his badge. "Detectives Denton and Gianelli."

"Is this about the kidnapping last night?" the kid asked.

I nodded. "It is. How did you hear about it?"

He smiled. "Mrs. Ortiz, across the street. She's already let everyone know about it. You don't need a newspaper with her around. Anyway, to answer your earlier question, my dad is sleeping. He works the night shift. And my mom is at work now. I can probably tell you more than either of them anyway."

"Why's that? You see something?" I asked.

"No, I didn't see anything, but like I said, Dad was working, and my mom was sleeping so she could get up for the early shift this morning."

"Why don't you tell us what you saw, or didn't see," Tip said.

He swung the door open wider. "Come on in. Just be quiet so you don't wake up the old man."

We walked quietly across the linoleum floors until we reached the kitchen table, where we both took a seat.

The kid reached his hand out to shake. "I'm Gregg," he said. "You want something to drink? I don't know how to make coffee, but you can do it if you want."

I laughed to myself. It would have been close to sacrilegious not to know how to make coffee in our house at his age. At least according to Uncle Dominic. "What can you tell us?"

Gregg leaned forward in his chair. "All the little kids were outside playing catch. And being noisy as hell I might add. When it started to rain, they scattered. I know because one of the thunderclaps was so loud I went to the window to look."

"What time was this? Did you see anything?" Tip asked.

"It was probably about seven-thirty, and yea, I saw a white van parked across the street. There was somebody just sittin' in there."

"How long was he there?" I asked.

"I don't know how long he was there? I just saw him when I went to the window. But the van had a name on it—Guinn Roofing, I think it was."

"Are you sure?" Tip asked.

"I'm not sure, but I think that's what it said. I remembered because I know a kid named Guinn."

"You ever see that van around here before?" Tip asked.

The kid shook his head. "I would have remembered 'cause I know a kid named Guinn, like I said."

"What time did the van leave?" I asked.

Gregg shook his head. "I don't know. I never looked outside again. All I know is that it was there when I looked out the window at about seven-thirty."

"Was it a new van? Old van? Beat up?" Anything else you can tell us about the van?"

"It wasn't new. And it wasn't old. I guess four or five years old maybe. And it wasn't beat up. I didn't see any dents or noticeable scratches."

I looked to Tip, and he nodded. "Okay," I said to Gregg. "I guess that does it for now. We'll be back if we need anything else." I handed him a card. "And call if you think of anything."

We started for the door, and Gregg said, "Hang on a minute. I just thought of something. I haven't heard Shane's dog barking all morning. Not even when y'all pulled up. And that dog *always* barks."

"Okay. Thanks," I said.

We went back to see Ms. Kimmler and asked if the dog was missing.

"Yea, that son of a bitch is gone. I figure he ran away after Shane left."

"Don't you think the kidnapper may have taken it?" I said.

"Taken the dog? What for? I hope he did, but if he's fixin' to try ransoming the dog, I got news for that kidnapper—I ain't paying a penny for that damn dog. I might pay whoever took the dog a few bucks to keep him though."

"Did you report the dog missing?" Tip asked.

"Hell no. I didn't know he was gone till you came this morning, and I didn't hear him bark."

"Okay, thanks," Tip said, and we left Ms. Kimmler's place again.

"By God, but that woman makes me sick," Tip said.

"Me too. But we can't let it bother us. We've still got people to talk to."

We questioned five more neighbors, but no one had much information to share. For sure no one had as much information as Gregg, not even Mrs. Ortiz. One person confirmed seeing the van, but they didn't have as many details as Gregg had provided.

We finished the questioning about noon, then we got in the car and headed back.

Tip drove down the beltway to I-45, then we went south toward the station. "We need to check that boyfriend out," I said. "I didn't like anything about him."

"We need to check 'em both out," Tip said. "I didn't like either one of them. Besides, it shouldn't be hard to prove or disprove his alibi. I know the people who run Buffalo Freds."

I looked sideways at Tip. "Is there anybody that you don't know?"

"Probably," he said. "I just haven't found 'em yet."

About half hour later, we pulled into the parking lot. We went inside and asked Julie to do a thorough investigation on Rudy Santiago and Kalee Kimmler. I had no doubts we'd turn up *something*. I was just curious as to what.

After spelling out what we wanted from Julie, we headed down to see Coop, as per the request on my desk. Cindy showed us in immediately.

"Coop, how the hell are you?" Tip asked.

"I'd be a whole lot better if Connie had come alone," she said.

"Come on, Coop. You know you love me."

She laughed. "What'd you find out? Is it the same guy?"

"I'm pretty sure it's the same guy, but I'd like to pin it on the kid's mother and her boyfriend."

"Why's that?" Coop asked.

"Disgusting types, both of them. They acted as if it was an inconvenience to answer our questions."

"What makes you think it was the same guy?" Coop asked.

"For starters, we don't get that many kidnappings. Also, one of the neighbors saw a van parked out front not long before it happened—a strange van, one he hadn't seen before."

"And you believe this kid?"

"He's credible," I said. "I believed him. Somebody else saw the van also, but this kid gave us more."

"We've still got a few neighbors to question," Tip said. "But unless we get lucky, I doubt we'll get much more."

"All right, finish up with the neighbors and check those two out. We can't leave a stone unturned. People are getting nervous about these kidnappings. They want the son of a bitch caught."

I stood and walked toward the door. "Nobody wants him caught more than me, Captain. Don't worry, we'll get him."

Chapter Twenty-Two

A TALK WITH UNCLE DOMINIC

I got up early, made my morning brew, fed the fish and the cat, and settled in to drink my espresso and eat a bagel. I savored the bagel, smothered with strawberry cream cheese, then walked over and plopped on the couch next to Hotshot. He meowed and smacked my shoulder when I sat down, his way of saying he wanted a treat.

"I just fed you," I said. "Leave me the hell alone."

Hotshot kept quiet, but he remained on the top of the couch, loafing as if he was still expecting to get more to eat.

After about two minutes, I succumbed to his charms and gave him some liver treats, which he loved. It was a good thing he wasn't a man because I did not have the will power to resist him.

With nothing else to do, I decided to call Uncle Dominic. What

Zeppe had said the last time I spoke to him was still bothering me. I wanted answers. I knew Uncle Dominic was hiding something. I just didn't know what.

Despite the not knowing driving me crazy, I was hesitant to find out. Uncle Dominic was a man who kept few secrets; if he was keeping one about me, I didn't know if I wanted to know what it was.

I scratched Hotshot's head, took a deep sigh, and dialed. I didn't have him on speed dial so his number wouldn't be on my phone, a leftover habit from living in Brooklyn too long.

Uncle Dominic answered right away, as he always did.

"Pronto."

"Uncle Dominic, it's me."

"Concetta, my favorite person. How are you? And what did I do to deserve a call?"

"I'm fine. And I don't know what you did, but I'm hoping to find out."

"What's that supposed to mean?"

"It means that I know you're keeping something from me, Uncle Dominic. I'm a big girl now. I've known you for more than thirty years, so whatever it is you have to tell me, you need to do it. I can handle it."

"Why do you want to know? What difference will it make?"

"Probably none. But I want to know anyway. I need to know."

A long silence followed. I could hear him breathing. Could picture him deliberating. "And you're sure you want to know? Even if what I tell you is disturbing?"

"Yes. Uncle Dominic, I've been through a lot in my life. I think I can handle one of your revelations."

"I'm sure you can picture what I'm doing. I'm sitting on the porch, sipping my espresso and deliberating whether to tell you or no."

"I knew that much, Uncle Dominic."

More silence ensued, then, "Are you sitting down?"

"I'm fine, Uncle Dominic."

"Maria was not your mother."

"What?" Uncle Dominic had been right. It was a good thing I was sitting down. "What do you mean? Of course, she was my mother."

"No, she wasn't," Uncle Dominic said.

I could almost see him shaking his head. "Then who was?"

"Somebody named Mrs. Gianelli. But she's gone. Has been gone since just after you were born."

"Why? Who was she?"

"She was married to your father, who was not a nice man. He beat her so badly that she left him. Even worse, she left you in his care."

"What happened to my father? Did he die from drugs like you said?"

For a moment, Uncle Dominic said nothing, so I repeated the question. "Did he, Uncle Dominic? Did he die from drugs?"

"No, Concetta. I lied."

I was stunned. Uncle Dominic never lied to me. "Then how?"

"I killed him."

"What? What?" Of all the responses I had been prepared for, this one shocked me more than the worst I had imagined.

"I said I killed him, Concetta. He worked for my boss, Vito, and he kept selling drugs to children in violation of Vito's orders. Vito told him three times to stop. When he kept it up, Vito gave me the order."

"You killed him?"

"I did. And after I shot him, I heard you crying from the bedroom. You were only a baby. A sweet and beautiful baby. I wasn't going to leave you there, so I took you home to Maria. I never told your mother that story. And yes, she was your mother. Maybe not your biological mother, but she raised you, and she loved you like any mother would."

"Oh, my God. Oh, my God. I need a minute, Uncle Dominic. I'll call you back."

"Concetta, before you go, know this. Your father was a horrible man. He was a drug dealer who sold drugs to children. He was a man who beat his wife so badly that she left her baby with him in order to escape. You would not have had a good life with him as your father."

"And what about my mother?" Where is she?"

"I don't know. I tried finding her several times to let her know what had become of you, but I could never locate her. She did a good job of disappearing."

"When was the last time you tried?"

"About two years ago, not long after you moved to Texas."

"And you never found anything?"

"Not a clue. And I did try. I had my best men on it."

"Okay. I need to digest this. It might take a few days."

"Concetta, whatever you do, don't hate me. I did what I thought best for you. And the only reason I didn't tell you was to keep you from the truth. I was trying to protect you."

I laughed. There wasn't much else to do. "Uncle Dominic, I could never hate you. I've spent my whole life loving you, and though this is disturbing news, it won't make me hate you."

"Okay, good. Ti voglio bene, Concetta."

"I love you too, Uncle Dominic. And thank you for being honest with me."

I hung up and sat on the couch petting Hotshot and wondering what to do when I heard Tip's horn. I had come to recognize the sound of his horn.

I walked out and got in the car. "Morning, Tip."

"Morning? Is that all you got to say? It's almost time for lunch."

"I'm sorry," I said. "I should have been ready."

"What the hell is wrong with you?" Tip asked. "Normally, you'd tell me to eat shit or something."

"I know. It's just... I don't know; it's nothing."

"Nothing my ass. What's up?"

I hesitated, then said, "I talked with my Uncle Dominic this morning, and he said something that has me on edge. That's all."

"What'd he say?"

"Nothing. Don't worry about it."

"I'm not worried about it, but it's obvious that you are."

I thought about what Tip said, and realized he was right. I was worried about it. And I didn't know if I should be. Yes, it was terrible that Uncle Dominic had shot him, but if what he said was true, he deserved it. Or at least it seemed so to me. Maybe I should tell Tip and get someone else's opinion.

"My Uncle Dominic killed my real father," I blurted out.

"What? What the hell? Are you serious?"

I almost laughed. Probably would have if it didn't involve me. "Yea, I'm serious. I have known for a long time that something was up, but I never expected this."

"How did you find out?"

"I asked him."

"And he just told you?"

"Yea, he said the only reason he hadn't told me before was to protect me from the truth of knowing my father was a drug dealer. And not just a drug dealer, but one who dealt to kids."

"And he has no problem telling you he killed someone, knowing you're a cop?"

I nodded. "He knows I won't do anything. Besides, knowing Uncle Dominic, I'm sure there was no proof."

"I'm not trying to be an ass or anything, but I don't see your problem. I know killing someone is nasty shit, but if the guy was dealing drugs, and especially if he was dealing to kids, I don't know if I blame him. I wouldn't kill him myself, but I wouldn't lose sleep over it."

"He said my father also beat my mother. Uncle Dominic said that's why she left."

"Shit. As far as I'm concerned, the case is closed. If he was that kind of son of a bitch, he'd have probably beaten you too. You should thank your uncle for what he did."

"But he's a criminal. He's killed people."

"Really? You know that Mollie shot her husband. He deserved it though. It's why I let her off. I couldn't see her going to prison for pulling the trigger on some scum-sucking pig like him. She should've done it sooner."

"And that's really how you feel?"

"Damn straight. I don't like Mafia men one bit, but I wouldn't go one block out of my way to slap the cuffs on one who did what your uncle did."

"But we're cops," I said. "How do we deal with things like that?"

"Same way you deal with anything else. There are technical crimes, and there is common sense. I despise having to lock somebody up for doing something that common sense says they should have done."

"And you think my uncle did right? You don't have a problem with that?"

"I'm not saying he did right. I don't know the details. But if you believe your father was the wife-beating, drug-dealing scum your uncle claims, then I've got no problem with what he did. If I wasn't a cop, I might have done the same."

"I guess I hadn't thought it through. I'm glad I mentioned it to you. Thanks, Tip."

"You're welcome. Now get your head out of your ass and focus on this case so we can kill another scum-sucking son of a bitch. 'Cause that's what I might do when we find him."

Chapter Twenty-Three

ROBERTS NEEDS CONVINCING

Justice sat in his van, parked outside the parking garage that serviced the building where Samantha Roberts worked on Milam Street. He got out and put more money into the parking meter, then opened the door and climbed back in. He wiped sweat from his brow and lowered the air conditioning, hoping it would cool down quickly. It had been a hot day.

Before long, he noticed Roberts come out of the building. Shortly afterward, she exited the garage.

Justice drove ahead to where he knew she'd be going—The Reporter's Dream—a quiet pub on Highway 290 not far outside the 610 Loop. He exited 290, pulled into the parking lot and took a space on the side, then crouched low, waiting for Roberts to show. He didn't have to wait long. About five songs into an old Johnny Rodriguez CD, she turned into the lot and found a parking spot near the front.

Justice wished she had parked in the rear, but so be it. The front would have to do. He waited about an hour before she came out, walking confidently toward her car. When she was about halfway there, he got out of the van, opened the side door, then leaned in, as if he were getting something, and began hollering. "Help! Help. Will somebody help me with my boy?"

Roberts came running. When she got to the van, Justice tossed a sack over her head and threw her into the van, where he tied her up with rope. Once she was secure, he got into the driver's seat and took off.

Samantha had some kind of cover over her head. At first, she thought it may have been a pillow case, but then realized it was too thick. In any case, she couldn't see. But that didn't mean she couldn't think. She paid close attention to the ride, distance in seconds between red lights, how many stops there were, and if she felt any of the bumps in the road that warned of lane changes or upcoming traffic signals. And she tried to commit to memory which way the van turned by the way her body shifted.

According to her calculations, they drove about forty minutes before stopping. A few seconds later, the side door to the van opened, and she was led outside, though still blindfolded.

They walked a long way, half a block maybe, then he opened a door using a key, then they walked another twenty-two steps. He opened another door, shouted "I'm home," then led Roberts in and led her to a seat on what she presumed was a sofa.

"I can't remove the sack," he said. "I can't let you see me."

"I understand," Roberts said. "But why am I here?" she asked.

"I need you to see the children and see how happy they are. As you'll see, the children are fine. You called me a sexual predator. Talk to the kids, and you'll see I'm not," the man said.

Roberts shifted into reporter mode. "Maybe they're afraid of you. Leave me alone with them, and let me see what they say then."

"Of course," Justice said. "If you want, you can stay and eat breakfast with them. In fact, now that I think about it, I believe it would be good for you to do that. I hope you don't mind sleeping on a sofa."

"I don't mind," Roberts said.

"Good. Tommy, when I leave, take the hood off Ms. Roberts head so she can see. And show her around, let her go anywhere."

Justice left and locked the door.

The next morning, Justice cooked a big breakfast—bacon, sausage, pancakes, toast, and scrambled eggs—then went down and knocked on the door. "Breakfast is served," he hollered.

"Tommy, put the hood back on Ms. Roberts and let me know when it's secure."

A moment later, Tommy yelled out. "Done, you can come in now."

Justice unlocked the door and entered, and was greeted by a rousing cheer.

He set the food on a table, then checked to ensure that Roberts's hood was fastened securely. "Good job, Tommy. I'm proud of you."

They spent the next half hour eating, Justice left the room so that Roberts could have her hood removed and had no trouble eating.

When they were done, Justice returned and told the kids to say goodbye to Ms. Roberts, then he helped her up, led her to the door, and out to the van.

~

On the ride back, Roberts tried her best to concentrate on road conditions, traffic signals, rates of speed, and other such things as her captor drove.

Within about forty minutes, she felt the van coming to a stop, then the side door opened.

"Time to get out," the man said, and helped her from the car and into the parking lot. "I'm leaving now," the man said. "If you—"

"—Where are you going? You can't leave me like this," Roberts said.

"I know you feel afraid, but there doesn't seem to be anyone here yet. I'm sure if you walk toward the sound of traffic, and wave your hands once you get there, someone will be sure to help you. Be careful not to step into the street."

"But I can't see. I'm blindfolded."

The man placed his hand on her shoulder and said, "I know you're blindfolded. I put it there, remember? I can't allow you to see me, but if you do as I say and are careful, everything will be fine. And don't forget to tell people I'm not hurting those children. I'm sure you saw that they were happy."

Desperate to keep him around a while so that she could get more information, Roberts scrambled for a thought. "Most of them seemed happy, but that one wasn't. I think his name was Shane. He seemed distraught."

"I don't know what distraught means, but if you mean he's not happy—you're right. He's the newest one. It takes a week or so to get used to something new. He'll get over it."

"Why are you doing this?" she asked.

"To give them a good home. The ones they had were bad. As you can see, the kids are happy and taken care of."

"Okay, what now?"

"Now you go home, as I promised. Have a good day, Ms. Roberts."

The man slid behind the steering wheel of the van and drove off.

It didn't take Roberts long to flag someone down, only a few moments. She was surprised it took her that long, but maybe that was a testament to how no one wanted to risk helping someone else anymore.

A stranger removed her blindfold/hood and then untied her hands. "Are you okay, lady? What happened?"

"I'm fine now. Thank you. I have a car in the parking lot of The Reporter's Dream, if you don't mind waiting until I get in."

"No problem. I'm right with you."

As they walked to her car, Roberts said, "I'm a reporter. If you don't mind, I'd like to do a short piece on you, maybe a Good Samaritan type piece."

The guy shook his head. "No thanks, lady. That's all I need is for my wife to see I stopped to help a fox like you. She'd have my ass. If you want to do something for me, forget we met."

Roberts laughed. "Okay, you've got a deal. But thank you so much. I was frightened."

She reached for her purse, which she just realized she still had, and pulled out her keys. "Here's my car," she said. "Again, I can't thank you enough." She leaned toward the man and pecked him on the cheek. "You don't have to tell your wife about that."

The man blushed. "No, ma'am. I won't. And thank you. I mean really thank you." The man turned and headed toward his car. Roberts got into hers, started the engine, and drove away. She should go home, take a shower, change clothes, and get some sleep, but she needed to get things done. This was huge. It gave her a chance to help break this case.

On her way into work, she called Tip.

Tip was almost to Connie's apartment building when the phone rang. "Damn, you're impatient," he said.

"It's not Connie if that's who you thought it was. This is Roberts."

"Roberts? What the hell are you doing calling at this time of the morning? I don't need this. I got enough women chasing me."

"They're alive."

"What? Who's alive?"

"The kids. The kidnapper grabbed me last night and took me to where he's keeping them."

"What the hell! Are you shitting me?"

"And I'm doing fine, thank you, Detective Denton."

"Shut the hell up, you soft shell. I knew you weren't dead 'cause you were talking. What can you tell me? What do you know?"

"Not much. He had a hood of some type over my head the whole time, but I figured out some things."

"Okay, listen. Hold on. Don't do anything. I'm on my way to pick up Connie now. We'll come right down and meet you at the coffee shop. Same place as before."

"How long?"

"I don't know. Probably forty-five minutes. One hour tops."

"Okay, see you then."

Roberts was already at the coffee shop when Tip and Connie arrived. She was sitting at a corner table, and from the looks of it, had already finished a few coffees.

Tip pulled out a chair and sat. "You don't throw away your empty cups?" he asked. "I'd hate to see your kitchen."

Roberts looked to Connie, with her eyebrows raised. "Is he always this sensitive? I just told him I had been kidnapped, and he's giving me shit about a couple of coffee cups on the table."

"That is Tip being sensitive," Connie said, then she and Roberts laughed.

"If you two are done yakking about nothing, let's focus on what matters, and that means you telling us what happened, Roberts."

Roberts told them how he had grabbed her from the bar and taken her to his "luir."

"Obviously, he knew who you were and where you'd be, or he followed you from work. Either way makes no difference. What else can you tell us? What was the ride like? Traffic? Freeway?"

"I tried to keep track; in fact, I was writing down what I remembered before you got here. We drove on the freeway for a few miles, then turned to the...right, I think." She shifted her body, mimicking a right turn. "Yes, it was right. Then we drove about ten miles or more before turning left. Then—"

"—Hold on a minute," Tip said. "Was that ten miles of freeway? Any traffic signals?"

Roberts shook her head. "Sorry, no. It was definitely freeway. No stops for red lights and all about the same speed."

Tip nodded. "So not much traffic either."

"Based on where he grabbed you, and you saying he turned right, that could only be the beltway between Highway 290 and I-45."

Roberts nodded. "I agree. And I think the left turn was onto I-45, because after he turned left, we hit some traffic, but no stop lights."

Tip looked to Connie. "That fits what we talked about, somebody in the north part of town."

Tip turned to Roberts. "What can you tell us about the roads after you left the freeway. And how long were you on I-45?"

"He drove about ten or fifteen minutes on the freeway, maybe more. I tried counting, but he kept talking, and it made me break concentration. When we exited, I think we went right, but I'm not sure. Then about five minutes later, he parked and took me out of the van. We went into a house, and he put me in a room with no windows and six kids. Oh, and some dogs too."

"Dogs?" Connie asked.

"Yeah. The dogs that belonged to the kids, or some of them anyway."

"One more thing. I can't be sure, but after we parked, we seemed to walk down to get to the room. Almost like walking down a ramp with a small slope."

"So it wasn't steps?" Tip asked.

"No, it wasn't steps, and it wasn't an elevator or anything like that. It was a gradual slope downward. At least it felt like it."

"And the kids weren't hurt?" Tip asked.

Roberts shook her head again. "Not in the least. In fact, they all seemed happy. All but one."

"Why's that?" Connie asked.

"I don't know. I mentioned it to the guy, and he said 'the boy was the newest one, and that it takes a week or so to get used to something new. He'll get over it.'"

"And then he just let you leave?" Connie asked.

"Well, I didn't just leave. He had to drive me back to where he abducted me. But he never harmed me or threatened to."

"Now what?" Tip asked.

"Now I'm going to do a story telling people that the kids are safe—at least not harmed. I don't know what this guy's agenda is, but I don't think we should antagonize him."

"I don't know about—"

"—Hold on," Connie said. "I agree with Roberts. And what she said has got me thinking about other things. Maybe we should meet to discuss this in more detail. In the meantime, I think Roberts should move forward with her article."

"All right, we'll meet at my house tonight. I want to get this over with," Tip said.

"If that's it, I'm going," Roberts said. "I've got a long day ahead of me."

"See ya later," Tip said.

"Yeah, see ya," Connie said as she stood. "And, Tip, don't forget to throw away your empty coffee cups."

Roberts laughed as she walked out.

"What are you thinking?" Tip asked.

"I'm not sure yet. Give me some time. We'll talk about it tonight."

Chapter Twenty-Four

TIME TO PAY THE PIPER

Justice waited outside of the Anadarko building, thanking God for the rain He provided. He loved the rain, and he loved nothing more than doing the Lord's work while it was raining, especially if it was raining hard.

The fierceness of the rain brought to mind his early days, when he would peer out the cellar window and see the other kids playing. He could still hear their laughter and taunts as they threw rocks in puddles to splash each other. And he could picture the dogs running and barking, playing right along with the kids. He wished he had been able to play in that rain, but his mama wouldn't allow him to. She said rain was for food for growing things and it wasn't their job to waste it by soaking it up with clothes.

"When it rains, it's best to stay inside," mama used to say.

Justice didn't know if he believed that, but it must be true because mama said it, and she didn't tell no lies. She's the one who told him about the Good Book and the Good Words, how you do unto others what others do to you. Mama said she lived her whole life that way, and she said Justice should too.

And Justice did live that way. He remembered the time that Helga Barker killed his pet toad, and how he put that same toad on her sandwich, then laughed while he watched her throw up after biting into it. And how he got even with George Sparks when George threw a rock at his dog.

Justice had thrown a rock back at George, but Justice's rock hit George in the head—not the hind leg—and George had to get stitches. Justice got in trouble for what he did, but that was all right. George didn't throw no more rocks at his dog.

Justice often wondered why mama had kept him in that cellar. He asked her one time, and she said, "Remember that time you put that squirrel in a cage? The Lord don't like nothin' in a cage, so I guess I need to teach you what it feels like."

Justice didn't mind her doin' what she did, but he'd been in that cellar for two years. It should have been enough time.

One time he told one of his teachers about it, and the teacher must have said somethin' to his mama 'cause that night she beat him with a hickory stick. After he was done bein' beat, she said if he ever said anything again, she beat him twice as bad but next time she'd use a mesquite stick that still had the thorns on it.

Justice figured she meant it 'cause Mama meant everything she said, like the time she had told Papa to shut up, or she'd hit him with a frying pan. Papa kept talking, and Mama *did* hit him with the frying pan, maybe a little too hard. It done killed Papa. Leastwise, that's what he'd found out later. He heard his mama talkin' about it with one of her friends.

Justice figured she'd buried him out back 'cause he'd seen a freshly dug patch of dirt near the back of the property. Justice never did tell nobody about Papa. He didn't guess it would do any good anyway.

Justice stopped his contemplation to focus on the rain. It was coming down harder now, and the employees were just leaving the building. A moment later, Justice saw him—Kent Richardson. A piece of shit if he ever saw one.

He followed Kent for about three miles until he parked in the driveway of his nice cushy house in The Woodlands.

Justice pulled to the curb in front of the house, rolled his window down, and hollered to Kent. "Excuse me, Mr. Richardson. Can you help me out with something?"

Richardson leaned forward, squinting, then he slowly walked toward the van.

"Over here," Justice said as he opened the driver's side door.

Richardson walked around the van, and, as he approached Justice, he said, "What do you want? Who are you?"

"I found a dog that I think is yours," Justice said. "Look." He reached to open the sliding door on the side of the van.

Richardson stepped forward to look inside, and when he did, Justice hit him over the head with a hammer, knocking him out. He pushed Richardson into the van, closed the door, then drove away.

After dropping him off and making sure he couldn't get loose, Justice went back to the neighborhood and looked for Richardson's son, Nate.

He drove around the neighborhood until he spotted Nate. He was playing with a group of other boys. It was not the ideal situation, but he'd try.

Justice stopped the van close by, leaned his head out the window and called to the boy.

"Hey, boy. I need directions on how to get to the Woodlands Parkway. Can you help me?"

"Sure. Turn around, take two rights, then follow that road about a mile or so. You'll run right into it."

"I'm confused. Will you show me? I'd be happy to pay you."

"No dice, mister. We're winning right now, and I don't intend to leave. Do what I said, and you'll be fine."

"Okay, thanks," Justice said, and drove off. Nate would have to wait for another day.

Richardson awoke, tied to a chair and seated in a dark room with no windows. After about two hours, Justice walked in and flicked on a light. He approached Richardson wearing a smile.

"Happy to see someone?" he said.

"What do you want? Who are you, and what am I doing here?"

"Let's just say that you can thank Justice for it." Justice laughed. "I don't think you know how funny that is," he said.

"What do you want?" Richardson asked again.

Justice held up a pair of pliers, squeezed a piece of Richardson's skin and yanked hard.

"Ow! Goddamn. That hurts. What the hell are you doing?"

"Just ripping a little skin off," Justice said. "But it seems resistant. Perhaps I'll have to help." He reached into a nearby toolbox and took out a box cutter, then he sliced Richardson's arm just above the elbow.

Richardson screamed, but while he was screaming, Justice took the pliers again and clamped them onto the same spot he'd just cut. This time, when he yanked, a patch of skin came off.

Richardson screamed louder and for a longer time.

Justice continued, doing the same thing on Richardson's other arm followed by his two thighs. Finally, Richardson passed out, and Justice stopped.

"Try to get some rest," Justice said. "We'll continue this later."

Chapter Twenty-Five

THEM BOYS IS ALIVE

I hadn't talked to Uncle Dominic since he told me he had been the one who killed my biological father. There wasn't any emotional shock, but it was still a surprise. It's not often someone tells you that they were the one who killed your father. The phone rang twice before Dominic answered.

"Pronto."

"Uncle Dominic, this is Connie."

I thought I heard a sigh followed by silence. "Concetta, did you come to terms with what I told you?"

"Uncle Dominic, I haven't thought much about that. I've been focusing on a case, and I'm stuck."

"And you need my help?"

"If you don't mind, yes. We have a series of kidnappings—six kids now and no clue as to why the kids are being kidnapped. He's taken boys, girls, and mixed nationalities, and he's taken them from a wide geography. But we know that he's not hurting them; in fact, he went out of his way to let a reporter spend time with the kids and talk to them."

"What else?" Dominic asked.

"I told him all I knew about the cases, then waited.

Uncle Dominic was quiet for a moment, then he said, "Concetta, it has been my experience that crimes are committed for a small number of reasons: sex, power, money, or revenge. Often, a person is crazy they are trying to do good, and the only way to do it is to break the law."

"I don't know if I buy it, Uncle Dominic. What about things like road rage, where someone is killed because a car cut in front of another car. That's not sex, or power, or money."

"No, but that could fall into the revenge category or the crazy category, or revenge driven by crazy. If you're not crazy, why else would you shoot someone for cutting in front of you?"

"What about if two people are arguing, and one shoots or stabs the other? Isn't that just a crime of passion?"

"It could be, Concetta. But chances are the argument was about sex or power or money. And if it wasn't, then one of them was likely crazy, probably the one who did the killing."

"How would you categorize these kidnappings?" I asked.

"I don't know enough about them," Dominic said. "But we can try to eliminate some of the possibilities and see what is remaining."

"What do you mean?"

"You said the children appeared to be treated well. That would imply that there is no sexual abuse on the kidnapper's part, so sex is off the table. He hasn't sold them for sex or asked for ransom, so money is off the table. You didn't mention a reason for revenge, and being the outstanding detective I know you are, you would have found a reason if one existed, so revenge is removed from consideration. Kidnapping children such as these would in no way give him power, so we can also eliminate that. He's not harming the children, and he's treating them well, so I think it's safe to say he's not crazy. That leaves only one option—he's doing it for a good reason. It's now up to you and your partner to figure out what that reason is. That's how you'll catch this person."

What he said made sense. It started the juices flowing. "All right, thank you, Uncle Dominic. You helped."

"I hope so, Concetta. I hope you catch this man before anyone is hurt. Buona notte. Ti voglio bene."

"Ti voglio bene, Uncle Dominic."

I got in the car and drove to Tip's house, thinking of what Uncle Dominic said the whole way. Before I realized it, I was turning onto the street where Tip lived.

I parked in the driveway next to Tip's car, and when I got out, I noticed Mollie's car on the side. I was glad to see she was there as that held promise for a decent meal.

Mollie was vacuuming the living room when I walked in. Flash raced to greet me, snarling the whole time.

I said my hellos to Flash, then Mollie. "Where's Tip?"

"He's in the shower," Mollie said. "I'm guessin' he's tryin' to wash that stink off. That man smells like a wet dog when he gets hot."

I restrained my laughter and took a seat at the kitchen table. "Need any help, Mollie?"

"I'm doin' fine," she said. "Just got to finish vacuuming, then swipe a couple of dishes and I'll be done. Ready to cook somethin' up for you two to eat."

I jumped up and moved to the sink. "I can do the dishes," I said and grabbed a wash cloth and a dish towel.

I was almost done washing when Mollie came in and snatched the towel from where it was hanging on my shoulder.

"Give me that damn towel," she said. "Least I can do is dry them."

"No need, Mollie. Sit down and have a beer. I'll finish these."

She cocked her head and stared, then tossed the towel on the counter and walked to the table and sat. "All right, girl. You talked me into it this time, but I'll have no arguing after dinner. I'll be doin' the dishes."

"You've got a deal," I said, then reached into the fridge and grabbed her a beer. "Sip on this while I finish. A cold beer will taste good after all your hard work."

A couple of minutes later, I dried the last dish, then sat in a chair next to Mollie. We chatted about a lot of things, but mostly about Tip. She loved that man like a son, though she'd never admit it.

We were talking about how she got to know Tip, when out of the blue, she said, "I think them boys are still alive."

Tip was just coming into the kitchen and must have heard her. "Why do you say that?"

"Because we ain't found no bodies, that's why. You can dispose of one body, but three is something else. And if you count the ones from Conroe, it's six."

Tip sneered. "And since when did you become the expert on body disposal? I thought your specialty was killing abusive husbands?"

"Better watch it," Mollie said. "If you keep it up, I might switch my expertise to poisoning smart-ass detectives. But go ahead, ignore my advice. You'll see."

"Judging by the way the last few dinners tasted, I'd say you already started practicing."

Mollie laughed, then reached over and smacked him across the back of the head. "You damn old scoundrel. If Connie wasn't here, I just might perfect it. But no sense in makin' her suffer for your sins." She got up from the table and walked to the fridge, took out some hamburger meat, and said, "Burgers all right? I didn't have time to plan much else."

Tip was still laughing, but he managed to say, "That'll be fine, Mollie. Thank you. And you're right, those kids are still alive."

Mollie spun toward Tip, surprise showing. "What? How do you know?"

The kidnapper grabbed a reporter and let her see the kids, then he took her back to her car, polite as all get out.

Mollie shook her head. "I'll be damned," she said. "I wonder what the hell he's doing." She finished off her beer, then grabbed the meat and took it to the grill, mumbling all the way. "Got no time to think about it now. Need to get these burgers cooked."

Tip waited for Mollie to go outside to cook, then he turned to me and said, "What about what you said earlier when we met with Roberts? You had a chance to think about it?"

"It was what Roberts said about the kids being happy," I said. "Then she said he had their dogs too."

"What's that got to do with anything?"

"I don't know, but it got me thinking. If this guy was so bad, why did he bother taking their dogs? It's almost like he did it for the kids—to make them happy."

"I don't buy it," Tip said. "He's kidnapping them. It's plain and simple, nothing good about it."

"My Uncle Dominic says that crimes are done for six reasons: sex, power, money, revenge, a person is crazy, or it's a crime where someone is trying to do good."

"I'll go along with most of that," Tip said. "But that doesn't give us anything."

"Don't be so sure," I said. "I talked to Uncle Dominic about it, and he concluded that the first five don't apply to these kidnappings, and I agree with him. That leaves us only number six—that someone is trying to do good. And if we believe Roberts about the kids' attitude, that theory fits."

Tip sucked on his beer and leaned back in the chair. "If we go along with that, what good is he trying to do?"

"I don't know," I said. "We'll have to find that out."

"And how do we do that?" Tip asked.

"We start digging into all their lives, even deeper than we have. Get Julie to find out everything: finances—who they owe, and who they used to owe; exes—where they live now and where they were when the kidnappings happened; boyfriends—where they work, sleep, and everything else. I want to know everything about these people and the people who are close to them."

"Sounds good," Tip said. "We'll get Julie on it in the morning."

"If we can figure out why this guy is taking the kids, maybe we can figure out who is doing the taking."

"That's what we're supposed to do," Tip said. "Let's hope we can do it."

"We'll do it," I said. "Though I don't like relying on gangsters for help."

"I'll take help any way it comes," Tip said. "Gino and Ribs used Gino's girlfriend to help with his last case. And she's the worst kind of criminal—one that got away."

"Who? You mean Marissa?"

"Yeah, you met her that night at the house."

"I like her. She's nice."

"Maybe it runs in the family," Tip said, then ducked the punch he knew was coming.

"You son of a bitch. I'll get you."

Tip was still laughing when Mollie walked in with the burgers. "Time to eat," she hollered.

"Sounds good to me," Tip said. "I'm as hungry as—"

"—It doesn't matter what you were gonna say you were as hungry as, it would have been a lie. So just get yourself another beer —'cause I ain't doin' it. Then you can sit down to eat."

I laughed so hard my side hurt. Mollie was the only one who could talk to Tip like that and get away with it.

Tip came back to the table holding two beers. As he took a seat, he squinted his eyes and said, "There was something Roberts said..." Tip gulped his beer, then set the empty can on the table. "I can't remember what it was, but it rang a bell with me."

"You'll think of it," I said, then took a bite of the burger. "Damn, this is good, Mollie."

"Of course it's good. I wouldn't cook a bad one."

"Mollie, you're gonna need to put on your thinkin' cap. We need you to help on this case," Tip said.

"I know you need my help, but I ain't decided if I'll give it to you or not. One thing's for sure—you got some kind of pervert out there taking these kids. Nobody but a pervert would take a kid from his mother."

"That's what we're going to figure out, Mollie."

"You better do it fast unless you want to lose more kids, 'cause I got a feeling this pervert isn't stopping."

"Don't you worry, old girl. We'll get him."

Chapter Twenty-Six

IT'S GOT TO BE HIM

We finished eating burgers, drank another beer each, then Tip suggested we try to figure the case out.

"We need to look at everything again, like we always do. I made up some charts earlier, so let's take a look."

We went into the living room, where he had two charts set up on a small table. One showed each kidnapping on the left side with what we knew about it on the right. The other was blank except for the word *conclusions* across the top.

Kid #1—Hendricks

- Taken from mall.
- Was with mother.
- Kidnapper had cat.
- Kidnapper talked slow.
- Hendricks smelled chloroform.
- Kidnapper called them, so he had phone number.

- Met her in dark-green van.
- Single mother. Ex is in Corpus Christi.

Kid #2—Salerno

- Taken from Little League game.
- Game crowded.
- Van seen at scene.
- Possibly taken by tall thin man with angular features.
- White van with plumbing sign was spotted.

Kid #3—Kimmler

- Taken from outside home.
- Mother home at time.
- Van seen on street.
- Roofing sign on van.
- Dog missing as well.

"The first thing I see," Tip said. "Is that in every one of these, there was a van seen on the night of the kidnapping. Not the same van, but a similar van. Hendricks says it was a green van, but a white one was seen on the night of the kidnapping."

"It's only not the same because of the sign," I said. "Suppose he's using those magnetic signs to change it up, make it appear different?"

"And they're all single women," Tip said. "Even though Kimmler had a boyfriend, he wasn't around. And he wasn't a live-in boyfriend."

"I know he wasn't a live-in, but I didn't like him," I said. "He gave me the creeps."

"I hear that," Tip said. "I already said we'd have Julie check him out. Hell, we'll have her check everyone out. We could have missed something."

"All right, let's move on to what we know and don't know.

CONCLUCSIONS:

Looking for a white van
May also be a green van involved
Kidnapper may be tall and thin
It has rained every time a kid was taken
He targets single mothers

QUESTIONS:

Why is he taking animals?
Why is he taking kids? What does he want them for?
How does he target them?
Why doesn't anyone see him?

"As you can see on the chart, if we take what witnesses have told us, we're looking for a white van, but according to Ms. Hendricks, he drives a green van."

"So maybe he has two vans. One to grab the kids with, and another one he uses for normal use."

"That's possible," Tip said. "We've got to presume that may be right, at least for now. We've also got a report that he may be tall and thin—this from the guy at the Little League game."

"What about the rain? Do you think it's a coincidence they've been taken on nights when it rains?"

"I've been thinking about that," Tip said. "I don't think it is a coincidence. I think he's using the rain to hide his activity. People tend to be more concerned with protecting themselves from getting wet when it's raining. They're not paying attention to what's going on."

I thought about what Tip said and had to agree. I was that way myself. If I got caught in a downpour, the first thing I did was tuck my head down and run for cover. I wouldn't notice it if a bank was being robbed next to me. "Okay, Tip, I buy that. What about the animals? Why the hell is he taking the animals? He's not killing them, not that we know of."

"That leads to the bigger question of why he's taking the kids to begin with. From what we know: he's not a pervert; he's not selling them into the sex slave trade; he's not asking for ransom; and as far as we can tell, he's not an ex or a family member who feels slighted."

"If you abide by Uncle Dominic's theory, that rules out money, sex, power, and revenge. It means he's crazy or he's doing it for good reasons or perceived good reasons."

"And if we believe what Roberts told us, he's not hurting the kids, so maybe that theory holds some water."

"You get anywhere on figuring out where he might be holding them based on Roberts' description of her ride."

Tip shook his head. "She did good, but it's tough to get close enough to matter. Even if she's off by two exits, we're screwed. That leaves a lot of ground to cover. From what she told us, he could be anywhere from a few miles north of the beltway to just south of Conroe. We couldn't search that amount of territory with fifty people to help."

"Well, he's doing something right. According to Roberts, the kids were all happy—all except that one."

Tip set his beer down and appeared to be giving that thought.

"What's up, Tip?"

He held up his finger in a gesture for me to wait, then he continued focusing on ... something.

Finally, he said, "I think I have something, Connie, but I don't know if I want to."

"What?"

"Remember what Roberts said about that kid? She said the kidnapper told her that 'It takes a week or so to get used to something new.'"

"Yeah, so what?"

"The guy who works at my vet's office uses that same expression—word for word."

I laughed. "Come on, Tip. We can't arrest a guy for using an expression. At least not that one. Maybe one of your expressions, but not something as simple as that. A hundred people probably use that expression."

Tip pulled out his cell phone and dialed. "Roberts, this is Tip. Remember what you told me about what the kidnapper said to you when you asked about the kid you said wasn't happy?"

"I remember."

"What did he say? Exactly."

"Hang on. I wrote it down when I got to my car. I'll get it."

Roberts set the phone down, then returned a moment later. "He said, 'It takes a week or so to get used to something new.' That's verbatim. At least it is if I recall it properly."

"Perfect," Tip said.

"Why? Does it mean something?"

"I'm not sure yet, but maybe."

"If it helps, the way he said it ... it was like he was stating fact, not surmising. You know what I mean, like he knew that it took a week or so, not like he was guessing or even quoting someone."

"Roberts, you've been a big help. I'll fill you in when we figure something out."

Tip turned to me wearing a shit-eating grin. "She confirmed it, Connie. It's him."

"Tip, I don't mean to bust your bubble, but someone using an expression as common as that doesn't mean shit. Do you think this guy could be the kidnapper?"

Tip lost his smile. "I wouldn't have guessed so. I even like the guy. He's the one who's been taking care of Sacco. But still ..."

"What do you want to do?"

"I think we should put a tail on him. See where he goes, and what he does. Either rule him out or make him suspect number one."

I laughed. "You're serious about this, aren't you?"

"Damn straight, I'm serious. I think there might be something to it. And we don't have anything else to go on. Hell, if we had three or four suspects, maybe I'd feel differently. Maybe I wouldn't be grasping for straws if we had three or four suspects, but we don't have three or four suspects; in fact, we don't have one."

I sighed. I'd seen Tip when he had his mind made up. There was no getting him off it. "How do you want to handle this?"

"No need for you to do anything. I'll follow him."

"You're gonna follow him by yourself?" I asked.

"Well, maybe you can help a little bit."

I laughed. "Just what I figured." I got up and walked into the kitchen, grabbed a notepad and pen and sat. "Let's get busy and map it out."

Chapter Twenty-Seven

FOLLOW THE SUSPECT

Tip waited in his car, situated about a block from the vet's office. Whenever Spoons left work, he'd have to pass there, so Tip was ready. He sat slouched down in his seat and pretended to be reading a book. Music was blaring. If Spoons had suspicions, the loud music might throw him off; he wouldn't suspect a stake-out car to be blaring music.

Around 6:15, Spoons left the building. Tip got his first disappointment a moment later when Spoons pulled away in a blue Honda Civic, not the van Tip had hoped he'd be in.

He waited for Spoons to pass, let him get a decent lead, then made a U-turn and followed. He called Connie. "He's heading toward the freeway. Get on the freeway going south. If he goes that way, you'll be ahead of him so he won't suspect anything."

"What about if he goes north?" Connie said.

"If he goes north, we don't care," Tip said. "He could go north, but I doubt it. Let's see what he does. And stop asking so damn many questions."

Connie laughed. "Yes, sir. Didn't mean to confuse you with such complex problems."

Tip laughed along with her when she said that. "Keep alert. I'm guessing he'll be passing you soon."

A few minutes later, Spoons turned south onto the freeway. "Headin' your way," Tip said. "He's in a blue Honda Civic. Looks like it might be two years old."

Within five minutes, he passed Connie, who was driving the speed limit in the right lane. "Got him," she said. "I'm going to pass him by now."

"That's fine. Pass him, wait a minute or so, then drop back and let him pass you."

Connie did this for several miles, then Spoons pulled to the right lane and prepared to exit.

"Looks like he's going to exit at the Woodlands Mall," Tip said. "Get in front of him. I'll stay back so he doesn't spot me."

Spoons exited the freeway at the mall, then made a quick left turn into the mall parking lot. He parked near the second-floor entrance. It placed him near the middle of the mall and provided quick access to the escalators.

"Enter by Macy's and make your way to the escalators. He's going in the top entrance. If he goes down to the first floor, you'll be there to pick him up. If he stays upstairs, you'll have to find him."

"Damn, such a well-planned stakeout," Connie said.

"Eat shit," Tip said.

I found a spot to park, then raced inside the mall and down to where the escalators were. I stood in line at a store to get pastries and put in my Bluetooth earbud while I waited for Spoons to show up. "What's the status, Commander?"

Tip laughed. "Screw you. He's going in now. If he goes downstairs, it shouldn't be more than thirty seconds or so. And put your phone down so he doesn't suspect anything."

"Already got my earbud in, Mighty Leader. Any other instructions?"

"Screw you again," Tip said.

A moment later, I spotted what I felt sure was him. "Tall guy wearing jeans and an orange shirt?"

"You got him," Tip said. "Now who's the smart one?"

"Me. I'm the one who spotted him. Anyway, I'll keep you posted."

Spoons turned right at the bottom of the escalator, and a moment later he walked into the Apple store. "He went into the Apple store," I said. "If he's just here to pick something up, I'm gonna kick your ass."

"Just follow him," Tip said.

I waited about ten minutes, then Spoons came out carrying something small in a bag, looked like it could have been headsets or a charger. He turned right again and headed toward Macy's.

I kept my distance, following nonchalantly about fifty feet behind him. I stopped to window shop for a moment whenever I got too close. After a stroll that seemed to take forever, Spoons went into Macy's. "He's going into Macy's," I said. "You think I should follow or wait?"

"I'd wait," Tip said. "He's not going anywhere from Macy's. I'm sitting with eyes on his car, and you're watching the only exit to the mall. I guess he could go upstairs to exit, but he'd still have to get his car. So stay put."

"Will do."

"Have fun," Tip said.

Half an hour went by, and Spoons hadn't exited yet. "No sign of him here, Tip. His car still there?"

"Right in front of me. And you're sure he hasn't slipped out, maybe with a crowd of others?"

"I've been watching. There's no way he came out. He's still in Macy's, doing God knows what unless he went upstairs to exit."

"Then I guess we let him stay in there. Maybe he's doing his yearly shopping."

"Yearly?"

"Did you see the way he dressed? Spoons is no clothes horse. I'd be surprised if he shopped more than once a year for clothes."

"Say no more. I'll hang tight and wait."

Another hour passed, then a few minutes later, Spoons came walking out of the store. I lowered my head and spoke into the mic. "He's here."

"About damn time," Tip said. "I was ready to fall asleep."

I let Spoons get fifty or sixty feet ahead of me, then got up to follow. "I'm on him. He's heading for the escalators again."

"I'm waiting," Tip said. "Let me know when he goes up."

I followed him for about fifteen minutes, pausing as he stopped to look into a few stores. Finally, he got on the escalator and rode it to the second floor. "He's on his way."

A few moments later, Spoons exited the mall and walked slowly to his car. He unlocked the door, got behind the steering wheel, and drove off.

"May as well come out, Connie. He's gone, and we've got nothing to show for it."

"I don't know," I said. "I saw a couple of blouses I may want to pick up. It wasn't a complete waste of time."

"Go home, Connie. That's where I'm going."

"You're not following him? He may be off to kill a few people or heal a dog or two."

"Screw you a third time," Tip said. "See you tomorrow."

Chapter Twenty-Eight

ANOTHER RAINY DAY

Justice sat in the van staring out the window. It was raining hard, raining fish and frogs as they say in certain parts of East Texas.

Justice didn't see any fish splattering on his windshield, and he didn't see any frogs, but it was raining so hard it would have probably washed them away.

He listened to a few songs that were playing on the radio while he watched the house across the street. It looked empty, though he knew it wasn't. He'd seen a young boy hurry inside with his dog a few moments ago. A woman Justice assumed was his mother was holding the door open for him.

The dog looked to have been a yellow lab, maybe 8-10 months old, and, like all labs, he seemed exuberant—and clumsy.

Shouldn't be long now, Justice thought.

When he finished singing along to an old song by George Strait, who must have been the boy's father pulled up and parked in the driveway. He was driving a new Infiniti, dark gray. They were nice cars, but they were expensive. *He should have spent that money on the boy.*

Justice was driving an old model Chrysler, a dark blue van with a dent in the left rear panel. He sat still, waiting for the rain to slow down. If he had been foolish, he'd be waiting for it to stop, but he knew better; this was a real rain, not a quick downpour or a short thunderstorm. He'd seen downpours that lasted no more than a few minutes, but he figured this rain might last a few hours, if not more.

Much to his surprise, the rain did slow after about ten minutes. It went from deluge to downpour, enough for the man to make a run for the house and not get drenched, which is exactly what the boy's father did.

The car door popped open and he made a dash for it, racing into the front door, slipping, and darn near falling in the process.

The rain continued for another twenty minutes, and as much as Justice wanted the rain to continue, he knew he had to get busy before people began paying attention.

Once the rain stopped, they would pay attention. They'd be looking out their windows and peeking through the blinds. He didn't know why people did that after a rain, but they did. As if they were looking for something besides wet.

Justice sneaked across the street, opened the man's car door and turned on the lights. He made sure he was wearing his latex gloves so he didn't leave any prints. When he was back to his van, he picked up his cell and dialed.

"Hello?"

"Bob," he said, making it sound as familiar as possible. "You left your lights on in the car."

"What? Oh shit. Okay, thanks," Bob said, without even asking who it was on the phone.

The front door opened and Bob ran out. He opened the door and reached for the knob to turn off the lights.

Justice crept up behind Bob and slammed a club into the back of his head. Bob went down, unconscious.

Justice picked Bob up and dragged him to the curb. He then pulled his van next to Bob and put him in the back, using the side door. After gagging him and tying his hands and feet, he pulled away.

He drove about three blocks, then pulled to the curb and hit redial. The phone in Bob's house rang.

"Hello?"

"Hi, is your mother home?"

"No, who's this?"

"You don't know me, but I found somebody named Bob on the side of the road. It looks like he's been hit by a car. I called for an ambulance already; they should be here any minute."

"That's my dad. Where are you?"

"Not far, judging by the address on his license. Do you want me to come and get you?"

"Yeah, please. I'll be waiting outside."

"Okay, I won't be long. And I'll be in a blue van."

Chapter Twenty-Nine

VICTIM NUMBER FOUR

I finished my espresso, then sat on the bench waiting for Tip to pick me up. I heard the sound of tires squealing around the corner and presumed that to be Tip.

A few seconds later, Tip pulled to the curb. "Get in," he hollered through the rolled-down window.

I hopped in next to him and said, "I was thinking before you got here that we should give more thought to what Roberts told us."

"About what?" Tip asked.

"About the kids being still alive. And about how the kidnapper treated them."

"What about it?" Tip asked.

"Why would someone risk kidnapping, if it's not for ransom or for the sex-slave trade? And he's not abusing them, so what the hell is he risking twenty years in prison for?"

"I don't know. After I shoot the son of a bitch, we'll ask him."

"I'm serious, Tip."

"I am too. This son of a bitch is driving those mothers crazy with worry. What would you feel like if someone stole your kid? I remember when you were missing that damn cat of yours for one night—you were about to call the Army."

I laughed. "I guess you're right. Still, I'd love to know what he's thinking."

"I'm not saying these are perfect mothers, but then again, nobody is."

My phone rang. "Hello?"

"Connie, it's Coop. We've got another one."

"What? Where?"

"Off of Rayford Road, east of the Woodlands. Technically, it's Montgomery County, but I already spoke to them, and they invited us in. They don't have the manpower to handle it, and since we're already on this case, I told them we'd be happy to investigate."

"Okay, Captain, text me the address. We're not far from there."

"Another kidnapping," I said to Tip. "Turn around. It's on Rayford Road."

Tip exited the freeway and made a U-turn at the intersection, then headed north. He got off on Rayford and turned right. "Where to?"

I looked at the map on my smart phone. "Looks like we turn left into Imperial Oaks, then right on Pincher. The name's Albus."

We got to the house in a few minutes and knocked on the door. A woman who appeared to be in her thirties answered.

"I'm Detective Connie Gianelli, and this is my partner, Detective Tip Denton. We're here about your son."

"Oh my God! It's not just my son. My husband is missing too."

I looked to Tip, then back to Mrs. Albus. "Your husband went missing at the same time?"

She opened the door wider and us in. "Yes, Bob called me on his way home. He said he was only about ten minutes away. I got home a few hours later, and neither one of them were here."

"What time did you talk to your husband?"

She reached for her phone. "It will be on here under recent calls." She scanned the list then pointed to a number and said, "Right there—he called at 6:45. See it?"

"When did you get home?" Tip asked.

She looked down at the phone again. "I called my neighbor right away when I didn't see Bob or Rusty. See, here it is, 8:20. So it was a little more than an hour and a half." She put her hands to her face and wept uncontrollably.

"Now they're gone. Where are they? Who took them?"

I placed her arm on Mrs. Albus' shoulder. "Would you like a glass of water, Mrs. Albus? Or some tea or coffee? I can make some if you show me where things are."

She sniffled, wiped her eyes with a cloth, then shook her head. "I'll be all right. Just find my boy. He's all I've got."

"We'll get him, ma'am," Tip said. "We'll get them both."

"Are you sure they were taken? That they didn't go somewhere?" I asked.

"Of course they were taken," she said. She almost shrieked it. "The car is still here, and Bob didn't leave a note. Neither one of them would do that."

"So they weren't planning on going anywhere or having anyone over?"

Mrs. Albus shook her head. "No. Nothing like that. We were going to cook hot dogs on the grill when I got home. That's what we had discussed earlier."

Tip looked at a picture in a frame on the coffee table. It was of a little boy and a dog. "Is that your son?"

She picked it up and stared, crying. "That's Rusty. And that's his dog or used to be his dog. His name was Max. Rusty loved that dog."

"Where is Max now?" Tip asked.

"He died," she said. "Not long after that picture was taken."

"Okay, we're going to talk to some of your neighbors to see if anyone saw anything that would help. Afterward, I'm sure we'll have more questions for you."

We made the rounds to the neighbors, starting with the house next door. A woman who looked to be in her fifties lived there alone, but she said she hadn't seen anything. "It was raining cats and dogs," she said. "I didn't even look outside."

She got up and opened her curtains. "Sun's shining now. Need to let the light in."

"What can you tell us about Rusty Albus or his father?" Tip asked.

"I can tell you that he was a no-good son of a bitch if that's what you mean. Won't be many people miss him being gone; leastwise not many I can think of."

"Why do you say that?" I asked.

"I say it because it's true. I can't think of anyone who knew the man who liked him. He was a nasty, ill-tempered, mean son of a bitch. And I'm being nice."

Tip gave me a look, then said. "What about the boy?"

"Rusty? Rusty was a sweetheart. A good boy. He was always ready to help you with anything. He had manners. He was a sweet kid."

"And Mrs. Albus?" I asked.

She waved her hand in the air. "She's a nice enough sort, but she should've thrown out that no-good husband of hers years ago. She and Rusty would have been better off. Not to mention that dog."

"What about the dog?" Tip asked.

"That man used to beat that dog something awful. Even when the dog didn't do nothing. I even called the cops on him a few times, but those damn cops didn't do nothing. Shoulda locked his ass up is what they shoulda done."

"Anything else you can tell us?" Tip asked.

"What? That ain't enough? I could talk all day about what an ass he was and just as long about how sweet that boy was. But I ain't got nothing to tell you about what happened because I didn't see anything."

I handed her a card. "If you think of anything, call us. It doesn't matter what time it is."

We went to four more houses asking questions. At house number three, we finally caught a break, a small one, but it was better than nothing.

"I saw a dark blue van parked in front of their house. It was raining like hell, but the van was just sitting there, some guy behind the wheel."

"Can you tell me what he looked like?" Tip asked.

The guy shook his head. "Not really. Like I said, it was raining like hell and that made seeing tough. I could make out his shape, but that's about all. No way I could pick him out of a lineup."

"Anything else?" I asked. "Did you see Mr. Albus or his son? Did you see the man get out of the van?"

He shook his head again. "No. I watched him in that van for a few minutes, then I figured he must be waiting out the rain, so I quit looking. Now, I'm sorry I did. I didn't much like Bob, but his boy was nice."

"We've heard that from others," Tip said. "What was wrong with Bob?"

"Nothing specific. He was just a horse's ass. Treated his wife and kid terribly. Used to have a dog, and he treated it even worse."

"What did he do that was so terrible?" Tip asked.

"He was always hollering at his wife. And he wouldn't let that boy play with any of the other kids. For the life of me, I don't know why. Rusty's a good kid."

"Did he hit them?" Connie asked.

"I can only guess. I never saw him do it, but he threatened to a lot. And they seemed scared of him like they knew he'd do it."

"Okay, thanks. We've got what we need for now. If we need more, we'll come back."

"I'll be here," he said.

As Tip got behind the steering wheel, he turned. "Doesn't sound like the world is going to miss Mr. Albus much."

"I wonder why Mrs. Albus didn't say anything."

"Some people are like that," Tip said. "especially wives that have been abused. Their husbands are sons of bitches right up until the time they're gone, then all of a sudden they did no wrong."

"It sounds like this one did plenty wrong. Now we've got to see if any of what he did wrong got him kidnapped."

Tip hit the gas and the car jerked forward. "Let's do it," he said.

Chapter Thirty

THE SEARCH NARROWS

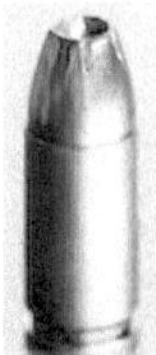

We got to the station just after lunch. We stopped at Julie's office on the way to our desks, and Tip said, "Julie, you got anything going on?"

"Just digging into those names you gave me—the kidnap victims and their families."

"Add the most recent victims to your list, especially the father. Albus is the name. I'm sure Coop has the particulars."

"Will do, Tip. I'm almost done with the others."

We then went to our desks and sat. "What do you think changed?" I asked. "Why did he take an adult? And, more importantly, what is he going to do with him? I don't imagine he'll be playing with the other kids in that room Roberts told us about."

"I don't guess he will," Tip said. "I'm just hoping he keeps Albus alive. Even assholes deserve to live. Well, maybe."

Coop walked into the office carrying a folder in her hand.

"What have you got?" I asked.

"What I've got is a report from the Huntsville Police Department on a body found that had been tied to a tree in the woods. Half his skin had been pulled from its body with what appears to have been pliers based on the markings. And according to the coroner, the person was alive while it happened."

"Holy shit!" Tip said. "That's a nasty way to check out."

"Not that any way is a good way, but yes, I'd agree with you on that, Tip. And I seldom agree with you."

"You said Huntsville, Captain. Why are we getting the report?"

"Because the body belonged to Kent Richardson. He lived in the Woodlands. Huntsville thought it might have something to do with our kidnappings. They sent the file to Conroe also. One more thing. There was a note pinned to the body. It read "Do unto others what they do to you." Sounds almost biblical."

"Sounds like revenge," Tip said. "Maybe Richardson did something to this guy, and this was payback. Richardson didn't have a kid that was taken, right?"

"No kid taken, but there may have been an attempt. Mrs. Richardson told Huntsville that a man driving a white van had attempted to lure her son inside by saying he needed help with directions."

"Smart kid for not going," I said.

"Smarter than the father," Tip said.

Tip grabbed the folder and walked toward Julie's office. "Got another one for you to check on." He handed her the folder. "Just copy the inside and get it back to us as soon as you can."

Tip got coffee while I settled in to get work done. When he

returned, I looked up at him. "You know the kidnapping last night puts a damper on your suspect number one."

"Why's that?"

"Because he has one hell of an alibi; he was under surveillance by two detectives while the kidnapping took place."

"But he was in Macy's," Tip said. "We didn't have eyes on him."

I cocked my head and stared. "What'd he do—fly to Rayford Road, kidnap the kid and his father, then drop them off and fly back? Let go of it, Tip. It's not him."

"All right, smart ass. If it isn't him, then who is it?"

"I don't know who it is. I'd like it to be Kimmler's boyfriend, but I don't think it is."

Julie walked up and handed me the folder. "Here it is," she said. "Pretty nasty stuff in there."

I placed the folder on my desk and opened it. Julie had seen a lot of gruesome pictures. If she was calling this nasty, then it must be bad. I looked at the first picture and shivered. "Oh my God," I said. "How could anyone do this to another person?"

Tip reached over and took the folder, then stared. "Shit in a bucket of piss," he said.

"What the hell kind of saying is that, Tip?"

"I don't know, but it means something disgusting. Shit is disgusting, and piss is disgusting, so if you combine the two, it's really disgusting."

"I'll tell you what's disgusting—you."

"See what I mean," Tip said. "You already think I'm disgusting just for saying it."

He shook his head numerous times. "I'm with you, how the hell could someone do this to another person? Look at it, half the guy's skin is ripped from his body."

"And somebody had to do the ripping," I said. "And the coroner said the guy was alive when it happened. That's worse. I can't imagine."

"A whole lot worse," Tip said. "Way beyond cruelty."

"It makes me more thankful that his son didn't get in that van," I said. "But it also makes me wonder about Albus. Why the kidnapper took him, and what is he going to do with him?"

"I hope it's something different than what this guy got," Tip said. "Nobody deserves this."

"I don't feel like discussing it, but we have to if we're gonna solve this case. Look at those pictures. It took someone a long time to do that. And if the guy was alive when he did it, you can bet your ass he was screaming. Which brings us back to our original theory that whoever is doing this must have some property and be isolated. If not, somebody would report it."

Tip nodded. "I'm with you on that, Gianelli. And I would guess it's a piece of property north of the city but south of Conroe. That would put it at the halfway point."

"We should get Julie to look into it," I said.

"Get Julie to look into what," said Julie as she approached.

"Don't go sneaking up on me like that, girl. I might shoot you."

"Tip, if you shot as many people as you said you were going to, we wouldn't have a population problem."

I laughed. "What's up, Julie?"

"I've got those reports you asked for earlier. You're going to be disappointed in the exes. They all seem clean. But the one guy—she looked through her papers—Rudy Santiago. He looks like trouble."

"Trouble in what way?" Tip asked.

"He's got no official arrest record, but I found two citations for domestic violence where they warned him. They should have arrested him, but they didn't. And he walked.

"Somebody needs to kick some ass," Tip said. "Domestic violence is nothing to shit around with. If a guy is beating his wife or girl-friend, he needs to be put away—in prison or the grave. Either one suits me fine."

"That's not all," Julie said. "After some deep digging, I found out he was a distant cousin of Ryan Salerno, and several years ago he was asked to leave a family gathering by none other than Ryan's mother, who was the gathering organizer."

Tip sat up straight in his chair. "What? Are you shitting me?"

"Not one bit," Julie said. "And get this. Four years ago, he worked at the same company as Ms. Hendricks. To top it all off, Hendricks was promoted before he was, causing him to make a big stink."

"Son of a bitch," Tip said, "This is all good, but it doesn't help. He was at Buffalo Fred's ice house when the Kimmler boy was kidnapped."

Julie shook her head. "That's the thing. He wasn't."

"Yeah, he was," Tip said. "I talked to the owners."

"Then they weren't honest with you," Julie said. "I have a receipt from his credit card that was used at a corner store not three miles from the Kimmler house when he was supposedly at the ice house. Unless he's the kind to lend out his card to someone else, that puts him quite a few miles from Buffalo Fred's."

Tip held his hand out. "Let me see," he said, as if he didn't believe her.

After staring at the receipt for more than a few seconds, he said, "Son of a bitch. Son of a bitch. Those pricks lied to me."

Tip grabbed his keys and stood to leave. "Let's go, Gianelli. I'm going to see those pricks in person."

On the way to Buffalo Fred's, I said, "You know if his alibi doesn't hold for the night of the Kimmler kidnapping, then he's tied to three kidnappings and with motive or some semblance thereof."

"I know, and nothing would give me more pleasure than to slap the cuffs on that scum-sucking son of a bitch. I didn't like him from day one."

"I'd love to pin it on this guy, but he doesn't seem like the type to do something nice for the kids. I don't picture him getting the dogs for them. If anything, I think he'd specifically not get them. He didn't strike me as the kind and thoughtful type."

"I'll agree with you on that," Tip said. "But there's still too much here to ignore. He needs to provide some answers."

Tip pulled into the parking lot at Buffalo Fred's, and we went inside. Tip headed straight for the kitchen. He walked up to Fred, grabbed him by the collar, and said, "You told me Rudy Santiago was here the night I asked you about. He wasn't. What the hell is going on?"

"He was here. He was drinking with his buddies."

"You're lying, Fred. If I don't get the truth in the next minute, I'm going to have three squad cars parked outside your place every night with instructions to administer breathalyzers to everyone who leaves."

"You can't do that."

"Watch me. And it doesn't matter if it doesn't stand up in court. The trouble that your customers will have to go through will make them steer clear of your place in the future."

"You can't do that, Tip."

"Consider it done, you lying piece of shit. A kid was kidnapped that night, and you provided an alibi for a guy we suspect of involvement."

Fred sighed. "All right. He wasn't here. I'm sorry. He's a good customer, and he knows a lot of other good customers. He asked me to vouch for him because he said he was with a different woman, and he didn't want his girl to find out."

"And you believed him?"

"I had no reason not to. He's never asked anything like that before."

Tip glared at Fred. "If this goes to court, and if you're called to testify, you better tell the truth, or I'll cut your balls off."

Fred gulped. "Yes, sir."

As we drove away, Tip looked at me and said, "We need to have a talk with Mr. Santiago. He's got a lot of explaining to do."

"I'm ready," I said.

EXPLAIN YOURSELF

We got in the car and headed toward Rudy's work—Drilco. Tip felt it would be a good strategy to embarrass him in front of his co-workers. I didn't have a feeling about it one way or the other, so I went along with it. Truth was, I'd be thrilled to see this son of a bitch be humiliated. It would make my day. Whether it would be good for the case, I didn't know.

On the drive over, Tip called Buffalo Fred's. "Fred, this is Tip Denton. Listen up. If you get a call from Rudy, refuse it. And if you happen to answer, tell him you've got to hang up, but do it quickly because I'm gonna pull your phone records and if you talk to him for more than a few seconds, I'll shut your ass down. Got that?"

"All right, good. Expect a call 'cause I'm on my way to see him now."

Rudy worked from the Drilco office on San Felipe, so we didn't have far to drive. It only took about fifteen minutes for us to get there.

The lobby was huge, with tiled floors, a ceiling several stories high, and it was decorated with an abundance of live plants. Tip approached the receptionist, a young blonde with what looked to be a permanent grin.

"Morning, darlin'. I'm Detective Tip Denton, and this gorgeous thing standing next to me is Detective Connie Gianelli. We're here to see Rudy Santiago."

"Sure thing, Detective. Do you have an appointment?"

Tip chuckled. "No, ma'am. This isn't an appointment kind of thing. You see, we're here to arrest him. Slap the cuffs on and whisk him away. And if for some reason we don't, it's only a matter of time."

"Arrest Mr. Santiago? For what?"

"I'm afraid I can't tell you that, sugar. I can say that he's suspected of some pretty heinous crimes, so if I were you, I'd keep my distance. I'm allowed to say that 'cause it's viewed as protecting the citizens."

"Oh, my. Thank you, Detective." She reached for the intercom. "I'll let him know you're here."

Tip laid his hand on her forearm. "I'd appreciate it if you didn't. Point us in the right direction or provide an escort, and we'll announce ourselves." He winked at her after he said that, then said, "Don't want to alert him."

The receptionist blushed. "Of course. I didn't think of that." She stood and called to a man standing to the side. He appeared to be a security guard.

"Josh, will you walk these detectives down to see Rudy Santiago? He's in #412."

"No problem, ma'am," he said.

We followed Josh around the bend to the elevators, then took them to the fourth floor. Room #412 was only a short walk away.

"Here it is," Josh said, stopping at an office in the middle of a long hallway.

Rudy was inside, standing behind his desk and talking on the phone. He furrowed his brow when he saw us, then held up his finger, telling us he'd only be a moment.

"Okay, I'll make sure we have a team out there by Friday," Rudy said. "We'll get it taken care of."

He hung up the phone, then turned to us. "What are you doing here? Any news on the boy?"

"The boy has a name," I said. "His name is Shane. And no, there is no news about him."

"Then what are you doing here?"

"We were hoping you could help us," I said.

"Help how?"

"By telling us where the hell you were the night Shane was taken?" Tip said.

Rudy looked at Tip, then me. "I already told you. I was at Buffalo Fred's."

"And I found out that was a lie," Tip said, "so you better come up with a different story. And if this one is a lie, it's over."

"What are you talking about? I was at Fred's."

"That's not gonna cut it," Tip said. "You need a better story because I already talked to Fred and got the truth. And this new story better match what Fred told me, or you're going to prison. Not jail for a night or two, but prison for a few decades 'cause I'll make sure you go down for these kidnappings."

Rudy stammered and stuttered and shuffled things around on his desk. "I don't know what you're talking about, but I think it's time you left. I've got meetings to attend."

Tip stood, signaling me to do likewise. "You've got meetings all right. One of them is going to be a court date. This isn't over. I'll be talking to you again and soon."

After leaving the building, Connie hit Tip on the arm. "Nice job, Tip. You had me convinced. If I were Rudy, I'd be calling Fred to sync the stories."

Tip hadn't even gotten to I-45 when his cell phone rang. "Denton."

"Tip, it's Fred. He called, but I told him I couldn't talk. He pressed hard, but I insisted. I told him to call later. What should I tell him?"

"Dodge him today, Fred. You can talk to him all you want tomorrow. But give me today."

"Okay. Don't forget this, Tip. I did you a solid."

"You know I don't forget, Fred."

Tip hung up from the call and mumbled,"Son of a bitch."

"Now what?" I asked.

"Now we drop by to see him when he's with his girlfriend. If nothing else, it should shed some light on his activities for her."

"It'll be a pretty harsh light."

"Exactly," he said. "That's what I'm aiming for."

We returned to the office, caught up on paperwork, then grabbed a burger for dinner before going to Kimmler's house.

Tip parked, then we walked up and knocked on the door. Mrs. Kimmler answered quickly. She seemed surprised to see us, and her face lit up in a hopeful expression.

"Did you find Shane? Any word?"

Tip lowered his head. "Sorry, ma'am, but so far we have nothing. We did have a few questions for your boyfriend though. Is he here?"

"Rudy? He's on the back porch. Come on in."

She looked confused by our request.

We walked through the house, following her, then she slid the patio door open.

"Who was that?" Rudy asked.

"Just us," Tip said, and stepped onto the porch.

"You? What the hell do you want? Haven't you pestered me enough?"

"Just had a few more questions," I said.

"I think I've answered enough questions," Rudy said. "If you want more answers, you'll have to call my lawyer."

"Lawyer? You're threatening to bring a lawyer in when we're trying to help your girlfriend find her son?"

Mrs. Kimmler stepped forward to stand beside Rudy. "I'm wondering what questions you have also. What could Rudy know that he hasn't already answered?"

"For starters, he could tell us where he was the night of the kidnapping," Tip said.

"What do you mean? He already told you. I was here when he did. He was at the ice house having a few beers with friends."

"Except he wasn't, ma'am," I said. "We spoke to Fred, the owner, and he said Rudy never came in that night. And we have a receipt from Rudy's credit card being used not far from here at about the time Shane was taken."

"What?" Kimmler screamed while turning to glare at him. "What? Where were you? You told me you were at the ice house? Were you with that whore bitch Shirley again?" She slapped at him several times.

"Settle down, Kaylee. I can explain," he said while holding up his hands to fend off her blows.

"You better start then, and it better be good."

"I was on my way to the ice house when I saw Carlos. He invited me to his place to watch a UFC fight and to have a few beers."

"Let's find out," I said, reaching for my cell. "What's Carlos's number?"

"I don't know. But you can't just call him."

"I can, and I will," I said. "Now give me the number."

"I have his number," Mrs. Kimmler said. "Hang on, I'll get it." She walked toward into the house, returning in a moment with a slip of paper. "Here it is. Carlos Fertiz."

I had only dialed two of the numbers before Rudy shouted, "Stop! I wasn't with Carlos. I was with Shirley."

Mrs. Kimmler showed her anger, face turning red. She ran toward him, hands slapping and scratching at his face. "You son of a bitch! You dirty son of a bitch. How could you?"

Rudy protected his face but didn't say much. I don't imagine there was much to say. I took hold of Mrs. Kimmler and stopped her assault on Rudy; meanwhile, Tip slapped the cuffs on him.

"You have the right to remain silent. Anything you say ... " He completed reading Rudy his Miranda rights, then we walked him to the car.

"What are you doing? Where are we going? My car is here. I've got a meeting tomorrow."

"Your car will be just fine where it is," Tip said. "I'm sure Mrs. Kimmler wouldn't think of doing anything to it. As for your meeting, you might want to cancel it. You can use your one phone call at the station to do that."

"You son of a bitch. I'll get even with you for this."

"Wow. There's a new idea. I've never heard that threat before. Now you've got me worried."

Tip helped him into the back seat, then we got in the car and drove off. "Enjoy the scenery," Tip said. "It's only about a forty minute ride, so don't get too comfortable."

"You sure know how to piss a guy off, don't you?" I said.

"I try," Tip said. "But there's always room for improvement."

"I need to use a phone," Rudy said.

"Wait till we get to the station. You have to wait if you need to piss too. If you piss in the car, I'll shoot your dick off."

"You're disgusting," Rudy said.

"Heard that before too," Tip said. "Try to come up with something new."

We dropped Rudy off at the station and had them hold him. We could keep him for a few days, but then we had to let him go or charge him, and right now we didn't have enough to charge him.

Tip rushed down the hall. "Where you off to, partner?"

"See if Julie is still here. We need some information on his other activities."

"I doubt she's here. It's already past quitting time."

I caught up to Tip by the time he reached the end of the hall, and to my surprise, Julie was still working.

"Julie," Tip said. "We need everything you've got on that guy, Santiago. Who he had a beef with at the family gathering, where he worked and in what position, all of it."

"I'll have it in a couple of minutes, Tip. Want me to bring it to you?"

"Darlin', that would be super. I'll be at my desk."

About fifteen minutes later, Julie brought by the papers. Several folders worth of information. "Here it is, y'all. Have fun."

"Thanks, Julie," I said. "I'll try not to have too much fun."

"Grab the folders, Connie. We'll take them with us and go over all this tonight. We need to find something to build a case on or the D.A. Is never gonna press charges. Not with the little bit we have."

Connie scooped up the folders and put them under her arm. "Let's go then. I'm hungry."

Tip stood slowly. "Is there ever a time when you're not hungry? I'm beginning to think you only partnered with me so you could eat my food."

"Don't think too hard on that, Tip. You might be right."

Chapter Thirty-Two

PLANNING THE QUESTIONS

We got to Tip's house in about forty minutes. It was either good timing or bad timing, depending on how you looked at it. Mollie was leaving, which meant that she wouldn't be cooking dinner. On the other hand, she wouldn't be yapping about the case either.

Tip rolled his window down as he was about to pass her car. "Where you going, girl? Not staying to cook for me?"

Mollie poked her head out the car window. "I got news for you. I don't live my life to cook, especially not for you. I don't remember sayin' "I do" or any such nonsense to the likes of Tip Denton, so until I say it, which would be a cold day in hell, you can prepare your own meals."

Tip laughed. "Damn, girl, but you've got a lot of sauce. I might have to test you on that "I do" shit."

Mollie laughed and brushed her hand in the air, then she drove off while rolling up her window.

Tip drove slowly down the driveway, still laughing at Mollie. "She's a saucy old gal, isn't she?"

"That she is," I said. "But more importantly, what the hell are we going to eat?"

"I should've known where your head was. If it's not up your ass, it's thinking about food. Don't worry. I'm not gonna let you starve. We'll order Chinese. Got a place not far from here that has the best Orange Chicken, and they deliver too."

"I'm up for Orange Chicken," I said. "Side of rice too."

When we got to the house, Flash did her usual, running to greet us and snarling as if she hadn't seen us in a year. Sacco did his usual too —lying on the floor, giving a customary two wags of the tail, but never bothering to get up. These dogs couldn't have been any more opposite.

I finished petting Flash, then took the folders to the kitchen table. "Let's order that food," I said.

"Already did, smart ass. But it'll take them about an hour to get here."

I opened the first folder, the one with the information on Rudy when he worked at Shell Oil Company.

"What'd he do for them?"

"He was a project manager with the drill pipe department. Looks like he worked there about seven years."

"And when did Hendricks work there? Does it say?"

I leafed through a few more papers, paying attention to Julie's notes. "She was in the same department, project manager also. She started one year after he did, but she was promoted to an assistant director after three years. He was still project manager."

"What happened after that?"

I read more of Julie's notes, then said, "He stayed in the same department for almost a year after she was promoted, then he requested a transfer to the Offshore Division. Six months later, he got the transfer. He stayed there until he left the company."

"Does it say why he left?"

"All it says is discharged."

"From my experience, that usually means fired. And not laid off, but fired."

"Guess we'll need to talk to a few of his former co-workers to find out."

"We should start with Hendricks. I'm sure she'll tell us something if she knows."

"What about the family gathering deal?"

"Julie said it was Salerno who asked him to leave. Since that's the case, I think we have another willing witness. She's sure to do anything to get her kid back."

"Sounds good. Let's get started early tomorrow. We'll go to Shell first, then see Hendricks, then Salerno."

"Hold on, Gianelli. We still need to discuss motive. Even if he is some kind of lunatic and still holds a grudge, do you think it's enough of a grudge to warrant kidnapping? That's a serious crime."

"I can't see it, Tip, but I don't claim to be able to think like a lunatic. I never have been able to understand why people like Santiago or serial killers do what they do. But that's not my job. My job is to catch them and get them off the streets."

"All right. Let's see if we can get enough to nail this bastard," Tip said.

"It's not going to be enough to paint him as a reprehensible person. We're going to have to show evidence that ties him to the crimes, and it's going to have to be a lot more than the circumstantial evidence we have now."

"A witness would help," Tip said. "We should take a picture of him to that young boy who spotted the van."

"Unless he can swear without a doubt that he saw Santiago snatch the kid, it won't hold up. Santiago's lawyer will swear that the kid is familiar with his features because he lives next door to him. And I'd find it tough to argue with that reasoning, despite wanting to see him rot in prison."

Headlights lit up the driveway and shined through the front window. "Must be the food," Tip said.

"About damn time. I'm starved."

Tip went to the door, paid the delivery driver, and returned with the food. I had plates on the table and accompanying silverware.

"Dig in," Tip said. "Grab any one you want 'cause they're both the same—Orange Chicken. And trust me, you're gonna love it."

I dug into the Orange Chicken, and took a spoonful of rice with each piece. "Damn, Tip, you were right. This is good. Especially the sauce."

"Best I've had," Tip said. "And they give you enough for two meals, though it is kinda pricey."

"But worth it," I said. "I haven't had Chinese take-out this good for years. A lot of years."

"So how are we going to get this guy?" Tip said. "If he did the snatching, he'd have had to take the kid, drive him to wherever it is he keeps them—and if we believe Roberts, that's somewhere between the beltway and Conroe—then he'd have to get the kid settled and return here to be with Mrs. Kimmler."

I took another few bites of food. "Pretty tight schedule."

"Damn tight," Tip said. "Let's hope we can do something with that timeline."

Tip slammed another beer down as he finished his meal. "Hey, partner. Don't forget you have to drive me home, so lay off the beer."

"I can drive that car blindfolded."

"And it usually look as if you do, but I don't want you driving me drunk. And I'm not spending the night here, so if that thought crossed your mind, scratch it out."

Tip laughed. "That's what I love about you, Gianelli. There's no bullshit."

"And don't forget we need to get an early start. Shell is down on I-10, almost to Katy."

Tip sighed. "All right, you convinced me. Pack up what you need, and I'll take you home."

I grabbed the folders Julie had given us, and I took the what was left of my dinner, then got into the car. Tip came out a moment later, and within fifteen minutes he was letting me out at my place.

"See ya in the morning, partner. What time?"

"I probably better pick you up at seven if we want to be there by eight or eight-thirty."

"All right, see ya then. Drive safe."

"Yeah, see ya tomorrow."

Chapter Thirty-Three

EVERYDAY IS A PARTY

Justice walked down to the room carrying a tray loaded with food—pancakes, scrambled eggs, bacon, and two cartons of orange juice. "Time for breakfast," he hollered as he approached.

He set the tray on top of a table in the hall, then unlocked the door and stepped inside. "Who's hungry?"

"Me!" they all yelled at once, screaming with joy.

"Guess what?" Justice asked.

"What?"

"I don't have to work today. That means we can play outside —with the dogs."

"And K.C.?" Tommy asked.

Justice smiled. "And K.C., of course."

They all cheered, then Justice said, "Get some balls to toss. We'll pick up a few sticks on the way. And don't forget, if I say hide, everyone is to look for a hiding place immediately. Is that clear?"

"Clear," they shouted.

Justice led them through the tunnel and up to the play area. When they got above ground, the kids cheered loudly. They immediately began tossing tennis balls and throwing sticks for the dogs to run and fetch.

"Be careful where you throw those sticks," Justice said. "You don't want to hit anybody."

For hours, they played catch, chase, and hide-n-seek. They only stopped to go inside and eat lunch. Afterward, they were ready again.

"Good gosh," Justice said. "You're gonna wear me to a frazzle. I'm plumb tuckered out already."

"You talk funny, Mr. Justice," one of them said.

He laughed. "I guess I do, but at least it gives you something to laugh about. Everybody should have something to laugh about."

After lunch, Justice took three of the kids with him to fly kites. The others continued playing with the dogs or kept playing hide-n-seek. K.C. didn't play catch or chase, but the cat was never far away from the activity. He seemed to be enjoying the fun, even chasing after one of the girls once.

"I didn't know cats were so fast," Emily said.

"K.C. Is lightning fast," Tommy said. "He outruns the dogs in the neighborhood. He can even climb trees."

"No way," another kid said.

"Oh, yeah," Justice said as he approached. "Cats are good climbers. I've seen cats go twenty or thirty feet up a tree." Justice knelt next to the kids and laughed. "They can't always get down, but they do get up."

Sheila fell and scraped her knee as she ran from a snake. She cried a little. Justice ran to her and patted her back. "No need to worry. We'll take you inside and get that fixed up in no time."

"But the snake is still there," she said.

"That snake will go away in no time. You probably scared it more than it scared you."

"Besides, it's time to go inside."

"Do we have to go in?" Emily asked.

Justice looked at the position of the sun, then nodded. "Yeah, I think we should. It's getting late in the day. Pretty soon it will be time for supper. Besides, we don't want anyone coming by here and seeing us playing when you should be in school."

"When are we going back to school?"

"No need for all of that," Justice said. "I'll teach you what you need to know."

"How about some games? Can we play games after dinner?"

"Sure thing," Justice said. "We can make castles with building blocks, or we can play Sequence."

"Building blocks!" Tommy shouted, and he was joined by two other boys.

"Sequence!" one of the girls said. "I've got blue. And I pick Shane as my partner."

Justice laughed. "How about we do both. Whoever wants to build with the blocks can do that, and whoever wants to play Sequence can sit at the table and play."

"What are you doing, Mr. Justice?"

"I'm going to do both. I'm big, so I get to do that. I'll build with blocks for a while, then I'll play Sequence. How about that?"

"Yay!"

"What's for dinner?" Emily asked.

"I thought we'd cook hamburgers and hot dogs on the grill. But everyone needs to pitch in and help. Is that okay?"

"You bet," Tommy said.

"I'll light the fire," said Shane.

"I'll set the table," said Emily.

"Okay, it's all set. We know who is doing what. We still have a ways to go, so let's see if we can find any snakes."

"Yuk!" said Emily. "Snakes are nasty."

"Snakes are no different than any other animal," Justice said. "You just have to understand them. I'll teach you. You'll see."

Shane lit the grill, Emily set the table with Chad's help, and Tommy helped do the cooking. After dinner, everyone joined to help with the cleanup, then they set about playing—with either blocks or with the Sequence game. Three hours later, yawns proved the predominant noise, and within fifteen more minutes, a few of them had fallen asleep.

Justice stood from the table and spoke quietly. "All right, kids. I think it's time for bed. We had a fun day. We'll do it again next week."

"Can we do it tomorrow?" Tommy asked.

"Not tomorrow," Justice said. "I have to work. But next week we can. In the meantime, pay attention to the rules and be nice to each other. Deal?"

"Deal," they said.

Justice opened the door and began to leave. "Goodnight," he said. "See you tomorrow."

"Goodnight," they said. "Thanks for playing."

"I had fun," Justice said. "No need to thank me."

As Justice lay in bed that night, he thought about what his mama had taught him—about the Good Words. According to her, he shouldn't be treating these kids so nicely, but it felt right to do so. If he listened to his mama, he'd be locking them up and beating them for every little thing they did wrong. It made him question what his mama had told him about the Good Words.

Chapter Thirty-Four

ASKING QUESTIONS

As promised, Tip picked me up at seven. We made it to the Shell Oil location by 8:15.

There were plenty of people bustling about, most of them making their way inside, no doubt reporting for work.

Tip walked to the receptionist's desk and flashed his smile—either famous or infamous, depending on which side of the law you were on. "Morning, darlin'. How's the day treating you?"

The receptionist—a gorgeous little brunette with bright blue eyes—smiled back. "Can I help you, sir?"

"You can help a lot by not calling me sir," Tip said. "Aside from that, I wanted to see if Lou Phillips still works here, and if he does, my parter, Detective Gianelli and I would like to speak with him."

She brushed aside his comment. As pretty as she was, I'm sure she was accustomed to lines that were a lot smoother than that one. She spoke into a microphone that she wore over her head, then looked back at Tip.

"Mr. Phillips will be right down to see you, Detective. You can have a seat over there," she said and pointed to a small cluster of chairs by a large window.

Lou Phillips showed up ten minutes later. He wore what appeared to be an expensive blue suit and displayed a smile that looked as if it had been painted on.

"Lou Phillips," he said. "How can I help?"

I shook his hand. "Connie GIanelli. And this is my partner, Detective Tip Denton. We're here about a matter that goes way back, Mr. Phillips. We're inquiring about a former employee by the name of Rudy Santiago. Do you remember him?"

Phillips nodded in recognition. "Oh, I remember Rudy. And I'm not surprised you're here about him. I'm more surprised it's taken this long for the police to show up."

Tip looked at all the people milling about. "Can we go somewhere private to talk?"

"Of course," Phillips said. "Follow me." He moved toward a small conference room in the far corner of the lobby. "In here should do. Can I get you coffee or tea?"

"Tea for me," Tip said.

"I'll have coffee, please," I said. "Actually if you have espresso, that would be better. If not, just tell them to make the coffee strong."

"Not to worry," Phillips said. "We have espresso, and it's pretty good too." He leaned to the side, hit the intercom button and said, "Janice, can you get us a black coffee, an espresso, and a hot tea, please?"

"Sure thing, Mr. Phillips. Be right there."

We sat at the end of the conference table, and I laid my folders out in front of me.

"What kind of trouble has Rudy gotten himself into?"

"We're not allowed to be specific, Mr. Phillips, but I can tell you we're not here because he ran a red light."

"I surmised that," he said. "They wouldn't send two detectives for something mundane. I'm guessing domestic violence or worse." Phillips raised his eyebrows in a questioning look.

"We still can't say, sir. I'm sorry. But perhaps you can help us. We've heard from other sources that there was an incident involving Mr. Santiago and a woman who worked here—Ms. Hendricks. We were told she was promoted before Santiago and he became upset."

"That's putting it mildly," Phillips said. "He was enraged. He lodged a formal complaint, he verbally assaulted Ms. Hendricks as well as his supervisor, and he even threatened Ms. Hendricks. That was the deciding factor. After he threatened her, we had him transferred. HR reports will show that he requested a transfer, but he was forced to transfer. We couldn't have him working in the same department as Ms. Hendricks after that. Couldn't risk it."

"Why'd you keep him on at all?" Tip asked.

"Because he was a good project manager and back at that time good project managers were difficult to find. We felt we could solve the problem with a transfer."

"And did it?" I asked.

"Did it what?"

"Solve the problem. We heard he was let go not long afterward."

"It was a while. A few years, I believe. The problems we had with

Mr. Santiago continued to accumulate. He had several sexual harassment charges brought against him by various employees. It got to the point where legal insisted he go."

"And?" I asked.

"And that was it," Phillips said. "We gave him a severance package and cut him loose. We haven't heard from him since."

"What happened to Ms. Hendricks?" Tip asked.

"Ms. Hendricks is still with us, and she's doing a great job. She's a director now with a large group of project managers reporting to her."

"Good to hear," I said. "That about wraps it up for us, Mr. Phillips. We appreciate your honesty. It's been a big help." I stood, pushing my chair back as I did.

Phillips reached to shake hands. "I hope this information helps. And if you can, do let us know what this is all about. The oilfield is a close community. We like to keep tabs on who is doing what."

"Do you think Ms. Hendricks may have something to add to the story, I mean considering she was involved?"

"I'm sure she would," Phillips said. "Wait here, and I'll have someone bring her. And you can tell Janice—if she ever gets here—to get you anything else you need."

Janice did eventually arrive, and Phillips had been right—the espresso was good—but it took Ms. Hendricks another fifteen or twenty minutes to arrive.

She pushed opened the door and stepped in, then stood with her mouth agape. "Detectives! Is something wrong? Did you find my boy?"

I reached out for her and took her hand. "No, ma'am. Sorry to startle you. We're going background work on the case, and we discovered that years ago you had an issue with a co-worker—a Rudy Santiago?"

"Rudy? Good God, I haven't heard his name in a long time. But what does he have to do with Tommy? Is Rudy involved?"

"We don't know anything yet, Ms. Hendricks. On cases like this, we investigate everything, look at all motives. Even though it was years ago, if he made a threat, we need to check it out."

Hendricks sat in a chair near the end of the table. "He made a threat all right. He said he'd kill me, my kids, my husband, and my dog. I never put much weight on what he said, but... Do you think he did this?"

I made what I hoped was a calming gesture, then said, "Ms. Hendricks, we don't know anything yet; we're simply investigating. We are looking into every possible angle, and this is just one of them. If it leads somewhere, we'll tell you. I promise."

She pulled a handkerchief from her purse and dried her eyes. "Thank you. It's been difficult—living like this. I think the not knowing is the worst. Not knowing what has happened to him allows my mind to wander and think of horrible things."

"Don't worry, ma'am," Tip said. "We'll get whoever did this. I don't often promise people but this time I will."

She patted Tip's hand and seemed to force a smile. "Thank you, Detective. I need some kind of hope; otherwise, it feels as if it isn't worth getting up in the morning."

My heart was breaking for this woman. Not only was she going through this horrible experience, but she was doing it alone. "You shouldn't think that way, ma'am. It's always worth getting up in the morning. And someday soon, you'll have Tommy to share breakfast with."

"You think so?" she asked.

"I know so," I said. "I'll add my promise to Tip's. We're gonna get your son back."

"Is there anything else you can tell us about Mr. Santiago?" I asked. "Did he ever do anything to make you feel as if his threats had substance?"

She shook her head. "At first, he seemed resigned to make my life miserable, spreading rumors, telling lies to my employees, but after his transfer, it stopped. It was like a light going off. One minute Rudy and all his troubles were there and the next they had disappeared. I presumed I had heard the last of him when he transferred, although I was still glad when I heard he had been let go."

"So he wasn't just laid off?" Tip asked.

"Oh, no. He was fired," Hendricks said. "Everyone knew that."

"And you haven't heard from him since that time?" I asked.

"Not a peep," she said. "But I didn't expect to. I presumed he was all fluff. He always was."

Tip stood and shook her hand. "Like I said, Ms. Hendricks. We're gonna get who did this."

"I pray every night, Detective. You don't know how hard I pray."

Tip nodded. "I think I do, Ms. Hendricks. And all that praying is bound to help. I want to say thank you for your time, and thank you for your input on Mr. Santiago. It helped."

"I didn't tell you much. But if it helped, I'm glad."

We were halfway across the parking lot when Tip turned to me and said, "We're gonna get this son of a bitch. I almost don't care whether he's guilty, he deserves to be locked up for being such an ass."

"Let's go see Ms. Salerno. We'll see what she can tell us about Santiago. All we need is something solid to go on. From there, we can build a case."

Chapter Thirty-Five

MRS. SALERNO

We drove up to Ms. Salerno's house and parked by the curb. Her car was in the driveway.

I walked up, knocked on the door, and waited for her to answer. Tip leaned against the brick wall. In less than a minute, she answered. When she saw us, her face lit up, but then she seemed to panic.

"Is this about Ryan? Is he safe?"

I stepped forward and took her by the shoulders. "It's not about Ryan. We're continuing the investigation, and we have some questions."

"Dios mío. Come in and sit. Get out of the sun."

Tip and I followed her inside and sat in chairs by the sofa.

"What do you need to know?" she asked.

"During the investigation, a name came up that we think you're familiar with—Rudy Santiago."

"Rudy! I'm more than familiar with him; he's my cousin. Did he do this?"

"We don't know that, ma'am. But why would you ask that?"

"Because he's a low-life and a pervert. And he swore to get even with me."

"Swore to get even with you for what?" I asked.

"Let me get a drink of water," she said. "You want any?"

"No thanks," we both replied.

She returned in a moment and took her seat again. "I'm from a big family. Many of them are first-generation from Mexico, and the rest are second- or third-generation. Anyway, every summer we have a family gathering so that everyone can mingle with their family— aunts, uncles, cousins, etc."

"How large is the gathering?" Tip asked.

"Large. I think last year we had almost 400 people."

"Damn, that is a big gathering," Tip said.

"Anyway, a few years ago, I was walking back to my car to get some things I had left inside when I saw Rudy sitting in the back seat of another car with my niece. She was only thirteen years old at the time."

"Disgusting," I said.

"I moved close so that I could hear what they were saying. His hand was on her leg, and I heard him say 'You sure look older than thirteen.'"

Mrs. Salerno's face tightened, and it colored red with anger. "As soon as I heard him say that, I yanked the door open and hollered. 'Get the hell out of here. Get out and don't come back.' I then grabbed Clorita's arm and pulled her out of the car. 'As for you, you're going to see your father.' She cried and pleaded, but I hauled her kicking and screaming to see her father, who had to be restrained from killing Rudy."

"What happened to Rudy?" I asked.

"Everyone agreed that he could never be allowed to attend a gathering again and that he could never be seen near Clorita again."

"And that was it?" Tip asked.

Salerno shook her head. "As he was leaving, he said he'd get even with me, no matter what it took. I laughed at him and he said it again. 'Go ahead and laugh, bitch, but I'll get you back for this."

"Did he ever do anything?" I asked.

"He never did anything. I had almost forgotten about it until you brought it up." She shifted sideways on the sofa. "Do you think he had something to do with Ryan disappearing?"

"We don't know, ma'am. We don't have enough information yet, but we're working on it. In fact, that's all we're working on."

"Also, I don't remember if we asked you before, but do you know anyone who owns a white van that may or may not have the name of a service or construction company on it. We've had reports of one showing Clausen Electric one showing Guinn Roofing, and others."

She shook her head. "I don't know anybody like that. I don't know anybody who owns any kind of van. Why are you asking? Did someone who owns a van do this? Did anyone see them?"

"We don't know anything specific, Ms. Salerno. All we know is that a van was seen parked by the curb while the Little League game was taking place. We're investigating because vans would be a good vehicle for someone to use if they were planning on kidnapping."

"But no one saw Ryan getting into the van?"

I smiled. "No, ma'am. No one saw anything. That's been one of the difficult aspects. It seems as if everyone was paying attention to the game and not what was happening around them."

"I can understand that," Mrs. Salerno said. "Most of those people are nuts when it comes to sports." She turned her head, then began crying. "Now I wish I had never let Ryan go."

I moved alongside her and held her close. "No sense in thinking like that, Mrs. Salerno. It's not going to do any good to blame yourself. You didn't do this; the kidnapper did. And we're going to get him and bring him to justice."

She continued sobbing for a moment, then used her sleeve to dry her eyes. "I'm sorry. Sometimes it gets hard to deal with. He's all I have."

"I understand, ma'am. Listen we have to go so we can get back to this case. I'll let you know if anything develops."

She stood and moved toward the front door. "All right. Please call me when you learn anything. Day or night. It doesn't matter."

"You've got it, ma'am. Bye now."

We exited the house and walked slowly to the car. Tip started the engine then drove off. "What did you do to comfort people before I came along?" I asked.

"I'm not very good at comforting," Tip said. "Unless you consider the people that want to hear that I'm gonna plug some son of a bitch full of holes."

"So you're saying that unless someone is looking for revenge, you're useless?"

Tip cocked his head to the side as if giving it thought, then said, "Pretty much, yeah."

"Tp, has anyone ever told you that you're not worth a shit?"

"I think you just did, damn you."

I laughed, and we drove on to I-45, on our way to the station.

Chapter Thirty-Six

INTERVIEW STRATEGY

I looked through the interview observation window while waiting for Tip to return from the rest room. Santiago was sitting in an uncomfortable chair on the back side of the table. He hadn't had a drink in hours, and I felt pretty sure he hadn't slept well the night before; it's pretty tough to get a good night's sleep in jail, especially on the first night.

I watched him for another few minutes, then Tip walked in. He handed me a cup of coffee.

"Anything interesting?" he asked.

"Not unless you like watching perverts," I said.

"Let's go talk to that pervert. I'm eager to hear what he has to say."

We went into the interrogation room and took seats on either side of Santiago, Tip on his right and me on the left.

"When the hell am I getting out of here?" he asked.

"I'm guessing about 2042, maybe longer if you don't get time off for good behavior."

"You're crazy as bat shit," he said. "I didn't do nothin'."

Tip leaned forward, within inches of his face. "Nothin'? Is that what you call threatening women who get promoted before you? Is that what you call swearing to get even with a woman who caught you molesting a child?"

Tip leaned back in his chair. "Yeah, Rudy, that's right. We know it all. And before long, everyone will know. People don't take kindly to child molesters—even in prison; in fact, I've seen cases where innocent men were sent to prison simply because the jury didn't like them, not because the evidence was overwhelming."

"And I don't even want to tell you what happens to them after they get to prison," I said.

Tip leaned forward and whispered. "The good thing is none of them had problems with constipation after that." He straightened in his chair and laughed.

Santiago looked my way. "Will you talk some sense into this Neanderthal? I need to get back to work."

"I'm afraid I agree with him, Santiago. I'd convict you of killing the president if I were on the jury. That is, once I heard you were a pedophile."

I must have hit a sore spot because he got angry and slammed his fist on the table. "I'm not a goddamn pedophile."

"Say that all you want," Tip said. "But when the jury hears how Ms. Salerno caught you in the back seat of the car with your hand on her thirteen-year-old niece's leg, they won't care what the facts say. You're gonna be guilty."

"I didn't do anything."

Tip laughed. "That's a son of a bitch isn't it?"

"How about the Hendricks woman?" I asked. "You threatened to kill her, her kids, her husband, and her dog."

Santiago lowered his head. "That was just talk. I was angry at the time. People say things they don't mean when they're angry."

"So instead of killing her you simply kidnapped her son."

"No way. No goddamn way. I didn't do anything."

"According to reports from co-workers, you did everything you could to make her life miserable—that is until they shipped your ass out of her department."

"I might have told a few tales, but I never hurt her or her family. I never did anything."

"*Anything* is a matter of opinion," Tip said. "There are some parts of the state where threatening to kill someone's dog will earn you a few nights in jail and a stick up your ass. Threatening to kill their kids ... now that's a different story. I've heard of people who never made it to jail."

"You're a sick son of a bitch," Santiago said. "I want a lawyer."

"I'm sure he'll be here at any moment," Tip said. "You did call one, didn't you?"

Santiago looked as if he were going to have a seizure. "I told you I needed a lawyer. I used my call to cancel meetings at work."

"And you say you told me? Darn, I must have misheard you. That's all right. When we leave here, I'll tell them that you need a public defender. I'll make sure you get a sharp one."

"You make me sick," Santiago said.

"Well isn't that a coincidence," Tip said. "Who'd have thought that?"

"Tell me, Santiago, why did you lie to us about where you were on the night of the kidnapping?" I asked.

"I told you, I was with another woman."

"Oh, yeah, I forgot. You were with the mystery woman, Shirley, the one we haven't been able to get in touch with. Are you sure you were with her? Or is that another lie?"

"I was with her," Santiago leaned back and sighed. "And now Kaylee knows it, which means I probably won't be with her anymore."

"What did you have against the Albus family? We know about Hendricks, Salerno, and of course, Kimmler. But what did Albus do to you? Was it the mother or father you were pissed off at? And why take the father?" I leaned toward him as I asked.

"I didn't take anybody. Tell me what night it happened. I'm sure I have an alibi."

"You mean like the one you had with missing Shirley?" Tip asked. "Don't worry, we're gonna find her and get the real story, then your ass is mine, or should I say it will belong to the inmates up in Huntsville?"

"I don't know anybody named Albus, and I didn't take anyone. And now I'm done speaking until my lawyer gets here."

"You mean you're afraid that your legendary temper won't hold up under interrogation?" Tip asked. "Is that it?"

Santiago made a gesture as if he were zippering his mouth shut.

I tapped Tip on the arm and whispered. "I think we're through getting information from him."

He nodded, led Santiago back to a cell, then we met in the coffee room.

"Looks like he's gonna sit this one out," Tip said. "I couldn't even goad him into talking on the way to his cell."

"What now?" I asked. "We don't have enough to charge him."

"I'll see," Tip said. "I'll talk to the ADA."

"Good luck with that," I said. "I'll be waiting."

"Stop by my place tonight," Tip said. "Around seven. I'll fill you in."

"Okay, see you then."

Tip got off the elevator and turned right, heading to the ADA's office. He approached the office, stopping to see Mandy, the ever-present admin who guarded the ADA's privacy.

"Mandy, how are ya darlin'?"

Her smile lit up her face. "Tip, you old charmer. What in the world brings you here? I haven't seen you in ages."

"I came here to see ol' Tall Beans. Is he busy? Don't bother telling me he's not in because I know he is. And tell him it will only take a minute."

Mandy laughed. "They don't give out those detective badges to just anyone, do they? Hang on, I'll check."

Jack "Tall Beans" Murchison was an assistant district attorney. He'd earned his nickname as a youngster because he was so tall and thin. Despite having put on an ample number of pounds, the name had stuck.

Mandy got up, walked over, and cracked open his office door. She poked her head inside. "Mr. Murchison, Detective Denton is here to see you. He said it would only take a minute."

Murchison sighed, looked around, then said, "Give me a moment to clear off this desk, then show him in. But make sure he doesn't stay long. Buzz me in ten minutes if he's not gone."

"Will do, sir. Thank you." Mandy closed the door and returned to her desk. "Have a seat, Tip. He'll be right with you."

Less than five minutes later, the door to the ADA's office opened. "Tip, come on in. Good to see you."

"I'll get right to the point, Jack. We've got a scumbag who we're holding as a suspect in these kidnappings, both here and in Conroe."

"Good news. What have you got on him?"

"That's the bad news," Tip said. "We don't have much on the kidnapping, other than what any good lawyer may call *coincidence*, but he should be locked up on principle."

"Tell me what you've got, and let me decide if it's enough."

Tip sat in a chair across from Murchison's desk. "To begin with, he's the boyfriend of the mother of the most recent kidnapping. And he lied to us about where he was when the kidnapping took place."

"That's not much, but it's a start," Murchison said.

"He tried molesting a thirteen-year-old girl who was one of his relatives, and he threatened to kill a woman who got promoted before he did. It just so happens that the aunt of the little girl he tried molesting and the woman who was promoted before him are the parents of the first two kidnapped kids. And he threatened both of them."

"Threatened them how?"

"He said he'd get even if he had to kill them, their kids, or their dogs."

Murchison shook his head. "Why wasn't the man arrested back then?"

"I don't know," Tip said. "I'd ask why he wasn't shot, but you might object to that."

Murchison sat back in his chair and folded his hands behind his head. "I agree that this makes him a no-good son of a bitch, but what it doesn't do is make him a kidnapper. We need concrete evidence that ties him to the kidnappings."

"But he's a goddamn scumbag," Tip said.

"Tip, I know it sounds good, but if I locked up just half the people who were scumbags, we'd have a million people in prison, and *you* wouldn't have any friends. I'm sorry, but you don't have enough evidence. You've got evidence to prove he's a scumbag, but not to convict him of the kidnappings. It's all conjecture. Get me something solid, and I'll charge him. Until then you're going to have to let him go."

"How long can we hold him?" Tip asked.

"I could reasonably say seventy-two hours from when you picked him up," Murchison said. "But I'm sure you knew that. Afterward, he's a free man."

Tip slowly shook his head as he stood. "All right, Murch, but the next kidnapping is on you."

"You think there'll be another one?"

"If you let this guy go, there will be."

"Then I'd suggest you watch him, Detective. Make sure that doesn't happen."

Chapter Thirty-Seven

MORE PLANS FOR NOTHING

I got to Tip's around 6:45. His car wasn't in the driveway, which surprised me. There's no way he was still with Murchison; Murch didn't spend that much time with his wife on their honeymoon.

Mollie's car was in the driveway though, which meant I was in for an earful of … something. A person never knew what the topic of conversation would be with Mollie, but sure enough, it would be opinionated. She's never been shy about expressing herself.

I walked in the back door, greeted the dogs, then sat at the kitchen table. "Need help with anything, Mollie?"

"That's a loaded question, girl. I need help with a lot of things, but cookin' this brisket ain't one of them. If you ever see me at the grocery store tryin' to buy steaks, jump on in. I'll need help then."

"I'm in about the same department as you are when it comes to that, Mollie. I haven't had a good steak in a long time."

"Shoot. Looks like we'll have to get old tight-ass to buy some steaks. He's got more money than the Lord allows. He can afford to treat a couple of fine young ladies like us to a good meal. I'll mention it to him next week."

"You don't have to do that. I'm fine with whatever you make."

Mollie swatted at a fly with the towel she had around her neck. "Missed that son of a bitch again."

I looked at her strangely, wondering what she'd have done with the towel if she had gotten the fly.

Mollie grabbed a beer from the fridge and handed it to me. "Here you go. Figure you might be thirsty. And don't think I didn't see the way you looked at me. Don't worry. If I'd have hit that little bugger, I'd have gotten a new towel. Never do get the damn things though; they're too fast."

Mollie walked back to the stove and checked on her gravy. "Anyway, I know you'll eat darn near anything, but there's no sense in them good steaks sittin' in the grocery store when Tip could have me cookin' them up. I'm gonna tell him so."

"No need to say anything, Mollie. You can't ask someone to buy steaks. If he wants to, he'll do it."

"Maybe you can't ask him, but I can. I'm gettin' tired of cookin' briskets and fajitas anyway."

I listened to Mollie rant about the evils of pharmaceutical companies, politicians, and about everybody else. Even when I had an opinion I was willing to voice, I never got a chance. Once she started, she didn't stop.

Thankfully, about ten minutes later, Tip walked in the back door. He said hello to the dogs, then came into the kitchen. "Hey, Connie, Mollie. Sorry I'm late, I was—"

"—You need to give me some money to buy steaks," Mollie said. "Connie said she hasn't had one in years. And it ain't right to treat your partner that way. Ain't right to treat me that way either, but I'm not complaining. Not yet."

I almost spit my beer out. "Mollie! It hasn't been years, and I thought you were waiting till next week to ask."

"I was goin' to, but it was festering inside me like a pimple that needs to be popped. I figured I might as well get it over with. No sense in waiting till next week. Hell, he might get himself killed in the meantime, then where would we be. Eatin' brisket instead of steak, that's where."

Tip laughed as he grabbed a beer for himself and another one for me. "Shoot, Mollie, you should have told me. I'll buy steaks. Get some tomorrow, and we'll cook 'em up." Tip pulled a wad of bills from his pocket and handed her three hundred dollars. "Get enough for Gino and Ribs in case they come by. We'll have 'em over and grill up a nice meal."

"If Gino's coming, you better count on Marissa. And if she's coming, you better figure on Rib's wife."

Tip reached into his pocket and pulled out another hundred, then handed it to Mollie. "You see the shit you started? I ought to make you eat hot dogs."

Mollie laughed while she stuffed the bills in her purse. "If I'd have known it would be this easy, I'd have asked you a long time ago."

Tip sat next to me and said, "Tall Beans said we didn't have enough."

I nodded. "Not like we didn't know that. Guess we'll have to let Santiago go in the morning."

She slugged the rest of her beer and said, "You know, I'm not too bothered by it all. I think the guy's a dirtbag, but I don't think he's the kidnapper. Don't get me wrong, I'd love to see him to go prison but not for this."

"Why don't you think it's him?" Tip asked.

"I can't see him doing it. For one, he's not thoughtful enough to treat the kids that nice—you know, bringing their animals for them. According to Roberts, he was letting their pets live with them. I'm not saying give up on him. Hell, we've got nothing else anyway. Let's at least see if his alibi with the mystery woman checks out."

"All of that points back to what we said to begin with—that whoever is doing this has to have a decent amount of property, or they'd be seen."

Tip got up and walked around the kitchen island. "I know we ruled him out, but I can't help thinking that Spoons has something to do with this. He'd definitely be the type to bring the animals. He likes animals."

"So now we're looking for anyone who likes animals?"

"Screw you," Tip said. "But I'm gonna check this out further."

I NEED AN ADDRESS

First thing in the morning, Tip called the vet's office.

"Conroe Veterinary. Dr. Umlang's office."

"Betty, this is Tip Denton."

"Tip! What are you doin' callin' Dr. Umlang's private number?"

"I need a favor. And I need it kept quiet. Can I count on you for that?"

"Of course. I won't tell a soul. What do you need?"

"I need something you're probably not allowed to do. Give me a person's address."

A long silence followed. "Whose address? And what do you need it for?"

"I need the address where Spoons lives. And all I can say is that I need it for an investigation. I promise, if it ever comes up, your name won't enter into it."

"Spoons!" Betty chuckled. "What'd he do? Run a red light? I can't imagine it being much more that."

When Tip didn't respond, she said, "Let me look through the files. But I'll swear I never gave it to you if it comes to that."

"No problem. It won't."

She was silent while she looked through the computer files. "Here it is, Tip. You ready? I'll read it to you. I don't want a record of a text or email."

"Sounds good," Tip said. "Shoot."

"It's in Spring, off Rayford Road: 438 Pinewood Ridge Drive."

"Pinewood? Isn't that in Imperial Oaks? Or close to there?"

"I believe it is, Tip. Not far from that big Kroger store."

"That can't be right," Tip said, almost to himself.

"Right or not, that's the address. Now forget I ever told you about it, and I'll be happy."

"What? Oh, okay, Betty. Don't worry about that. I won't tell a soul."

Before going in to the station, Tip decided to pay a visit to Spoon's house. He picked up his cell and called Connie. "Gianelli, I'm gonna be late today. Real late. So you better drive in yourself. I'll probably be a couple of hours."

"Anything I can help you with?" she asked.

"No, I'm good. I'll see you later."

After hanging up, Tip turned around and headed toward Spoon's house. If Spoons hadn't left for work yet, he soon would. Tip stopped at a local coffee shop and got a pastry and tea, then he waited about half an hour to ensure Spoons had left the house.

When he felt sure the timing was right, he drove to the address Betty had provided. It was a modest two-story house in a crowded neighborhood, much as he had anticipated. Definitely not the kind of house where you could keep a half a dozen kids and animals a secret.

Tip called Betty on his way back. "Betty, you sure that address you gave me was the right one?"

Tip could hear her accessing the computer. "It's the right one: 438 Pinewood Ridge Drive. It's where we send his W-2 and everything else."

"Okay. Thanks, Betty."

Tip drove the rest of the way to the station in silence no radio and no cell phone. When he arrived, he walked straight to the coffee room for more tea.

Connie followed him in. "Where the hell have you been, partner? You look like the grim reaper kicked your ass."

"I feel like it too. I thought I might have something figured out, but it didn't work."

Connie laughed. "Those goddamn animal lovers again?"

"I'm getting tired of saying 'screw you,' but you keep making me say it."

"All right, spit it out. What went wrong?"

"I thought I'd check Spoon's place, but he lives in a regular house in a subdivision that no way could be the kind of place we're looking for."

"Have you considered the possibility that it's not Spoons? Houston's got a few more people living here."

Tip took a drink of his tea and sighed. "I guess we need to start over. We'll remind Julie to focus on what you said about looking into property north of the city. Ask her to dig into larger tracts of land. We need to concentrate on that."

"And tell her I want addresses with satellite views. I want to see what we're looking at from above. It gives a different perspective."

"And while I'm doing your dirty work, what are you going to be doing?"

"I'm going to be figuring out how this son of a bitch is beating us at every turn."

Connie grabbed a new coffee cup, filled it, and left. "Good luck with that, partner. See ya later."

ANOTHER BODY

Deputy Rawlins was finishing his second cup of coffee when the phone rang. "Rawlins," he said.

"Deputy, this is Fernandez. I'm up here south of FM 1097, and we got a mess."

"What are you talking about, Fernandez? What kind of mess?"

Fernandez's voice cracked. "Sir, we got a body tied to a tree off the feeder, and it's ... I mean it's ... Well, it's a mess, sir. You need to come see."

Rawlins sighed. "All right, Fernandez. Where exactly are you?"

"North of FM 830—Seven Coves Road—on the feeder south of FM 1097 and east of I-45."

"All right. I"ll be there in ten minutes. And keep everyone away from the scene."

"Got it, sir."

Ten minutes later, Rawlins pulled up to the scene and got out of his car. Fernandez and the county medical examiner were standing next to what looked to be a large oak tree about fifty yards east of the feeder road. Rawlins walked in that direction.

A moment later, he saw what Fernandez had been so revolted about. A man's naked body was tied to the tree, but half his skin had been removed. It looked to have been torn off.

"Good God in Heaven! What the hell is that?" Rawlins said.

Fernandez turned his head to the side. "I ain't never seen nothing like it, sir. Somebody ripped this man's skin from his body. I mean, for Christ's sake, look at it!"

Roger Kemphorn, the medical examiner, looked at Rawlins. "I haven't seen anything like it either, and I've seen some gruesome stuff; I served two years in Chicago before coming here."

Rawlins shook his head. "You got anything you can tell me yet?"

"I got a note that was pinned to his body—'This one's for Tip.' You know what that means?"

Rawlins nodded. "I sure do. I'll be calling him in a minute." Rawlins ventured a few steps closer. "You know anything else? Even if it's a guess."

Kemphorn shook his head. "From what I can see, whoever did this, used some kind of knife to cut him, then yanked his skin off in patches. It must have been damn painful."

Rawlins almost puked. "You mean he was alive while the guy did it?"

"I'll be able to confirm it later, but from what I see, coagulation had begun which means he was still alive."

"Lord have mercy," Rawlins said. "What kind of sicko would do that?"

"The kind we need to find before he does it again," Kemphorn said.

"I don't mind a simple shooting or stabbing, but this is a little much, especially when it's first thing in the morning."

"Let me know what else you get," Rawlins said. "And look hard for tire tracks. It'd be nice if we could match imprints to a make and model."

"I'll have 'em look harder, but so far we haven't seen any. No footprints either."

Rawlins dialed his cell phone as he walked toward his car.

"Tip Denton."

"Tip, this is Deputy Rawlins up in Conroe."

"Yeah, Rawlins, what the hell are you doing?"

"Just left the scene of what used to be a man's body. And it had a note pinned to it that had the words 'This one's for Tip' on it."

"What?"

"You heard me. The guy was tied to a tree by the freeway. One of the most gruesome sights I've seen."

"Don't tell me. Skin torn from the body, cut out in patches."

Rawlins opened the car door and slid in. "You got it," he said. "Don't tell me you got one like it."

"Huntsville does. If yours is like I said, it sounds exactly alike. And their victim was tied to a tree also. And it was by the freeway too."

"Son of a bitch. I can't believe no one saw him. You know how many cars pass by here every day?"

"How long has it been there?" Tip asked.

"I'll check, but I'm guessing it had to be put there last night. Three of my officers go home that way, and thousands of cars pass there.

This body was in plain view, not fifty yards from the feeder. No way that body was tied there for long."

"I guess that provides an alibi for my scumbag," Tip said.

"What?"

"Nothing. I had a suspect in custody, but he was in jail last night, so he sure as hell didn't do it."

"You like him for it?"

"Not really. I wanted him to be guilty, but I was afraid he wasn't. This kind of proves that. By the way, are there any back roads that can access that spot? I mean, if a guy knew the area, could he get there without being seen?"

"That's a good point, Tip. I'll have some people check that out and let you know."

"Okay, thanks. And, Rawlins. Give the okay for your medical examiner to share with me. I need to find this prick."

Chapter Forty

MORE PROOF

Tip picked me up around 8:00, and filled me in on what Rawlins had told him.

"I guess that provides an alibi for this scum," I said.

Tip hit the accelerator and moved to the left lane. "According to Conroe PD, there is no way that Albus's body was there early last night. In fact, Rawlins said that three of their officers go home that way. One of them—or one of the thousands of cars that pass that way—would have surely seen it. It was in plain sight of the freeway."

"How do you think he gets them to the tree without being seen?" I asked.

"I don't know. That's a good question. How the hell does anybody tie up a dead man to a tree in plain sight of everyone and not get seen? Good question, Connie."

"I don't know how he does it," I said. "but it doesn't matter because he didn't do it from jail. Which means it wasn't our friend, Santiago. As much as I would have liked it to have been him, it wasn't."

Tip sighed. "I can't argue with that."

We drove a couple of miles in silence, then I asked, "What do you think is going on, Tip? That's the second body this week."

"Don't I know it. And trust me, Coop's gonna let us know it too."

"Should we tell her? Or let her find out on her own?"

"Let her find out. Hell if we tell her we knew, she'll want to know why we don't have it solved."

I laughed. Tip was full of shit, but he was pretty close on this one; Coop was a tough nut.

We got to the station before 9:00. As we climbed the stairs, he said, "Gotta go see Julie. Why don't you get some tea and that shit you drink and meet me back at the desk."

By the time Tip returned, Cindy had already called. "Coop wants to see us ASAP," I said.

"Figures. That goddamn Rawlins probably called her to make things proper. Chicken shit."

Cindy was sitting behind her desk shaking her head when we rounded the corner. "I'd be polite today, Tip. She's not in a good mood."

"Coop? Not in a good mood? Surprises never end."

Cindy laughed, then hit the buzzer. "They're here, Captain."

We pushed through the door, and I took a seat on the far left. Tip took the seat on the right.

Coop removed her glasses and glared. "Don't even try to tell me you didn't know about this, 'cause Rawlins already told me he talked to you."

"If you'd answer your goddamn phone, you'd have known," Tip said. "I tried calling you earlier."

Coop grabbed her cell and pulled up the "recents" call list. "There's no call from you. Not a damn one."

"Fuckin' Apple," Tip said. "Can't count on them for reliability anymore. I called you as soon as I hung up from Rawlins."

"And you're trying to blame this on Apple?"

"Apple or AT&T. One of them."

Coop shook her head. "Connie, please forgive me for sticking you with this asshole of a partner? I swear one day, I'll make it up to you."

"No need, Cap. Just knowing you realize the hell you're putting me through is enough."

Coop leaned back in her chair. "All right, so tell me what the hell we're doing about this. It's escalated beyond kidnapping now. We're into full-blown, gruesome murder, and I don't like it. And I know the mayor isn't going to like it."

"You mean Mayor Cybil? When the hell are you going to stop being concerned with what she thinks?"

"Joke all you want about Cybil, but she does more for this city than Rusty ever dreamt about. In fact, I doubt he dreams about anything other than the size and shape of the stripper's **ass** at the club he visited the night before."

Coop turned to me and said, "Connie, I'm guessing this gives a "get out of jail free card" to the suspect you have in custody?"

I didn't want to answer, but I felt I had to. "Yes, ma'am. Santiago couldn't have committed the murder last night, not while he was in jail. And it matches the one in Huntsville almost exactly."

"Looks like you'll have to find a new suspect then. Guess it's time to work instead of drinking coffee."

"I don't drink coffee," Tip said.

"Then I guess it's time to get to work," Coop said. "I don't want to see you until you have a suspect—a viable one, not some cowboy who happened to be sitting at the end of the bar."

"Damn," Tip said. "I should have listened to John. He said you were a mean son of a bitch."

Coop laughed. "Yeah, I guess you should have listened. Now let your suspect loose and find out who's doing this."

As we walked back to our desks, Tip said, "We're back to square one. We need to find something."

"I say we ask Julie to double her efforts on searching properties north of the city. Maybe she'll find something."

"Yeah, but what do we have her look for? Can't just search for all property more than a few acres. It would be too many. I already told you, there are places like over on FM 1488 where entire communities require a minimum of five acres to build a home, so every person living there would be a suspect."

"Yeah, but that's west of I-45. If we believe Roberts. She was taken right when she exited I-45—when he took her to see the kids. There aren't many communities, if any, on that side of the freeway. It's mostly larger tracts of land that have been in families for years."

Tip nodded. "I'll buy that so far. What do we look for?"

"I say we start with property that has changed hands in the past few years. I'm not saying an old-time resident couldn't be doing this, but I'm guessing it's somebody new. Then we get Julie to use the Google maps for satellite view and look at the area that way. She'll be able to see if a property is secluded enough to work for this kind of sick operation. That should limit the number of properties we need to inspect. It will still be a lot, but it will be manageable."

"That's still going to be a lot of properties," Tip said.

"Knock on every door."

"What?"

"'Knock on every door.' That's what my old boss used to tell us when a crime took place in an apartment building. We may have had a hundred or more tenants, but he'd tell us to talk to everyone. 'Knock on every door' he'd say."

"How's that help us?" Tip asked.

"This is no different. We may end up with a few hundred properties, but if we do, we get some help and visit each one just like we did in New York. 'Knock on every door' so to speak."

Tip was quiet a moment, then said, "Shit, I might even like that idea, Gianelli. Who said people from New York were stupid?"

It took Julie two days to get a big enough list to start with.

"If you add in the older property, it's going to make the list a lot longer," Julie said. "People have been buying up property on that side so they can find a convenient place to live that isn't so expensive. The Woodlands is not only getting crowded but pricey."

"Where are most of them located?" Tip asked.

"There are some around FM 1960 and a few more north of there, but you don't find most of them until you get north of Rayford Road."

"All right, listen up. I want you to make six copies of this list. I'll be back and give you names of who to distribute them to. We're going to split that list up so that six teams can check it out. And I'm gonna want you to brief them too."

True to his word, Tip returned within the hour, and he had the names, which he handed to Julie. "I've got everybody waiting in the coffee room to go over things. Bring your list or properties and distribute them to each team. I'll tell them which sites to visit. I want them knocking on doors."

"What are we looking for?" Julie asked.

"We're looking for any sign of kids," Tip said. "Tell that to the homeowners and make note of their reactions. If something looks wrong, report back to me, and we'll check it out further." Tip slapped his hand on the desk. "We've got seven kids missing counting the ones in Conroe. Seven goddamn kids! We need to find them, and we need to do it now. Make it good. This is your ballgame. Go solve a crime."

Julie already had the list divided into equal parts. She handed them out to each team, then instructed them on what to do. "Don't slouch off on this," she said. "I'm a mom, and I know most of you have kids. You would want to find them quickly if they were missing. I know I would."

An officer in the second row raised his hand.

"Yeah?" Tip asked.

"You said to look for signs of kids, but most of these places will have kids. We need more than that to go on."

Tip nodded. "You're right. Julie is going to give each of you a packet before you leave. Inside the packet will be pictures of all the kids, plus the dogs and cats we know to be missing. We have a report from Samantha Roberts that the kidnapper is keeping the animals with the kids. And she thinks they were underground."

"Underground"

"Yeah. She was blindfolded when the kidnapper took her to this place, but she felt certain that they went downward. Not in an elevator, and not using steps, but downward as in how you might go down a ramp."

"You saying we're looking for a damn dungeon?"

"Not a dungeon. Just a room or two underground. Someplace where the kids wouldn't be noticed."

"Sort of like how the houses up north have basements. Sounds like somebody may have done something similar," I said.

Someone near the rear of the room cracked a joke. Tip slammed his fist on the table. "Listen up, assholes. This is not a joke. We've got little kids who have been stolen from their parents, and we've got two damn gruesome murders. I don't want any loafing on this. I want you working this case like it's your kids or your nieces and nephews who are missing. Got that? I want them found. And I want them found quickly."

"You got it," the officer said, and everyone echoed his comment.

"We'll get started on it first thing," an officer said.

Tip glared. "First thing? You think those parents are gonna stop worrying about their kids after work? You think those kids are gonna stop wondering when they're getting home because the work day is over?"

Tip stared at each person in the room. "I'll answer that for you, 'cause I'm guessing a bunch of you are morons. No! The parents won't stop worrying. And no! The kids won't stop wondering. So get your asses out there and find them. Nighttime is the best time to reach these people at home so get out there and get it done."

Chapter Forty-One

WHO OWNS WHAT?

Tip had split the teams up into daytime and nighttime shifts. The daytime groups weren't getting much in the way of results, but the nighttime teams were. They were finding more than half the people home when they called on them. The problem was that despite more than a dozen inspections, no one had been identified as a potential suspect. There had been no sign of kids or dogs at any of the houses, save a few teenagers and a house or two with one dog or cat and one house that had a few horses.

"This isn't getting us anywhere," Tip said. "We need to crank things up."

Connie was about to respond when her cell rang. "Gianelli."

"Connie, it's Julie.

"Hey, Jules, what's up? Before we start, let me put you on speaker so Tip can hear."

"I've been doing more digging on the victims who were killed, and I stumbled across something on the internet. It wasn't in the files, but I found an accusation on social media about Mr. Albus being involved with dog fighting.”

“Involved how?”

“As in he was using his dog to fight, and that was reportedly the reason the dog died.”

“Where’d you see this?” Tip asked.

“On a Twitter post, though the person who accused him no longer has an account.”

“Find whoever it was who did the accusing. I don’t care what you have to do, find them.”

Connie hung up the phone and looked at Tip. “That puts a twist on things.”

“You bet your ass it does. It makes me wonder about Richardson. We need to interview the Richardson boy and see if there was any instance of animal abuse."

“The kidnapper didn't take the Richardson boy," Connie said.

"I know he didn't," Tip said. "But he supposedly tried to. And he probably would have if the kid had gotten into the van with him."

“If that’s what you’re thinking, he may try again. We better get there first.”

Tip turned the car around and headed toward The Woodlands. He parked in front of Mrs. Richardson’s house, and he and Connie walked to the door and rang the bell. A moment later Mrs. Richardson answered, wearing jeans and a sweatshirt and looking as if she’d been cleaning.

“May I help you?” she asked, eyebrows raised.

"I'm Detective Denton, and this is my partner, Detective Gianelli," Tip said. "We have a few questions if you don't mind."

"About what? I've already spoken to the police."

"I know that, ma'am, but we've had another killing and we're trying to see if we can find any links," Tip said.

She opened the door wider and said, "Of course. Come in and have a seat."

Tip and I sat on the sofa, and she sat across from us in a love seat. "What do you need to know?" she asked.

"Has your son said anything else about the man who asked him to get into the van? Any further descriptions? Or has he seen him since?"

She shook her head. "Not to me, he hasn't. He may have talked to his friends, knowing kids, but not me."

"And you haven't seen the van since?" Connie asked.

"Definitely not. I look at all vans now with a suspicion I never had. I don't know if I'll ever get rid of that."

"I know it's an odd question, Mrs. Richardson, but do you own a dog or did you own a dog?"

She looked at Tip with her head cocked to the side. "We did a long time ago, maybe six years ago, but he died. We haven't had one since, why?"

"What kind of dog was it?" Tip asked.

"It was a pit bull. Why do you ask?"

"Just a random question. We had a few reports of people who had their dogs stolen near here, but they weren't pit bulls."

"My husband did say he thought he was being followed."

"Followed?" Connie asked, leaning forward.

"Yes, followed by someone in a green sports car. He mentioned it to me twice."

"Did he call the police?" Tip asked.

She shook her head again. "Not that I know of. But that wasn't Kent's style. He would've sooner stopped the car and confronted the man. I wonder if that's what happened. That, or something like that."

"Hard to say right yet," Tip said. "But we'll find out. And just so that you know, we'll be talking to some of your neighbors to see if they saw anything."

"Nobody said they did," Mrs. Richardson said.

"I realize that, ma'am, but a lot of times, people hold back. Information has to be dragged out of them."

"Whatever you think," she said. "I want this over with so my son and I can get on with life. I don't want him bothered by all this."

After a few more questions, we left Mrs. Richardson and went to the house next door, then the two after that. We didn't learn anything new, so we kept it up. On the fifth house— one across the street from Richardson's—we struck gold. It belonged to a Mr. Saxon.

"How long have you known the Richardson's?" Connie asked.

"Going on ten years," Saxon said. "Since right after the boy was born. He wasn't even a toddler when I moved in."

"So you knew him when he had his dog," Tip said.

Saxon looked up and down the street, then nodded. "Wish I didn't, but I did."

"Why say that?" Tip asked.

"He treated that dog like shit."

"Such as?"

"Just treated him badly. You know, always yelling at him, making him follow orders like a damn soldier, that kind of stuff."

"Nothing else though? He hit it?"

Saxon thought a moment, then said, "Not that I saw, but it wouldn't surprise me if you told me he did." He looked at Connie, then me, and said, "Hey, why all the questions about the dog. That dog's been dead for years. I thought you were looking into Kent's death."

"We are looking into it," Connie said. "But that often involves asking about peripheral things like this. Anything else you can tell us?"

Saxon shook his head and started to close the door. "Nothing else. Sorry."

"How did the dog die?" Tip asked.

Saxon got an irritated look on his face. "How the hell do I know how it died. It wasn't my dog."

"When did it die?" Tip asked.

"I have no idea," Saxon said, then he began to close the door and step back inside his house.

"Well shit on you too," Tip said.

Connie grabbed Tip's arm and started down the sidewalk. "He knows a lot more than he's telling."

"I agree, but why do you think that?"

"The tone of his voice when he answered you about the dog dying. He seemed irritated, like a little kid defending a lie."

"So what do you want to do about it?" Tip asked.

"I want you to sit in the car while I go back and explain why we need this information."

"And what makes you think he'll be any more cooperative for you?"

Connie laughed. "Because I'm prettier," she said, and turned toward the house.

I knocked on the door and waited.

A moment later, Saxon opened the door. "What the hell do you want now?"

"The truth."

"What's that supposed to mean? I told you what I know."

"May I come in, Mr. Saxon?"

He looked as if he might say no, but then he stepped aside as he opened the door wider. "Come on in," he said with a reluctant tone.

I sat on the sofa and looked straight at him. "It seemed to me as if you knew more than what you said about Mr. Richardson's dog."

"The damn dog again? Good God. What is it with the dog?"

"That's what I want to know, Mr. Saxon. And I'm not leaving here until I do."

Saxon sighed. "I'm not gonna get in any trouble for what I tell you, right?"

"I don't know. I don't know what you're going tell me. If you tell me you killed someone, you'll get in trouble. If you tell me you ran a red light—no."

He sighed again. "Okay, I'm trusting you."

"Go ahead."

"When I first moved in, Richardson and I became pretty close. He liked to golf, and so did I. He liked fishing, and so did I. Then one night at a local bar, he asked me if I'd ever seen a dogfight."

Saxon looked at me and shifted on the chair. "I told him no, and that I didn't want to."

"'Suit yourself,' he said. But it's a hell of a show. You can make damn good money too."

"The dogfighting didn't get my interest, but the mention of money did. I had just moved in, and the new mortgage was pretty high."

"Go on."

"Anyway, he took me to a place where they fought dogs and bet on them. The betting was pretty heavy. I listened to Richardson, and we walked away that night a few thousand richer."

"A few thousand?" I asked.

He nodded. "And that was nothing. Richardson did twice as good 'cause his dog won."

Saxon got up to get water. When he returned, he picked up where he'd left off. "Anyway, I went with him a few times and made darn good money, but it got to be I couldn't stand watching those dogs tear each other up. It was horrible. And if a dog got hurt bad, they just killed it."

"Is that how his dog died?" I asked.

"I don't know for sure, but I suspect so. Richardson kept fighting long after I quit going, but then they got busted one night. He managed to get off because he knew one of the cop's brothers, but I thought he quit after that experience."

"Where did this take place?" I asked.

"The fighting took place up in Conroe somewhere, and don't ask me to find it, 'cause I can't. But he always went with some guy who lived off of Rayford."

"You know his name?"

He shook his head. "I don't know his name, and I'd be hard-pressed to describe him. It's been a few years, and I've been trying to forget. I like dogs, and I still have nightmares about what I saw."

"Anything else?" I asked.

"Nothing I can think of. I'm sorry I didn't say this at first. I guess I was scared and embarrassed both."

I placed my hand on his arm. "I understand, Mr. Saxon. Thanks for telling us now. This helps."

"Did him being killed have something to do with this?" Saxon asked.

"It may have," I said as I stood to leave. "That's what we're checking out."

"But it won't come back on me, will it? I mean nobody will know I said anything."

I almost laughed. "No, Mr. Saxon. Nobody will know you said a word."

On our way back to the station, Tip

said, "You know what this means?"

"What?"

It means we've got a new suspect list. In other words, we're shit out of luck. We need to brainstorm this. I'd like to have Gino and Ribs over. Maybe they can help."

"You ought to invite Marissa too. She helped Gino and Ribs on their last case."

"Yeah, I guess she did. Okay, you take care of inviting her, and I'll call Cataldi."

Chapter Forty-Two

A NIGHT OF PLANNING

I got home and called Marissa. "Marissa, can you and Gino come to Tip's for dinner tonight? I know it's late notice, but it was spur of the moment."

A pause followed, then, "You sure you want me there? If you only want Gino, I can go shopping or something."

I laughed. "We can do without Gino. Not that I don't enjoy his company, but it's your brains I want to pick."

"What? Why? What's going on?"

"Tip and I have been working these kidnapping cases involving little kids. We're up to four kids now—and that's Houston only. There are three more in Conroe. And to make matters worse, there are now two bodies associated with the kidnappings."

"Oh my God!"

"No. Kids weren't killed, but parents were. And what the guy does to them is pretty disgusting. I know you don't like talking about your past, but any insight you have might help. I'd appreciate it."

"Of course, I'll come over. I don't know if I can help, but I'll try."

"That's all any of us can do," I said. "Can you make it by seven?"

"Assuming Gino is home on time, I can."

"And just wear jeans or whatever you're comfortable in. I don't want you dressing up; you're too gorgeous as it is."

Marissa laughed. "You're full of it, Connie, but thanks."

"Okay. See you there."

I got to Tip's place before anyone—anyone but Mollie, that is. Sometimes it seemed as if she lived there.

I took a seat at the table and said hi to Mollie, who was washing dishes.

"Still waitin' on those steaks," she said. "Haven't seen anything better than a hamburger since you were here last."

"What do you mean, Mollie? I saw him give you the money for it."

"Yeah, he gave me the money, but he hasn't said when he wants to do it."

"I got news for you. I think he wants to do it tonight. Ribs and Gino are coming over. And Marissa too."

Mollie stopped and leaned on the counter. "What? That damn fool didn't tell me anything about it. I don't have enough food for that many people."

"If you want, I'll go to the grocery store with you. We can pick up those steaks you've been wanting and a few potatoes."

"I'll go myself," Mollie said. She put the dishtowel on the counter, grabbed her purse, and headed out the door. "Tell that tick turd I'm buying him a steak with lots of fat."

"He hates fat, Mollie."

"I know. It'll serve him right for springing this on me at the last minute."

"Mollie, you can't do that. You know Tip goes crazy over the tiniest piece of fat."

"All right. But if he does anything like this again, he's in for it," she said, and walked out the door.

Five minutes later, Gino and Ribs pulled up with Marissa in the car. Tip was still in the shower, so I walked out to greet them.

"Ribs, where's your wife?"

"She said she had too much to do, and we were having a tough time finding a babysitter anyway. Looks like you're stuck with just me."

I kissed him on the cheek. "Lucky us," I said, then greeted Gino and Marissa.

As we were walking inside, Tip was coming out. "Hey, Gino, good to see you." He looked at Ribs with a questioning gaze. "Ribs, what are you doing here? I didn't invite you."

Ribs hit him in the arm, then turned to me. "Connie, if you ever want a real partner, give me a call. We'll let Gino and Tip have each other."

"You got a deal," I said, then we all took seats at the table. Mollie came in about twenty minutes later.

She stood in the doorway with her hands on her hips and looked at everyone. "Tip, if I'd have known you wanted me to cook for a banquet, I'd have been better prepared."

Tip handed a beer to Ribs and Gino. "There goes Mollie, running her mouth again. She's not happy unless she's bitching about something."

Mollie turned and glared. "No need to worry then, 'cause working for you gives me plenty to bitch about—enough to last several lifetimes."

"Come on, Mollie," Gino said. "You know you love having us over."

"That ain't the point, Gino. The point is he makes me seem like a complainer when I'm just speaking my mind. If I wanted to complain, you can bet your sweet ass you'd know it. And so would old turd head."

Everyone laughed, then Mollie set a notepad on the table. "Write down how you like your steaks done, so I know how to cook 'em."

"What kind of steaks you did you get?" Ribs asked.

"I got filets for everyone. Tip paid for them, so money wasn't the issue. All I need to know is how everyone wants them cooked."

Everyone placed their orders, then Mollie went outside to cook.

"What have we got?" Ribs asked. "It must be a tough case if you need me."

"Ribs, nobody needs you. Your kids don't even need you. I only invited you to get Gino and Marissa to come along. Hell, the last time I worked with you, you almost got me killed."

"Some people see it differently," Ribs said.

Tip shook his head, then leaned over the table while resting on his elbows. "We've had all these kidnappings, and now we've got two bodies to go along with 'em."

"They're connected?" Gino asked.

"I think they've got to be," I said. "The bodies are of men who both had a history with dog fighting, and they were both killed the same way."

"We can't prove they're connected," Tip said, but like Connie says, we feel pretty sure they are. We've got no DNA and no other evidence, but whoever is taking the kids—and the animals—according to Roberts, he isn't hurting them; in fact, she swears they seemed happy."

"So nobody's been hurt?" Ribs asked.

"Not until recently," I said. "But now we've got two dead bodies. Not kids though. They're fathers whose kids the kidnapper tried getting but failed. And, I might add, these are the first two cases where a father was in the picture. The other ones were all single moms."

"You think the fathers interfered with the kidnapper getting the kids?" Gino asked. "Maybe he witnessed it happening and tried to stop it."

"That's a possibility," Tip said. "A remote one, but a possibility."

"Why remote?" Ribs asked.

"Nothing solid, Ribs. Just a gut feel. When we interviewed the neighbors of the one guy, he didn't come across as a loving and caring type. Don't get me wrong; I'm not saying he wouldn't defend his kid; I just don't know if he cared enough to be watching what his kid was doing."

I glanced over at Marissa. She hadn't said a thing. I could tell she was listening, but she was doing it quietly. "Marissa, what do you think."

My question startled her. Gino shifted in his seat, obviously uncomfortable by her being put on the spot.

"Me, oh, I don't know. It's not for me to say."

"Sure it is. This is an everyone-contribute party. Have no fear;

Mollie will be throwing in her two cents once she's done cooking. She always does."

"Four cents is more like it," Tip said. "That woman can't keep her mouth shut."

"Come on, Marissa. I'd love to hear your opinion," I said.

She smiled, but straightened in her seat and looked to Gino. He smiled and nodded. "How did he kill the fathers?" she asked.

"Tortured them," I said. "Yanked the skin from their bones, and when he was done, he tied them to a tree in a public location."

"I'm sure you know it, but that has to be the key. If it had nothing to do with the fathers, he would have either left them alone or killed them quickly. If they had simply interfered with the kidnappings, he wouldn't waste time with torture. A quick shot to the head would be easier, quicker, and safer."

Marissa leaned forward and rested folded hands on her legs. "What have you found out so far about the fathers? If you haven't found anything, keep digging. I'd bet that's what will solve this case."

"I like that. I like that a lot, Marissa," Tip said. "In fact, I like that so much, I'll drink a beer to you."

Everyone laughed as Tip popped the top on another beer and gulped it down. When he was finished, he tossed the empty into the trashcan and hollered. "Mollie, we're hungry as hell and short on beer."

"I'm workin' on dinner, and you can get your own damn beer, you old fart."

"Is Elena coming, Tip?" Marissa asked.

"She was supposed to, but she called today and said she had to go to Dallas for some fashion show or some such nonsense. I'd be half wondering if she didn't have another man somewhere if I didn't know she already had the best."

"Well ain't that a crock," Mollie said, standing with a tray of steaks in her hands. "Get seated where you want to be. Supper's ready. And be careful where you step; you'll have to wade through all the bullshit Tip's spitting out."

"I'm not arguing that the killings are tied to the dog fighting, but how does that connect them to the kidnappings?" Ribs asked.

"For one thing, the guy had a note taped to one of the bodies that read 'This one's for Tip.' And since Tip is the lead on the kidnapping case, that would make sense. Add to that the fact that the bodies were found in Conroe and Huntsville—and we've had kidnappings there—any you've got more evidence."

Gino finished chewing his meat, then said, "I say follow the dog fighting leads and see where it goes. I'm with Marissa and Connie. It has to be connected and I think that will be the quickest way to get to the guy."

"Sounds like we're all in agreement," Ribs said.

"Sounds like you're all a crock of shit," Mollie said. "Everybody knew the killings were connected to the kidnappings. A damn ten-year-old could've told you that. What you've got to do is find out who did the killings, then you'll have who's doing the kidnappings."

Tip coughed and almost spit out his beer. "Well shit, Mollie. Now that you've solved the crime for us, would you mind making some coffee?"

"Yes, I would mind. I got a damn life of my own to live, and it's time I got home and lived it." She grabbed her purse and headed toward the back door. "Good night, all. Don't stay up too late 'cause you got crimes to solve, and it looks like you need a lot of help."

We sat around talking for another hour or so, then Tip said, "I think Mollie may have been right. I'm convinced we're on the right track, but we've still got to figure out how to nail the son of a bitch. But thanks to everyone for coming over and bringing your good advice."

Marissa hugged me and kissed my cheek. "Don't thank us. We didn't do anything but agree with your assessment. And eat Tip's good steak, of course."

I laughed. "Hang on, Marissa. I'll walk out with you."

Chapter Forty-Three

MORE THINKING

Tip sat across the desk from me, wearing a scowl half as big as Texas.

"What's up, partner? I don't often see you in a sour mood."

He took another sip of tea, then said, "All night long, I was thinking of what you said. Now it's bothering me more."

"What did I say? Something to bother you? When?"

"Not last night. It was a while ago. You said something about the animals that got me thinking. Suppose we're looking at this wrong? Suppose the kidnapper isn't grabbing the animals to keep the kids happy, but he's grabbing the kids to keep the animals happy?"

I looked at him as if he were crazy. "What are you talking about? You're saying this guy is kidnapping kids so that their animals won't miss them?"

"Not exactly, but sort of," Tip said. "I don't know what I'm saying, but I know we're looking at this whole case wrong. We're missing something."

I got skeptical. "Are you back on your theory of the guy who works at the vet?"

"I've never been off that theory because it's right. I just haven't been able to prove it. Besides, you're the one who got me thinking this way."

"What's that supposed to mean?"

"When you were talking about what your Uncle Dominic said about people committing crimes for good reasons. Maybe that's what we've got here. The more I see of this case, the better it fits. This guy loves animals. If anyone is gonna take the animals and let the kids have them, it's him. In fact, like I just said, I wouldn't be surprised if he's taking the kids to comfort the animals."

"Okay, let's assume you're right. How do we go about it?"

"We find out about the killings like we talked about last night. Both those guys being hooked up with dog fights isn't a coincidence. No way it's a coincidence. The killer knew about the dogs, and he knew about the connection between Richardson and Albus."

"The question is how did he know," I said.

"Which brings me back to Spoons. He works at a veterinary office. What better place to find out about hurt dogs?"

I tapped my pencil on the desk as I thought. "And what better place to find out about missing dogs or cats," I said. "Didn't several of those kids have dogs or cats that were stolen or missing?"

"The faxes!" Tip said. "The goddamn faxes."

"What are you talking about?"

"I just thought of this. It's been in the back of my mind, but I kept missing it. When I was at the vet picking up Sacco, they had a pile of faxes with missing dogs, cats, you name it. And each one had a picture of the animal plus the owner's name and address. If the kidnapper is Spoons, he could have used that information to target his victims."

"And you saw the faxes? Did you see the kidnap victims' addresses?"

"I recognized a few from Houston and Conroe. The vet gets faxes from a place in Houston that sends notices of all the dogs and cats that are missing from about a fifty-mile radius. I saw a stack of them while I was there."

"We need to look through them," I said.

"I'll call Betty."

"Can we count on her to keep quiet?"

"She'll find it difficult, but I think we can count on her."

"Dr. Umlang's office."

"Betty, this is Tip Denton. I need a favor."

"What do you need, Detective? I hope it's not another address."

"Do you keep copies of the faxes of the missing animals? Like the ones you showed me."

"Yes, we keep them for six months, then they're shredded."

"Okay, good. If you don't mind. I need copies of the last six months, everything you've got."

"That's gonna be a lot, Detective; besides, didn't I already send you these?"

"You sent me a few," Tip said, "but I need the last six months. How long do you think it will take before you have 'em ready?"

"I don't know, let me look at the calendar." She put Tip on hold, then picked up a moment later. "I could probably have them ready for you by tomorrow. Is that okay?"

"That'll be great, Betty. And same as before, don't tell anyone you're doing this."

"You got it, Detective. I'll keep quiet."

"Good. I'll send someone to pick up the faxes tomorrow afternoon. I don't want to be seen there."

"All right, Tip. I'll have them ready."

Tip had an aide named Sharon pick up the faxes because she lived near the vet's office. She brought them with her the following morning and gave them to Tip.

He walked into the office carrying an armload of papers. "Looks like we got some work to do, Gianelli. Must be more than a hundred faxes here."

"Shouldn't be too tough," Connie said. "All we've got to do is compare names and addresses on the faxes with the names and addresses for the kidnap victims."

Tip handed Connie half the pile and took a seat. "Let's get started then. The sooner we find this bastard, the better."

By noon, they had everything sorted and double checked. They found records of every victim—every victim's pet, that is. In each case, the pet—a dog or cat—had gone missing sometime in the months before the kidnapping. And in the cases dealing with the dead bodies, the animals had never been found, although in the descriptions of the animals was language that indicated scars found on the dogs had likely been from fighting.

"This supports your theory, Tip. If anyone wanted to place blame on the guy from the vet's office, this would help their case."

"Help the case, yeah, but it doesn't do anything to prove it. All it does is show us that anyone who works at any vet's office that receives the faxes would have had access to the information."

"So all we've got to do is prove that your guy is the one doing it."

"I thought that's what we've been trying to do," Tip said.

"Let's start again. Why did he kill those people the way he did? Ripping their skin off."

"Because that's what happens when dogs fight," Tip said. "They tear each other's skin and rip it off, so the killer did the same thing to them."

"The note from Huntsville!" Connie said.

"What note?"

"The one pinned to the body. It read 'Do unto others what others do to you.' Remember?"

"Shit," Tip said. "This would fit. The skin was ripped from their bodies."

"Just like a dog fight," Connie said.

"Tip, thinking about this more, it fits better than what we thought."

"How's that?"

"The kids who were taken all had missing animals at some point, right? Now, he's taking the kids, making them 'missing' from their parents."

"Son of a bitch," Tip said. "I told you it was Spoons."

"We don't know who it was yet, Tip. It could be anyone who works at a vet's office within fifty miles. Or it could be someone else altogether, and we just haven't figured out how they're getting information."

"I say we follow him again," Tip said.

"That didn't work the first time or the second time."

"I'll ask Coop if we can yank everyone off the property canvassing and then take Simmie and Lancon for surveillance. We'll sit on his ass all night if we have to, but we'll nail him this time."

"And if it isn't him?"

"It's got to be him," Tip said.

"The alternative is, it isn't. And I think we better have a backup plan."

"All right. We'll keep canvassing the properties, but we still take Simmie and Lancon and follow him. We won't give him room to breathe."

"Deal," Connie said. "Get the okay from Coop, and we'll get started tonight."

Chapter Forty-Four

ANOTHER TAIL

I waited for Tip and thought about how we were doing this operation. It wasn't much different than what we did before, other than the personnel being different. Tip had Simmie and Lancon briefed on following Spoons from the time he left work to the time he tucked in. They had strict orders not to leave him.

As I thought more about it, Tip pulled up. He rolled the window down and shouted, "Gianelli, stop loafing and get in the car. We've got work to do."

I got in the car and buckled up. "You hear anything from the canvass?"

"Not a damn thing, and I already talked to Coop. No one uncovered a thing. This guy's a ghost."

"He's not a ghost. We just haven't found him yet. Remember, we still have a lot of property to look at. He could be in any one of them."

"He better be 'cause we're running out of ideas. And before you ask, yes, Simmie and Lancon are tailing Spoons. I've got Hartak, Mennil, and Crow on the canvass tonight."

"Together or separate?"

"They goddamn better be separate. We don't have time for them to be partying and telling jokes."

"You're driving awful slow today. Not that I mind, it's just got me wondering why."

"I'm thinking. I can't think right when I drive fast."

"I'm glad to hear that. You should have told me a long time ago, then I wouldn't have been so worried."

"Why, you want me to speed up?"

"Hell no. Keep thinking, partner. Keep this up, and I may be able to stop wearing diapers to work."

Tip laughed. "You asshole."

For three nights, Simmie and Lancon sat on Spoon's house, and he went nowhere. On the fourth night, he drove home from work and left fifteen minutes later. Simmie called Tip as he followed from a few blocks.

"He's on the move, Tip."

"Don't let the son of a bitch out of your sight. And don't let him make you either. Stay a good distance back."

"Will do. This isn't my first surveillance, you know."

"I don't care if it's your hundredth surveillance, do what I say. And let me know where he goes. I'll have my cell with me."

Simmie followed at a safe distance, ensuring that Spoons didn't spot him for a tail. He headed south on I-45, then exited at the Woodlands Mall. He parked at the entrance near the escalators on the second floor and walked in. Simmie waited about fifteen seconds, then he and Lancon followed.

By the time they got inside, Spoons was nowhere in sight. "Take the second floor to the right," Simmie said. "I'll take the escalator down and go right also. If we don't find him, we'll go the other way."

"Tip's gonna have a cow if we lose him," Lancon said.

"Fuck Tip. We'll find him."

Within ten minutes, Simmie called Lancon. "Got him. He's heading toward Macy's."

"I'll be right down," Lancon said.

"No. You stay up there and watch the Macy's exit on the second floor. I'll watch it from down here."

"What about if he goes out the back?"

"I doubt he'll go out the back of Macy's, then walk through the parking lot to his car. Just do what I said."

After half an hour, Simmie got nervous. After an hour, he panicked. He called Lancon. "Anything? Any signs of him?"

"Nothing," Lancon said. "I think we should call Tip. It's been too long. Hell, my wife doesn't take this long to shop."

"I don't give a shit about your wife, and forget about calling

Denton. I'm not doing it. Give him another half an hour, then we're going in."

"He might spot us."

"Fuck him if he does. We're going in thirty minutes."

Thirty minutes later, Lancon's cell rang.

"Time to go," Simmie said. "Check the men's department first."

"What about if he's somewhere else and slips out?"

"Then he slips out. I'm not waiting any longer."

Ten minutes later, while walking past the suits, Lancon spotted Spoons trying on a jacket. He walked by casually, then when out of sight, called Simmie. "Got him. He's in the suit department trying on clothes."

"Are you shitting me? You mean this asshole was here all this time shopping?"

"I don't know if he was here all this time, but he's here now."

"All right, go back into the mall and wait by the entrance. Call me if you see him leave, and I'll do the same."

Around ten o'clock, Tip got a call. It was Coop.

"We've got another one. Kid in Montgomery County."

"What time did it happen?" Tip asked.

"About 8:00 as best as we can tell. Sounds like the same person though. Did you have eyes on your suspect?"

"I'll find out. Simmie and Lancon were supposed to have him. I'm gonna call them now."

Tip hung up from Coop and dialed Simmie's number.

"Simmie."

"Where are you?" Tip asked.

"I'm home," Simmie said. "Where the hell do you think I am?"

"Did you follow our man all night? Did you have eyes on him at all times?"

"Yes and no. Yes, I followed him. But no, I didn't watch him go to the bathroom or change clothes in Macy's."

"Did you follow him into Macy's or did you wait outside?"

Simmie paused. "I waited at the mall entrance, but Lancon was upstairs."

"Good job, Simmie. A kid was kidnapped tonight."

"Hey, fuck you, Denton. That's not on me. No way that this guy snuck out did a kidnapping, and snuck back in, without us knowing."

"Is that right? I think that's exactly what he did. Right under your nose, you fuckin' rookie."

Tip hung up and called Connie. "A kid's gone, and those assholes lost Spoons. They didn't have eyes on him. I'm gonna recommend that Coop take their badges. Hell, I oughta shoot them."

"Easy goin', partner. Settle down. I know you're upset, but remember that we did the same thing. A kidnapping happened while we were tailing him."

The line was quiet for a moment, then Tip said, "Goddamnit, you're right, Connie. You're right, and you shouldn't be. No way that's a coincidence. Two kidnappings on the very nights we had him tailed. Get your ass over here so we can figure this out."

"Now?"

"Hell yes, now. I'm not letting this sit any longer than I have to."

Chapter Forty-Five

HOW DOES HE DO IT?

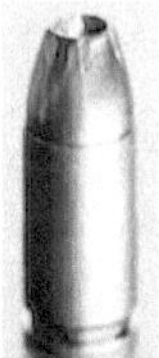

I got to Tip's in about ten minutes. He had cold beer waiting, but he also had coffee, or at least what he called coffee. Being an avid tea drinker, he didn't grasp the nuances of a good cup of coffee or how important the brewing process was.

"You want beer or coffee?" he asked when I sat down.

"Despite your inability to brew a good cup of coffee, I'll opt for that. I need it."

"Did Coop call you?" Tip asked.

"She called when I was on my way over here. When I told her where I was going, she said to get the details from you."

"I don't know much," Tip said. "A kid off Sawdust Road went missing around 8:00. That was when Spoons was in Macy's by himself, and goddamn Simmie and Lancon were loafing near the entrances to the mall."

"We've already been through this, Tip. We did the same thing. It's more important to figure out how Spoons kidnapped the kid if he was in Macy's."

"If I've got to think that hard, I need another beer," Tip said, and he went to the fridge and got one.

"I just realized this might only be the second time I've been here when Mollie wasn't here."

"Thank God for small favors," Tip said.

I sipped the coffee and tried not to make a scowl. "So how'd he do it?"

"If we presume it's Spoons, and since we know he went into Macy's and didn't leave—at least by way of the mall—and he didn't take his car, then he must have had another car in the parking lot. There's no way around that logic. Either he had a car, or someone picked him up."

As I was giving that theory consideration, Tip said, "What time is it?"

I looked at the clock on the wall. "According to your own damn clock, it's five of ten. Why?"

Tip reached over and grabbed his keys off the counter. "We need to drive to the mall and look in the parking lot. It should be mostly empty by now, so we'll be able to spot an extra van if there is one."

We drove to the mall and headed straight for the parking lot by Macy's. Sitting about five rows from the entrance was a white van with a Calcon Fencing sign on the side panel. "That's it," Tip said. "We've got the son of a bitch."

For the next few days, we had teams following Spoons, and every team had specific instructions on what to do.

For two days, he went straight home from work, then on the third day, Tip and I drew the detail, and he ended up going to the mall. We worked it as we had before, with me going downstairs and waiting for him by the escalator. The exception was we had a third person with us, and he staked out the van outside of Macy's.

I waited by the escalator as before, then followed him to Macy's when he made his appearance. This time, I followed him into the store.

He shopped for almost an hour, looking at socks, pants, shirts, and other things. Then he went to the kitchenware section and stayed for half an hour, then he left and headed back into the mall and up the escalator to his car. He got in and drove home.

Tip insisted on following him all the way home. "Are you gonna tuck him in?" I asked. "I'm sure he's tired from all that shopping."

"Screw you, Gianelli. Maybe he didn't do anything tonight, but that doesn't mean he's not the guy."

"Tip, maybe you should give up on this guy. You must have considered other options."

"I have."

"Well, those options are still options. It's possible that Spoons is not the guy."

"Yeah, I know. But it's also possible he is the guy. And for now, I'm going with that. By the way, have you seen Julie? I've left her two messages, and she's never gotten back to me."

"She's on vacation. Why?"

"Goddamn! She never got back to me on that van in the parking lot. I told her to run the plates."

I took out my cell phone and lifted it to my mouth. "Siri, remind me to check on plates at nine tomorrow morning."

Tip looked over at me. "Does that shit work?"

I laughed. "What, the phone?"

"I know the phone works. I'm talking about that voice shit."

I laughed more. "Tip, you're such a dinosaur. Of course, it works. I use it all the time. I use the voice to text to send emails and texts too. It saves me tons of time."

"I don't know why the hell people don't pick up the phone and talk."

"It's called technology, Tip. It's the same reason we don't still ride horses."

"Is there anything new on the canvass? I didn't check today."

"Not that I heard of. We haven't gotten a thing from it, and we've put a lot of man-hours into it. I'm sure Coop will be reminding us of that soon."

Tip pulled into my apartment complex and let me off. "See you in the morning," he said. "Let's figure this thing out tomorrow."

I turned to look at him as I got out of the car. "What a good idea. I hadn't been trying to solve this case, but now I will."

Tip laughed. "Okay, Gianelli. Point made. I'll see you in the morning."

Chapter Forty-Six

WHO OWNS THE CAR?

Tip picked me up early, and we drove to the office, getting there before eight. As we climbed the stairs, he said, "I'm going to see Julie."

"She's on vacation. I told you that last night."

Tip slowed down. "Shit, I forgot. Do you have those plate numbers? We've got to get them run."

"I don' have them. You copied them down and gave them to Julie. Maybe you should have copied them onto your phone or taken a picture of them, then you'd still have them."

Tip turned and sneered. "How many times do I have to say 'screw you' before you get the hint?"

"As soon as you catch up with the rest of the world, I'll stop, partner. Until then you're fair game."

"I'm gonna look through Julie's desk and see if I can find those plate numbers. Be right back."

Tip walked up to his desk ten minutes later. "Find it?" I asked.

"Shit no. Her goddamn desk is so orderly you couldn't find anything."

I almost fell out of my chair, mostly because he was serious. "You realize what you just said, right? If a desk is organized, you should be able to find things."

"Not if you don't work that way. I don't like orderly desks. If you're so good at it, you find the damn plates. Go on. I dare you."

"I'm not falling for your tricks, Denton, but I am going to get some lousy coffee. You want any tea?"

"Yeah, please? As long as you don't spit in it."

"Does that mean I can piss in it?" I said as I was walking away.

"I guess. But stir it up before you serve it to me."

I laughed all the way to the coffee room. Tip was an ass, but he was fun to work with.

I stopped at Julie's desk on the way back just to see if I could find those plates. I looked on top of her desk, which was easy to search as it was as clean as Mollie's counters. Then I turned her computer on and entered her password, which she had given me previously. I went to the "things to do" folder, but it wasn't in there. Next, on a whim, I looked in the "projects completed" folder, and near the top sat Tip's request. Next to it was a note that read "delivered on Tuesday."

I wore a smile all the way back to the desk; in fact, by the time I reached the desk, it had turned into a shit-eating grin. "Guess what, Mr. Denton? I stopped at Julie's desk on the way back, and in her very-organized computer, under "projects completed" was a note that mentioned she had delivered your request for the plates on Tuesday. Based on that and Julie's well-deserved reputation for efficiency and reliability, I recommend you search your very-unorganized desk thoroughly."

For ten minutes, Tip looked through piles of papers and shuffled stuff around. Finally, under a stack of notes from Coop, he found what he was looking for. He laughed, but it was an embarrassed laugh. "Well, shit. I guess I should have looked harder," he said.

"And I guess you better figure out a way to delete those nasty messages you left on Julie's phone too."

"Oh, shit. Can I do that? Is there a way?"

"You'd need to know her password, but I'm sure she's already listened to and ignored your comments. I would have."

"Just show me who owns the plates," Tip said.

I pulled out the notepad where I had jotted it down and set it on Tip's desk.

"Permian Basin Construction. Who the hell is that?"

"That's the name the van is registered in," I said. "And since Julie didn't have it noted, I'd say the plates are not stolen."

I wrote down a phone number and handed it to Tip. "Before you ask, here's the number for Permian."

Tip dialed the number and waited. A woman answered, "Permian Basin."

"This is Officer Drexel in The Woodlands. Security at the mall contacted us about a van left in the parking lot. They said it's been there a long time. When we ran plates, it came back to you."

"Oh, yes. I'm sorry, Officer. Our foreman for fencing said it wouldn't start when he came out of the mall. We had a repairman go over there, but it wouldn't jump either. He said he thinks it's the alternator. We're waiting on a tow truck now."

"When do you expect the tow truck to pick it up?"

"They said tomorrow, but I don't know what time."

"All right. Thank you," Tip said.

He hung up the phone and slowly looked over to Connie. "It checked out. They said it was broken down and waiting to be towed."

"Seems like a long time to wait on towing," Connie said.

Tip nodded. "It does, but she said they had a repairman go there first, and he couldn't fix it; besides, I can't see the kidnapper planning this out so well that he'd have a fake line set up for Permian Construction."

"I have to agree with you there, Tip, and you know I hate doing that."

Tip sat in his chair, staring at the wall and obviously pondering something.

"Are you thinking about who else it might be, or are you still trying to figure out a way to pin this on Spoons?"

"I think I'm gonna follow Spoons one more time."

"And you think this will be different?"

Tip shrugged. "I don't know. I guess I'll see."

Chapter Forty-Seven

FOLLOW THE LEAD

Tip positioned his car so he couldn't be seen from the vet's office, but also so that he could easily tail Spoons no matter which way he went. The only direction he wasn't situated for was "east," but he didn't think Spoons would go that way. North or south was his bet.

Spoons exited the building shortly after six, got in his car, and headed south. Tip let him get a good start, then followed. He was driving a different vehicle tonight, having traded cars with Ribs, a precaution in case Spoons knew his. And he was wearing sunglasses and a hat to further hinder identification. The sunglasses and hat weren't enough to disguise him in a close-up situation, but for long-distance recognition, they were.

Tip followed him south on the freeway until he exited at Research Forest Drive, where he turned left, heading east. What the hell? Tip thought. Where's he going?

He followed cautiously for a few miles, then Spoons turned into an older subdivision, took a few left turns, then drove down a driveway marked "private drive."

Tip stopped the car, pulled into a neighbor's empty driveway, and waited. He sat there for three hours with no sign of Spoons. When the person next door pulled into their drive, Tip approached them. He showed his badge, and asked, "Is there a way out of that driveway, or is a dead end?"

"That's a dead end, Officer. Nothing but one house down there."

"Okay, thanks," Tip said, then he got into his car and drove home.

About ten that night, he got a call from Connie.

"There was a kidnap attempt tonight. Just an attempt though. He didn't get the kid."

"Son of a bitch! When?"

"About 7:30. This one was in the Woodlands."

"Are you sure about the time?"

"Tip, the boy's mother told us what time it happened, and a neighbor verified it. The kid was playing close to his house, and a man in a white van tried forcing him inside."

"How'd he get away?"

"The boy was struggling to break free when a neighbor walking his dog came by. He intervened and the kidnapper left."

"Did he get a plate?"

"He got a partial," Connie said, then read the numbers off. "But don't get excited. We've already run the plates, and they were stolen; in fact, they were stolen months ago."

"Son of a bitch. Son of a bitch. That would be one sick fuck if he planned it that far in advance."

"Were you sitting on Spoons at that time?" Connie asked.

After a momentary pause, Tip said. "Yeah, I was sitting on him until about an hour ago. It couldn't have been him."

"Glad to hear that's finally out of the way. Now we can focus on finding out who's doing this."

"We need to go back over the files on Richardson and Albus. I still agree that the key is with them, and I further agree that the dog fighting is the key to finding their killer."

"I figured you'd say that," Connie said. "Julie's bringing the files in a few minutes."

"Julie?"

"Yeah, she's back from vacation. And don't worry, I already apologized for you, and I told her how humiliated you were."

"You're an ass, Gianelli. Did anyone ever tell you that?"

"Never! I'm appalled you'd say that."

"You're a double ass."

Julie delivered the files, and Tip and I got to work analyzing them. After hours of work, we did find one connection. Both of them had made calls at one point to a guy named Benson. He had different phone numbers, but he owned the lines. And with further digging, we discovered that Benson had served six months in prison for cruelty to animals, and he was just released a few months ago.

"Shit, maybe it's not Spoons after all," Tip said. "Although that would mean the cases are probably not connected."

"Not all cases are connected, Tip."

"I know that, but these cases seem like they're connected—both dealing with animals and such."

"Connected or not, we've got to get to the bottom of it. I say we check out this Benson guy."

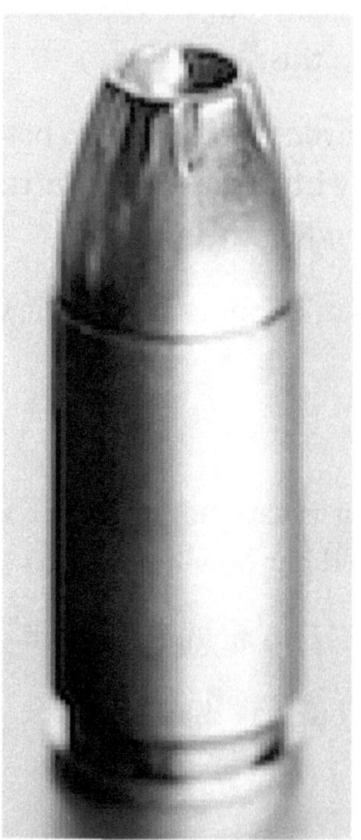

We drove to the address given us by Benson's parole officer, and after a few knocks on the door, he answered.

I showed my badge, then said, "Detective Connie Gianelli, and this is my partner, Detective Denton."

"What do you want?" he asked. "I been reporting on schedule, and I ain't done nothing else. So what are you here for?"

"Heard you've been fighting dogs again," Tip said.

"Bullshit! If someone told you that, they're lyin' their ass off. I've barely looked at a dog since I've been out. Ain't gonna be fighting 'em anymore."

"So you admit you were fighting them before?" I asked.

"What the hell you think I was in prison for?"

"Did you know Kent Richardson and his buddy Albus?"

"Knew of 'em. I wouldn't say I knew them. At least not well."

"Did you know they're both dead?" I asked.

He turned his head toward me quickly. "What? How?"

"Killed just like a dog dies in a fight. Skin yanked from their bodies."

"Son of a bitch," Benson said.

"Got you worried?" I asked.

"I didn't have nothin' to do with that."

"I didn't say you did. I asked if it had you worried. The way I see this is you're screwed either way you look at it. Either you had something to do with killing Albus and Richardson, and if you did, we'll find out. Or you had nothing to do with killing them, and whoever did it may be targeting you next."

"That's bullshit," Benson said. "You better get me some kind of protection or something."

Tip laughed. "Good luck with that. Protection is only for decent people. That's not a category you fit into."

"You can't just leave," Benson said. "I might be in danger."

"Ain't that a pisser," Tip said as he walked away.

"Be thankful we're not hauling your ass in for being a douchebag, Benson. And if I were you, I'd watch my ass. Somebody's out there torturing people who fight dogs. And we both know who fits that category."

Chapter Forty-Eight

CHECKING THE LEADS AGAIN

Tip dropped Connie off at her house, then drove north on I-45. He had plenty of time before Spoons would get off work. At least he thought he did. While he drove, he called Julie.

"Hey, darlin', how was vacation?"

"I got your ten thousand messages, Tip. Did you ever think to ask anyone where I was? And did you ever think to look for what I had already given you?"

"Sorry, Julie. Anyway, now that we're best buds again, I need another favor."

She laughed. "What do you need?"

Tip gave her an address. "Check on this for me. I think Flanagan checked it off his list as okay, but please confirm that for me."

"Please. Darn, you sure are being nice, Detective."

"Shut the hell up. There. Is that better?"

"Much more like it. Hang on, and I'll check."

Julie came back on the phone a moment later. "You're right. Flanagan signed off on it as being checked and clean."

"Son of a bitch. Okay, can you give me Flanagan's cell number, please?"

"Darn, you used please again. I'm gonna have to go on vacation more often."

"Just get me the number. And I'm not saying please."

Julie gave Tip Flanagan's cell, and he dialed it immediately.

"Hello?"

"Flanagan, you horse's ass. Do you do anything right? Do you take your goddamn job seriously?"

"Who the hell is this?"

"It's Tip Denton. And I'm calling because one of the addresses you signed off and marked as checked is not okay. Our suspect is in there."

A long silence, then, "Tip, I'm sorry. I know the one. Nobody answered the door, but it was listed as belonging to an older lady, and there were no animals or kids running around. I checked it two times, then signed off on it."

"And you think that was a good idea? Signing off on it?"

"I don't know, Tip. It was getting late, for Christ's sake. And like I said, there wasn't any sign of anything suspicious."

"Well, just so you know, asshole. There've been two more kidnappings since then, and we're pretty sure our main suspect is holed up there."

"But the tax records say it belongs to an older woman—a lady about 70."

"Maybe he's got her kidnapped too. Ever think of that. Maybe he's holding her hostage and using her place."

"I guess I didn't think of that. I'm sorry, Tip."

"Yeah, well sorry and three dollars will get you a cup of coffee." Tip hung up the phone. If it had been a desk phone, he'd have slammed it.

He drove to the address where he'd followed Spoons to before and parked in a neighbor's driveway. He got out of the car and knocked on the door. A middle-aged woman answered, curiosity showing on her face.

"Ma'am, I'm Detective Tip Denton with the HPD. We've had reports of possible prowlers in the area, and I'd like to use your back yard to go down through the woods to see if I can spot anything out of the ordinary. Is that all right?"

She smiled and swung the door open. "Of course, young man. You can walk through the house and go that way. It'll save you from climbing the fence. But you better watch out for the mosquitoes; they're terrible this year."

Tip walked about halfway to the woods and had to swat three or four mosquitoes away. The lady was right about them being bad, but then again, when weren't they? Tip had lived here all his life, and despite what people said about them being bad this year, they were bad every year."

When he entered the property where he'd followed Spoons to, the woods grew thicker, and the underbrush was covered in devil's thorn, an invasive species of plant that seemed to have won the war for survival. The stuff was almost impossible to navigate once it grew in and that didn't take long.

Tip swatted at a few more mosquitoes as he made his way through the trees. He was thankful for the dense woods that provided him cover. No way anyone would see him coming. Every now and then, he'd catch a glimpse of the house through an opening in the trees, but he still needed to get a lot closer for observation.

Spoons heard the alarm go off—someone or something had crossed the fence and was on his property. He grabbed his rifle from the front closet, the one with the 5-12x42 scope. The scope had a range of 5x to 12x magnification, meaning the image you saw through the lens would be at least five times larger than it would appear to a naked eye. From this distance, with this scope and gun, Spoons could shoot the beak off a crow.

He scanned the woods and noticed a few branches moving. He zoomed in on that location and focused. It was Detective Denton. *Interesting. What's he doing here?*

He thought about pulling the trigger. It wouldn't take much, just a squeeze of the finger. But killing a cop would bring a lot of inquiry, and that was something he didn't need. That wouldn't be smart. And if anything was true, it was that Justice Spoons was smart. He'd let Detective Denton have his fun. For now.

But maybe he better lay low for a while. Keep things quiet. Let things rest.

Tip got near the edge of the tree line and stopped. He didn't want to venture into the clearing. No telling who might be watching. He peered through a pair of binoculars, but he saw nothing of interest —no kids and no animals.

If they weren't here then where were they? And how did he get out of here that night to attempt that other kidnapping? That was something Tip would have to figure out.

Chapter Forty-Nine

HOW DID HE DO IT?

Tip picked me up at the usual time, and things seemed normal for a millisecond, then I noticed he was not himself and was thinking about something. "What's on your mind, Tip? And don't say nothing because I've seen that look before."

Tip stayed silent for a moment, then said, "Goddamnit, Connie, I was certain he'd exit the back of Macy's and take that van. I was positive."

"Tip, we checked the van and got an answer. You said so yourself; it would be damned difficult to arrange an answering service that far in advance. And you persisted, following him and waiting at the end of his drive. Against my advice, I might add."

I reached over and turned off the radio. "But you said, 'It couldn't have been him.' You said it yourself. You were sitting on his place. You may as well been playing cards with him."

"But I wasn't playing cards with him," Tip said. "I didn't have eyes on him. It's no different than the Macy's deal."

"Yeah, and look where that got us. Nowhere. We wasted three night's tailing him, and when he did go to the mall, he went shopping, for God's sake. What are you gonna arrest him for—buying bad socks?"

"Suppose he has a setup like the situation at Macy's, a back way out?"

"You're the one who said his drive is a dead end, that there is no way out. You even have a satellite view of it; besides, you never tied that van to Spoons. It was some construction company wasn't it?"

Tip looked at his notes. "Yeah, Permian Basin Construction."

"And what did the secretary say when you called?"

"That the van was used by one of their foremen who did side jobs doing fencing, and that it had broken down while he was shopping. It was waiting to be towed."

"All right, let's deal. Julie's got a report that Benson has been in contact with some former associates. I'll check that out, while you finalize Spoons. But this is it. He's either our suspect, or he isn't. We've got to get this thing solved."

"Deal," Tip said. "He's either in or out by the end of the week."

I gave him a look. "I'm gonna hold you to that."

I started following up on the leads for Benson. One of the leads was a phone number that Richardson had called several times, and now Benson had called the same number.

I went to visit the guy the next day at work. "You know a Tanny Benson?" I asked.

He opened his mouth forming a denial, but then he stopped. "Yeah, I know him. Or knew him before he went to prison. I don't have much to do with him anymore, but he did call the other night."

"What did he want?" I asked.

"Said he needed ID to skip town. I told him I couldn't help him. I used to do that kind of stuff, but I quit."

"Is that so?"

"On my mother's grave," he said.

"Is your mother even dead?" I asked.

The guy stared. "That's a cruel statement. Yes, she's dead."

"Just checking," I said. "You know where Benson was going?"

He shook his head. "Not a clue. I didn't ask 'cause I don't want to know. Benson is trouble. Always has been trouble, and I suspect he always will be."

"Okay. Thanks," I said, and walked back to the car.

Chapter Fifty

ONE LAST CHANCE

Tip was pulling into the parking lot just as Connie was leaving. He slowed the car and rolled down his window. "Gianelli, call me tonight. I'm giving Spoons one last shot."

"That's fine, but you've only got two days, partner. Make it work, or we're moving on."

"I'll make it work. You'll see."

"I'll call when I get home. See ya."

Tip had thought about how to approach the Spoons situation all morning. He'd already stopped by the mall to check on the van, but it was gone. Maybe it was just a slow tow job.

He worked all day trying to figure out how Spoons could have done the kidnappings, but every time he thought he had something, it didn't fit. Tip reworked the case files, going over all the testimony, all his notes about the kidnappings, the interviews with the parents, and his notes about Spoons, but nothing stuck out. If he looked at the evidence, Spoons was innocent. But his gut told him differently.

Around five o'clock, he looked at the clock and realized it was almost time to go home. It crossed his mind to tail Spoons from his work again, but he opted not to do that. It hadn't gotten him anywhere yet.

When quitting time arrived—and lacking a better solution, Tip decided to simply walk up to Spoon's house and knock on the door. If it turned out he was wrong, he could always apologize. He'd done that more than once.

With his decision made, he packed up and headed north toward Spoon's "second" house.

Thirty-five minutes later he took the exit toward Spoon's house, but this time, instead of sneaking through the woods, he drove down the dead-end driveway and parked.

He got out of the car on full alert, and walked up the front side-walk, then knocked on the door. All the while, he searched for signs of kids or animals.

He waited half a minute, but when no one answered, he knocked again, louder. The door opened about fifteen seconds later. Spoons looked surprised. "Detective! What are you doing here?"

Tip feigned surprise also. "Spoons, what the hell are you doing here? I thought you lived off Rayford."

"I do, but I live here also. This house belonged to my aunt, but she's taken ill and went to live with her sister, so I'm watching the place for her. But don't stand there with the mosquitoes, come in. Let me fix you some coffee or tea."

Tip was confused by his pleasantness, but he wasn't about to pass up an opportunity to get a look inside the house. "Don't mind if I do, Spoons. It's been a long day."

"Coffee or tea?"

"Make it tea, please. I've had my quota for coffee."

"Coming up in a minute. In the meantime, let me show you around. It's a great little house. I don't like the way I came into it, but ill-will aside, it's a beauty. Puts my house to shame."

Spoons walked Tip through the living room, dining room, family room, and all the bedrooms, then they sat at the kitchen table, drank tea, and talked. Spoons talked mostly about animals he'd taken care of at the vet's. But he got verbose when Tip asked about a picture of him and two crows he had on the windowsill.

"They're my babies," Spoons said. "I found them six years ago when they were blown out of their nest during a storm and have had them ever since. After you finish your tea, I'll take you out to see them if you want."

"I'd love to," Tip said, still wondering why Spoons was being so cooperative.

Spoons showed Tip the crows, then he showed him around the property, even the barn, which his cats had free roam of.

"You got a hell of a place here," Tip said.

"Well, it's not mine yet, but if my aunt doesn't improve, she said she'd be leaving it to me. I can't say I'm unhappy about it. She owns this place free and clear, so I'll be able to sell my place and use the money to do some fixing up, though it doesn't need much."

Tip nodded. "Not much to be unhappy about—except your aunt's health, that is."

"How about some more tea?"

"No thanks, I've had enough. I need to get home anyway. The dogs will be expecting me."

Spoons laughed. "Well then, don't let me keep you. I wouldn't want to keep them waiting."

Spoons walked Tip to the front door. "Good night, Detective. Thanks for stopping by." Then he furrowed his brows. "By the way, Detective, why did you stop by?"

Tip was caught off guard for a moment but quickly regained his composure. "This kidnapping case we're working on. We're checking all the houses in the area that have land. Looking for anything suspicious."

"I see. Well, good luck. I hope you find him soon."

"We will, Spoons. You can count on that," Tip said, then he left and walked to his car.

On the drive home, Tip thought about his visit with Spoons. Something wasn't right, but there was no denying that there were no kids or animals being kept there.

I called Tip when I got home, and he picked up right away. "It's me, Connie. Find anything?"

"Nothing. Not a goddamn thing. And I was sure that I would."

"Maybe he had them hidden?"

"No. There wasn't anybody there. I'm sure of that. He showed me around the whole damn place, and he let me wander on my own too."

"So he wasn't hiding anything?"

"Not that I could see. In fact, it was almost like he was showing me it couldn't be him," Tip said. "Like he knew what I was there for."

"And?" I asked.

"It hurts to say this, but I guess he's right. If there's a hidden room,

I couldn't see it. He walked me through the whole damn house, let me use the bathroom, took me outside to see his two pet crows. Nothing looked suspicious. *Nothing.* And I didn't see a van anywhere. All I saw was his blue Honda Civic. He even took me into his barn, and if he had a van to hide that would have been the place to do it."

"Maybe it's time you gave up on him. You said yourself you couldn't picture him as a killer."

"I can't picture him as a killer," Tip said. "But that's because I like him. I imagine it's hard for you to picture your Uncle Dominic as a killer."

I flinched, appalled that Tip would say such a thing, but then I realized it was true, and I also realized that he was right. I couldn't picture Uncle Dominic as a killer because I loved him, and all I saw were the good things. I *knew* he was a killer. I knew he'd killed men. Hell, he even told me he had Carlos killed, and he admitted he'd killed my father. But I still couldn't put him in the killer category. "Well, you've got one more day, Tip. Maybe…"

"No. There is no maybe. If he had those kids at this property, they were dead and buried. I guess I've got to admit that it isn't Spoons. Trouble is unless *you* got something today, that leaves us nowhere."

"I may have gotten a lead or two, but nothing that looks promising. Worth following up on, but I'm not excited about it."

"A lead is better than nothing. I'll pick you up in the morning."

"Okay, see you then."

Chapter Fifty-One

IT TAKES S CRIMINAL TO CATCH A CRIMINAL

I got up earlier than usual and put on a pot of espresso. I was going to need it. I hadn't slept much the night before, mostly because I was thinking about the case. Something about Spoons was nagging at me. Maybe it was what Tip said about Spoons showing him around like he was trying to prove it wasn't him. Why would he do that?

And there was a lot of circumstantial clues, not evidence per say, but things that could add up to motive and opportunity—like the faxes on the missing animals at the vet's office. And the fact that Spoons is such an animal person.

I needed to call Uncle Dominic. Maybe he could help.

"Pronto."

"Ciao, Zio Domenico, it's Concetta."

"Concetta! You're using your Italian, so it must be important. What do you need?"

"I need your help on a case I'm working. We're stumped." I gave

Uncle Dominic the details of the kidnappings and the murders, including the grisly details.

"Ah," Dominic said. "And we know that the children are safe?"

"According to the reporter who saw them, yes."

"Concetta, when you think about a crime, you must understand why it was committed. So ask yourself—were the children kidnapped for profit or personal gain? Since the reporter said they were safe, and since no ransom was demanded, and since they weren't sold for the slave trade, then it wasn't greed."

I could hear Uncle Dominic drinking his espresso. I could almost see him smiling.

"Now ask yourself—were the children kidnapped for the thrill of it? I would say no. People don't usually kidnap for thrills, and according to your reporter, the children are well-cared for."

"So you think it's that he feels he's doing good?"

"Based on what you've told me, I would think this fits into the last scenario of crimes I described to you. I said there were four reasons for crimes, but for murder and kidnapping, there are usually only three. First is greed, to gain power or money. If he's not kidnapping the children for ransom, then greed is out of the question. Second is a perversion, and if he isn't abusing them, then that is out of consideration. Third is for a good purpose, or what the person believes to be a good purpose. Your case seems to fit that."

There was a pause. "This is all, of course, assuming the most likely scenario has been ruled out—that a parent or relative did the kidnapping."

"We're pretty positive that's not the case. But what about the murders They were gruesome."

"We didn't talk specifically about murder the first time we spoke about crime. We talked about the 'greed, thrill, convenience, and justified factors.' When it comes to murder, there is a factor that replaces the 'convenience' factor: revenge."

"I'm not sure I follow."

"From what you've told me, I'd say the murders were committed for revenge, but the kidnappings were committed because the person felt justified in doing so. Revenge is usually found as a motive only in acts of violence. A person doesn't rob a bank or steal a car for revenge, but they might kill someone for revenge."

"Revenge for what?"

"The way they were killed tells you that. Sending signals or warnings when someone is murdered is as old as murder. You should know that. People who rat out a gangster may be found with their tongue cut out. People who steal from the mob may be found with hundred-dollar bills stuffed into their mouth—or other places."

"What do you think of the way these people were killed?"

"I think, Concetta, that you knew the answer to that before you called me. Learn to trust your gut."

I laughed. "You're right, Uncle Dominic. I guess I just wanted someone to agree with me."

"Now you have it. So hang up and go catch him."

"Okay, I will. And thanks for helping."

"Anytime, Concetta. Ti voglio bene."

"I love you too, Uncle Dominic. And tell Uncle Giuseppe I said so too."

"He'll be sorry he missed your call. Take care."

I was finishing my last cup of espresso when I heard Tip beeping the horn. By now I recognized not only the sound of the horn, but the annoying way Tip had of beeping it.

I rinsed the espresso cup, grabbed my gun, and headed out the door, locking it as I left.

I opened the car door and got in. "You know, one simple beep of the horn would suffice. You don't have to wake the whole damn neighborhood."

"The whole damn neighborhood should be up anyway."

"Maybe some of them work the night shift, or maybe it's their day off. Ever think of that?"

"I've thought of it, yeah. Damn, but you're a nice neighbor. Will you move in next to me?"

"I'll tell Elena if you don't watch out."

Tip got a serious look on his face as he left the complex. "Okay, what have you got? We need to get something going, or Coop is gonna have our asses."

"You've got one more day to decide on Spoons."

Tip shook his head. "It wasn't him. No sense in wasting time."

"Do you believe that? Or is it just that you haven't figured out how he did it."

"Anybody ever tell you that you're a son of a bitch?"

"All the time, but you haven't answered my question."

"I guess I still think he should be a suspect, but we don't have any evidence. Why are you asking? I thought you wanted to move on."

"I do want to move on, but I'm not sure we should. I called Uncle Dominic this morning to see what he thought."

"What? You shared the case file with a goddamn gangster?

"Yes, I did, and he agreed with you. He thinks we should keep looking at Spoons. Go with our gut."

"He did? Damn, your uncle's a smart man. You didn't by chance ask him how the hell Spoons disappeared while we were watching him, did you?"

"Tip, we've got today and the weekend—if we want to stretch it— so let's not waste time. I say we review everything and see if we've missed anything."

Tip turned south on the freeway. "Sounds good to me. Call Julie and tell her to get the files ready. We don't have a lot of time. Tell her we'll be there in twenty-five minutes."

"I'll make a deal with you. I'll call Julie if you slow down enough to make it thirty-five minutes."

Tip laughed. "All right. Deal."

Chapter Fifty-Two

ANOTHER LAST CHANCE

Tip slowed down enough to allow me to hold onto my breakfast, and forty minutes later we arrived at the office. Julie had the case files ready, spread out on Tip's desk in chronological order.

"Damn, would you look at that," Tip said. "That girl's good."

"You should tell her that, not me."

"I told her last month how good she was. I don't want to give her a big head."

"Other than yourself, I don't think anyone who works with you is in danger of that."

"All right, Gianelli. Now let's get to work. We've got a lot to do."

We spent hours poring over case files, looking particularly for things that pointed to Spoons: the first victim had described a pattern of speech that seemed to match Spoons; a person at the Little League game provided a description that was similar to Spoons; the vans that had been spotted matched the basic description of the van we had seen parked behind Macy's; and the faxes sent to the veterinary offices would have provided the information a kidnapper would need as far as names and addresses go.

"None of this by itself is enough to even get a warrant," I said. "There are plenty of people who speak with the same cadence as he does; there are tens of thousands who fit the description provided at the ball game; there are thousands of vans that look like the ones described; and there are hundreds of vets that the animal information was faxed to."

Tip nodded. "I know. I know."

"But if you add it all up, it makes him look guilty or at least suspicious," I said.

"I realize that," Tip said, "but looking suspicious isn't good enough. Remember, I had his driveway staked out the night of the attempted kidnapping, and there is no way out other than that driveway."

I thought for a minute, then said, "If we assume Spoons is the kidnapper, then the only option is that there is another way out, and we don't know about it."

Tip sat up straight and stared. "Just like Macy's. He went into Macy's, and we lost sight of him. A kidnapping happened, then he re-appeared. We presumed it couldn't have been him because we thought he was in Macy's."

"But what if he wasn't? I'm not saying the van was his, but what if he had some other means of leaving the mall?"

"Get Julie. Never mind, I'll get her." Tip dialed her extension. "Julie, I need satellite images of Spoon's property. Not his real property, but the one Flanagan screwed up on. On second thought, forget about that. I can bring it up on the computer."

"So what do you need, Tip?"

"I need everything you can get me on Spoon's real property, and more importantly, the one I gave you the address on and the property surrounding it."

"And I suppose you want it today?"

"Before lunch would be great, Julie."

"You gonna give her a pat on the back for this one?" I asked.

"Of course—if what she provides proves to be of use."

Tip pulled up the satellite images on his computer, and It didn't take long to see a possibility. The property bordering Spoon's on the east side had an exit to another road.

"He could have gone out that way," I said. "And if he exited onto that road, you'd have never seen him leave."

Tip shook his head. "Doesn't explain how he got a van from his place to that other road. There are fences between the properties and no gates. I saw that when I was there."

"Maybe he had a van parked at that house. Who knows? All I know is that we need to look into it."

As we were studying the road layout and the potential exits to the freeway, Julie walked into the office. "Here are the tax records for both houses. I think you need to look into this."

"What have you got?" Tip asked.

"The properties are listed as being owned by different people, but the taxes are being paid for by the same person."

"Who?" I asked.

Julie leaned against the desk. "Are you ready for this? Permian Basin Construction."

Tip turned quickly. "What?"

"You heard me right, Tip. Permian Basin—the company that owned the van you found at Macy's—is the one paying the taxes on both of those houses."

"Son of a bitch. Son of a goddamn bitch. He did it. This was all Spoons."

"Hang on, Tip. It's one thing to suspect he did it or even to know he did it, but we've got to prove it. At this point, it's still circumstantial."

"Then we stake the son of a bitch out again. This time, we'll be ready though."

"In what way?" I asked.

"We'll put a team on the main drive while you and I sit on the back exit. If he comes out, either way, we follow him."

Tip and Connie sat in the car until 11:00, but there was no sign of Spoons. Tip had checked every half hour with the other stakeout team, and they hadn't seen anything either.

"I guess it's time to call it a night," Tip said. "It's long past the time for any kid to be taken."

"Don't get frustrated, Tip. We'll come back tomorrow night."

"And with our luck, we'll have the same results—nothing."

"Think positive, Tip. Just because we haven't caught him yet doesn't mean we won't."

Tip sighed. "I know, but it gets frustrating. The worst part is I don't even know if I blame him. None of those kids seemed to have a good life, and the men who were killed deserved it."

"Careful, Tip. You're starting to sound like Uncle Dominic. He lives by his own set of rules."

"Maybe he's not so wrong. Sometimes I don't agree with who we lock up. I do my job, but I don't necessarily agree with it."

"You can't agree with what he did to Richardson and Albus."

"Can't I? I know the law says I can't, but my heart tells me differently. If I'd have taken a different path in life, I might have done the same; in fact, part of me doesn't want to catch him now."

"You like this guy, don't you?"

"I do. I like him a lot. He seems like a nice guy, and he has a way with animals. I put a lot on what animals think of a person. They're usually smarter than we are when it comes to sensing things in people."

"Why don't we leave him alone then? Leave the case unsolved."

Tip shook his head. "We can't do that. For better or worse, we took an oath. Sometimes it's for worse, but we've still got to go through with it."

"So what are we gonna do?"

"We'll come back tomorrow. And if we have to, the next night. We'll keep coming back until we get him."

"Whatever you say, partner."

Tip started the car and headed off. He dropped Connie off at her place twenty minutes later.

"You need any company?" Connie asked.

Tip shook his head. "Elena should be there. She said she was coming over tonight but thanks anyway. I'll figure it out by tomorrow."

"Call if you need me," Connie said. "I'm only a few minutes away."

Elena greeted Tip when he got home, and so did Flash and Sacco. He knelt and paid special attention to the dogs, then got up and hugged Elena.

"About time," she said. "The dogs got a better greeting than I did."

"They deserved it," Tip said. "I'm working this case, and it's related to dog fighting. It's got me pissed is all."

"Dog fighting? I thought that went out years ago."

"It should have, but it hasn't. Anything someone can make money on is never out. If the heat's bad enough, it may go away for a while, but it always comes back."

"So the guy you're after runs dog fights?"

"No. The guy I'm after is killing the ones who do the fighting."

"I can see why you're pissed. I might let the guy go."

"You're the second person who's said that tonight."

"Then maybe you should listen," Elena said. "There are a lot of bad people in this world. Sometimes the best way to take care of them is in an unorthodox manner."

Tip grabbed a beer from the refrigerator. "Do you hear yourself, Elena? You're condoning murder."

"Yes, I am. But how many times did I hear you say you were going to kill that man who had Kassie shot? And no matter what I said to calm you down, you were determined. I'm convinced that you would have killed him if you'd caught him. Go ahead. Deny it."

After a long pause, Tip said, "Maybe I would have. Who knows? But there's a difference—Carlos killed my dogs."

"And these people used them for fighting. I don't know which is worse. Your dogs suffered, but only for a few minutes. Those fighting dogs suffered a lot longer, possibly years."

"All right. I can't go on thinking like this. It's too confusing. I need to catch this guy and get it over with."

"Whatever you say," Elena said. "Now get another beer and rub my shoulders. That will take your mind off things. Well, off some things."

Tip smiled and went to get another beer. "God, but you're an evil woman."

"And you love it. Now get to work. And when you finish my shoulders, I'll tell you where else to rub."

"I'm beginning to forget what we were talking about."

"That's the point or at least half the point."

"What's the other half?" Tip asked.

"Making me forget what we were talking about."

Tip began rubbing lower on her back. "Let me see if I can accomplish that."

Elena smiled. "I'm sure you can if you try."

Chapter Fifty-Three

ANOTHER EXIT

I didn't see Tip until about four o'clock on Saturday. We grabbed a bite to eat and discussed what we planned on doing. "How are we playing this?" I asked.

"Flanagan and his partner are going to take the driveway, and we'll be on the back side again. Maybe he'll try something tonight. If we see him leave, we'll call Flanagan to back us up while we follow. I don't want Spoons to see us tailing him, so we'll switch off with Flanagan."

"You're hoping to catch him in the act?"

"Unless we find the kids or get some irrefutable evidence, catching him in the act is the only way I see of nailing him. We sure as hell aren't going to get him with what we've got."

"Then let's hope he tries something," I said.

"Or not," Tip whispered.

"I checked on Benson before you came by. There's been no activity, and according to the teams assigned to watch him, he hasn't left the house. I think he's clean."

"It's good that you checked, but I never thought it was Benson anyway. It didn't feel right."

"Yea, I know what you mean." I looked at the time and said, "Tip, we better get going. It's almost six-thirty."

We found a house close to the only exit from the road that bordered the back of Spoon's property. Tip knocked on the door and got permission to use their driveway as a stakeout point, and after that, we pulled in and settled in for the wait.

For about an hour, we played games on our phones, then Tip tapped me on the shoulder. "Check out the van coming down the street, Connie. I think it's him."

I slid lower in the seat. "Get down, Tip. Don't let him see you."

Tip got lower in the seat but kept peeking above the dashboard. "It's him, Gianelli. It's the same van he had behind Macy's—Calcon Fencing."

"Call Flanagan," I said. "Tell him to be ready to get on I-45 heading north or south. He's got to be prepared to go either way."

"Flanagan, this is Tip. It's on. He's heading toward the freeway. Go park somewhere that allows you access to the freeway going north or south. I'll call when he's close, but in case I miss it, he's in a white van with Calcon Fencing on the side panels."

Tip sat up and turned to me. "Okay, Gianelli. Time to go. Let him get far enough ahead, but not too far."

I looked at Tip and smiled. "I've tailed people before, partner."

"Sorry, just nervous."

We stayed a safe distance behind Spoons and called Flanagan when he got close to the freeway. Flanagan picked him up heading south and we fell back a short ways. After a few miles, we took over and let Flanagan fall back. This continued until Spoons exited on Louetta Road. He headed west.

Flanagan took the first turn at tailing him on Loretta, which would be more difficult than the freeway. Fortunately, we didn't have long to wait, as Spoons turned into a subdivision on the south side shorty afterward.

Tip let him get a few blocks ahead, but when he made a turn, Tip quickly followed. We parked on the side of the road and watched from about a block away. For almost half an hour, nothing went on, then Spoons got out and knelt by the side of the street. He called to a dog, who stopped and came to him. As soon as the dog got close, Spoons patted it on the head, then picked it up and tossed it into the back of the van.

"That's it!" Tip said. "Let's nail the son of a bitch."

I grabbed Tip's arm. "Hang on, Tip. All he did was put a dog in a van. We've got nothing to get him with yet."

Tip nodded. "You're right. We'll wait and see what happens."

Fifteen minutes later, a young boy walked down the street calling out—apparently for his dog.

"Mugsy. Mugsy boy. Where are you? Where'd you go?"

When he got close to the van, the door opened, and Spoons stepped out. "You looking' for a dog?"

"Yea," the kid said. "You seen him? He's a brown shepherd dog about yay big." He held his hand about two feet off the ground as he said that.

Spoons laughed and nodded as he walked toward the back of the van. "I figured he was lost. I got him in the back of the van. I bet he'll be glad to see you."

The kid ran across the street, smiling all the way. "Thanks, Mister. I thought I'd lost him."

Spoons opened the back door of the van when the boy was close, then he grabbed the boy and tossed him inside and quickly got in with him.

"Okay," I said. "Now, we've got him."

I opened the car door. "I'll approach on foot from the rear. You pull in front of the van and block it in."

"Got it," Tip said.

I unholstered my gun and approached at a fast walk while Tip pulled in front of the van. By the time Spoons was in the driver's seat and ready to leave, Tip and I had guns drawn and pointed.

"It's over, Spoons," Tip said. "Come out slowly, and keep your hands in the air."

The door opened, and Spoons got out. "I guess it's over, huh."

"It's over," I said, and pulled my handcuffs. "Put your hands behind your back and turn around please."

After I cuffed him, Tip got the boy and his dog from the back.

"I've got a few bottles of water and some snacks for both of them in the front seat," Spoons said. "They might be thirsty or hungry."

"Where are the rest of the kids, Spoons?" Tip asked.

"They're in the house behind mine. They're fine. They've got plenty of food and water, and they've got games to play or TV to watch."

"I'll need the key," Tip said.

"The door's not locked. Walk on in, Detective. You'll see the kids are fine."

Tip called in the report while he and Connie drove Spoons to the station. As they were heading south on the freeway, Tip asked him. "Why'd you do it, Spoons?"

"Because they'd have been better off with me. Their parents didn't give a damn about them. Didn't care for their animals either."

"Did you kill Richardson and Albus?"

"Were those the names of the ones who fought the dogs?"

Tip nodded.

"I won't say I killed them, but I read in the paper about what those men had done, and I can't say I'm sorry they died."

"That was a horrible way to die," I said.

"Are you talking about them or the dogs?" Spoons asked.

After driving a few miles in silence, Spoons said, "You know, Detective Denton, I could have killed you. I thought about it that day you were sneaking through

the woods. Had you in my sights. It wouldn't have been hard. I can shoot the beak off a crow as it flies by. Not that I'd ever do that, but I could if I wanted."

Tip turned and nodded to Justice with a look of respect. "I believe you, Spoons. Not just about whether you could shoot the eyes from a crow, but that you'd never do it. I truly believe you."

"How is Sacco?" Spoons asked.

Tip smiled. "He's fine, Spoons.

Thanks to you, he is. I appreciate what you did for him."

"Of course, Detective. He's a good boy. He deserves to live a long and happy life."

Tip parked, and then he and Connie led Spoons to be processed. "I wish it didn't have to end like this," Tip said.

Spoons nodded. "Everyone has a job to do, Detective. I did mine, and you did yours. I have no hard feelings."

"Why'd you do it, Spoons?"

Spoons thought for a moment, then said, "Because that's what the good book says. 'Do unto others as they do to you.'"

"Spoons, you know that's not how the saying goes?"

"That's not what my mama said."

I shook my head, then opened the door and walked to the front desk.

After we got him processed we called it a day. On the way home, I said, "Want to stop for a beer, partner?"

Tip shook his head. "Not tonight. I think I'm gonna go home and crash."

This didn't sound like Tip. "Bummed out?"

"He doesn't deserve to be put away, Connie. I know what he did was wrong, but prison is not the answer."

"Then what is?"

"I don't know," Tip said, "but it's not prison."

Chapter Fifty-Four

AFTERMATH

Two months later

Tip picked up Connie, like normal, and on the ride in, she said, "Tip, you all right? You haven't been the same since Spoons was convicted and sentenced."

"I'm fine, Connie. I just can't help thinking of him in that damn prison. He' s gonna be out of place there."

"Maybe he can do something where he won't be in with the other prisoners every day. You can't worry about it. You already did more than your part when you recommended leniency. It was mostly your testimony that shaved years from his sentence."

"You might have hit on something with the segregation, Connie. I'm gonna go see the warden."

"What? When?"

"As soon as I drop you off. Tell Coop I'm taking a personal day, and I'll call you when I get back."

Tip drove to the prison, which was only about an hour north of his house, and within half an hour he was sitting in the warden's office.

"What can I do for you, Detective?"

"You recently got a new prisoner named Justice Spoons, the one convicted of kidnapping."

The warden nodded. "If I remember correctly, he was also suspected of two murders, though the district attorney couldn't prove it."

"I know what he did, and I know what he was suspected of. It was my case. But I know the man. He doesn't belong here, despite what he did."

"The law says differently."

"I know what the law says, but your job is to rehabilitate people, and the best thing you could do with Spoons is to let him work with animals."

"Are you talking about our new program?"

Tip nodded. "The one where you let prisoners out to do community service. If you let him work with animals, you won't regret it. I've seen him work with animals, and I don't believe you could find anyone better. And you'll make a happy prisoner to boot. In fact, you may damn well make an actual reformed man some day."

"I don't know, Detective. He couldn't be approved for..."

"Forget regulations. He's more than qualified, and he'd be better than anybody. I stake my reputation on it. Give him a shot. You'll see."

The warden leaned back in his chair. "You feel that strongly about it?"

Tip nodded again. "I do."

The warden wrote a few notes on a tablet sitting on his desktop. "All right, Detective. I'll see what I can do, but if it doesn't work out, you'll hear from me."

Tip stood and shook the warden's hand. "Thanks. I owe you for this. And don't worry. It'll work out great. Spoons is a good man."

"For your sake, I hope so because I'm logging this in as your recommendation. If he does a good job, it will look good on you. But if he doesn't..."

Tip smiled. "I understand, and I'm not worried. Thanks for the help."

Tip drove back to the station and picked up Connie just before quitting time.

"I wasn't expecting you to get back so soon. Everything go okay?"

Tip smiled. "Yea, it did. Went well."

"You look like you feel good about yourself," Connie said.

"Feel good enough to let you buy me a beer," Tip said. "Hell, maybe I'll let you buy me two."

Connie grinned ear-to-ear. "Good to have you back, partner."

ACKNOWLEDGMENTS

It is with great honor that I give eternal gratitude to my wife and all four of my grandkids. They give me the inspiration to keep going.

I also need to give great thanks to Rose,

Giacomo Giammatteo is the author of gritty crime dramas about murder, mystery, and family. He also writes non-fiction books including the No Mistakes Careers series, No Mistakes Publishing, No Mistakes Grammar, and No Mistakes Writing.

When Giacomo isn't writing, he's helping his wife take care of the animals on their sanctuary. At last count they had forty-five animals —eleven dogs, a horse, six cats, and twenty-six pigs.

Oh, and one crazy—and very large—wild boar, who takes walks with Giacomo every day and happens to also be his best buddy.

nomistakespublishing.com
gg@giacomog.com

ALSO BY GIACOMO GIAMMATTEO

You can see all of my books here.

And you can buy them on the platform of your choice.

This brings up a thought: with more than fifty books out now, it is becoming difficult to try to update the list in the back of all of them. If you want to know what books I have out, use the link above, which takes you to my website, or download the latest copy of my GG recommended reading list, which is free.

Nonfiction :

Careers:

No Mistakes Resumes, Book I of No Mistakes Careers

No Mistakes Interviews, Book II of No Mistakes Careers

Grammar:

Misused Words, No Mistakes Grammar, Volume I

Misused Words for Business, No Mistakes Grammar, Volume II

More Misused Words, No Mistakes Grammar, Volume III

Visual Grammar (this is a compilation of volumes I–III with a bit of new information added. It also includes pictures. The world's first visual grammar book)

Misused Words and Then Some, No Mistakes Grammar, Volume V

More Grammar:

No Mistakes Grammar Bites, Volume I, Lie, Lay, Laid, and It's and Its

No Mistakes Grammar Bites, Volume II, Good and Well, and Then and Than

No Mistakes Grammar Bites, Volume III, That, Which, and Who, and There Is and There Are

No Mistakes Grammar Bites, Volume IV, Affect and Effect, and Accept and Except

No Mistakes Grammar Bites, Volume V, You're and Your, and They're, There, and Their

No Mistakes Grammar Bites, Volume VI, Passed and Past, and Into, In To and In

No Mistakes Grammar Bites, Volume VII, Farther and Further, and Onto, On, and On To

No Mistakes Grammar Bites, Volume VIII, Anxious and Eager, and Different From and Different Than

No Mistakes Grammar Bites, Volume IX, A While and Awhile, and Envy and Jealousy

No Mistakes Grammar Bites, Volume X, Could've and Should've, and Irony and Coincidence

Writing:

No Mistakes Writing, Volume I—Writing Shortcuts

No Mistakes Writing, Volume II—How to Write a Bestseller

No Mistakes Writing, Volume III—Editing Made Easy

Publishing:

How to Publish an eBook, No Mistakes Publishing, Volume I

How to Format an eBook, No Mistakes Publishing, Volume II

eBook Distribution, No Mistakes Publishing, Volume III

Print on Demand—Who to Use to Print Your Books, No Mistakes Publishing, Volume IV

Other nonfiction

Uneducated

Whiskers and Bear—Volume I, Sanctuary Tales *A Collection of Animal Stories, Volume II*, Sanctuary Tales

More Animal Stories, Volume III, Sanctuary Tales *Surviving a Stroke—or Two*

Life and Then Some

Fiction:

Friendship & Honor Series:

Murder Takes Time

Murder Has Consequences

Murder Takes Patience

Murder Is Invisible

Murder Is a Promise

Blood Flows South Series:

A Bullet For Carlos: A Connie Gianelli Mystery

Finding Family, a Novella

A Bullet From Dominic

The Good Book

Redemption Series:

Necessary Decisions: A Gino Cataldi Mystery

Old Wounds

Promises Kept, the Story of Number Two

Premeditated

Rules of Vengeance Series: (Fantasy)

Light of Lights (the beginning, a novella)

A Promise of Vengeance

Undeniable Vengeance

Consummate Vengeance

Note. The Light of Lights is a novella. It's about 100 pages long and sets the stage for the series. The other books in the series are about 800 pages long.

OTHER BOOKS

You can always see the current and coming-soon books on my website.

Fiction:

Memories for Sale (mystery/sf)

The Joshua Citadel (SF novella)

Children's Books:

No Mistakes Grammar for Kids, Volume I—Much and Many

No Mistakes Grammar for Kids, Volume II—Lie and Lay

No Mistakes Grammar for Kids, Volume III—Bring and Take

No Mistakes Grammar for Kids, Volume IV, "Would've, Should've" and "Your and You're"

No Mistakes Grammar for Kids, Volume V, "There, They're, and Their" and "To, Too, and Two"

Shinobi Goes to School—Life on the Farm for Kids, Volume I

Fiona Gets Caught, Life on the Farm for Kids, Volume II

Coco Gets a Donut, Life on the Farm for Kids, Volume III

Squeak Gets a Home, Life on the Farm for Kids, Volume IV

Biscotti Saves Punch, Life on the Farm for Kids, Volume V

Coming Soon:

The Adventures of Adalina, Volume I, Adalina and the Five Tiny Bears

The Adventures of Adalina, Volume II, Adalina and the Underwater Bears

Get on the mailing list and you'll be sure to be notified of release dates and sales.

Mailing list

And don't forget to leave a review!

9 781940 313887